Remake the Song

by

Flo Fitzpatrick

Fiona Belle's Time Travels

Remake the Song

COPYRIGHT © 2025 by Flo Fitzpatrick

Cover Art by *Lisa Dawn MacDonald*

The Wild Rose Press, Inc.
PO Box 708
Adams Basin, NY 14410-0708
Visit us at www.thewildrosepress.com

Publishing History
First Edition, 2025
Trade Paperback ISBN 978-1-5092-6240-3
Digital ISBN 978-1-5092-6241-0

Fiona Belle's Time Travels
Published in the United States of America

Acknowledgements

Big "thank-yous" to Jim McLean and Fredda Kaufman for graciously allowing me to use their names. Jim and I met when we were in college and have enjoyed a close friendship ever since. And yes, we've harbored this fantasy of being Olympic skating champions for years. The fact that neither of us skate has never deterred the dream.

I haven't yet had the pleasure of meeting Fredda Kaufman in person. Actress Suzan Perry (the inspiration for Fiona Belle and my real "BFF" since we met doing theater in Dallas in 1991) introduced us online. I've enjoyed exchanging messages and emails with Fredda and am still hoping one day the three of us can sit down to tea and cranberry-orange scones in the same room.

I'd also like to acknowledge, with more than a few high-fives, my brother, Don Wendorf, a retired psychologist who's also been a professional musician since he was a teenager. He currently uses his talent and love of music to guide sing-alongs at several respite care centers in Birmingham, Alabama.

The "obscure" quote Marcus uses when explaining why he titled his album Remake the Song comes from an untitled poem found in the 1908 volume "The Collected Works in Verse and Prose of William Butler Yeats."

Chapter 1

August 1975

Someone was singing the spiritual "Didn't My Lord Deliver Daniel?" It's a great song, with its dual message of strength and hope, not to mention a neat, almost jazzy, feel to the tune. I've always liked it. I was about to join in on the chorus when I realized the someone singing was, in fact, me.

I was sitting on a park bench in Riverside Park overlooking the Hudson River in New York City. I'm a dancer who can whip off triple pirouettes with my eyes closed and finish in the right spot, yet everything around me seemed unbalanced, as though the universe was tilting. My world view seemed off.

Focus. I needed to focus on an object and get my bearings back. I glanced down at the sheet music I was holding, an arrangement of "Didn't My Lord Deliver Daniel?" with handwritten musical notes on the page penned by folk singer Marcus Kennedy and dated August 21, 1975. I had no clue where it came from or how I came to own it or what I was doing singing it. However, since I was nuts enough to be belting out gospel tunes while sitting alone on a park bench, I was glad I was doing so on the Upper West Side of Manhattan. Not a soul was paying me the least bit of attention.

Something was also off about my outfit, which consisted of an ankle-length multi-tiered cotton skirt in hues of green and blue, with a cream-colored peasant top. The dark-brown faux-suede wide belt encircling my waist was a perfect match for my knee-high boots. All normal. But something wasn't right. I could swear I'd bought everything, from boots to blouse, at a vintage stall in Oak Cliff, Texas…this morning. I recalled changing into a skirt, blouse, and boots from cotton capris, sleeveless tee, and sandals in a makeshift dressing room at the stall. The recall did not include stepping onto a plane wearing the new threads and flying to New York City.

The top was long-sleeved, yet I was shivering, an action that had nothing to do with the temperature. After all, it was August and not exactly cool. Nope. This was fear. I was scared. I didn't remember my name. I didn't remember how I got to this bench. I didn't remember where I'd gotten a copy of this sheet music, emblazoned with the name of my favorite musical artist.

An oversized canvas duffel bag with the logo "Retro Records" stamped on the front took up the rest of the space on the bench. I didn't recognize it either, but I figured, what the heck, open it and check out the contents. If the bag was mine, perhaps there'd be some kind of I.D. tucked away in a pocket and I could find out who I was. And yes, I was aware I sounded ridiculous. I unzipped the bag and discovered an eclectic, jumbled, messy, hodge-podge of items scattered inside. There were two pairs of jeans, two leotards, one pair of black tights, one pair of pink tights, one pair of jazz dance sneakers, a black T-shirt, a blue T-shirt, and a very flirty black lace dress clearly meant for dancing at a nightclub.

Tucked inside a sturdy cardboard case was the rare "ghost train" cover copy of folk singer Marcus Kennedy's vinyl recording, *Remake the Song*. Several torn and abused magazine articles, more like clippings, all of them missing names and dates of publication, all of them with scratch-outs from a purple-inked pen, were also tucked in the cardboard case. Intriguing and not helpful. Something to explore later. Nearly hidden beneath the black dress I found a file folder holding sheet music to "The Yellow Rose of Texas." The date of publication for this particular arrangement was August 21, 2025. There was a note at the top next to the date with the cryptic phrase, *For December, if you choose to go back*, also written with purple ink. Like the clippings, interesting, but unhelpful in my quest for answers.

A second note was stuck to the cover of a brand new daily planner. I skimmed it, searching for a name, and found an entry, dated August 28, 1975, in the same handwriting (and, yes, purple ink) as the odd message about December: *Open Auditions for dinner theater production of Dames at Sea at Thirty-Ninth Street Studios. Ten a.m. Go!* At the very bottom of the duffel bag was a pocketbook-slash-coin purse.

Jackpot! I opened the pocketbook and stared at the Texas driver's license photo of Shiloh Meridien, who looked to be about eighteen. The expiration date was June 24, 1975. I felt certain the girl was me. I knew my birth date was June 24, 1955. But there was something out of sync with the picture and the dates, because I also knew I was older. By fifty years and two months.

What had started as bewilderment now became sheer panic. I stared down at the ground and tried to breathe.

"Shiloh, look at me."

I lifted my head and stared at the chubby woman standing in front of the bench. She'd encased her short frame in a striped yellow-and-black bumblebee costume, complete with yellow wings on the shoulders and little yellow antennae balls behind her head. They were bobbing, although she hadn't moved.

"Oh, man. I know you. You're Fiona Belle Winthorp Donovan, yes?" I said. "Wait. You hate the Winthorp part. Sorry."

She growled, "I despised that man."

"Why?"

She glared at me.

"Okay. Never mind. Not vital to the problem at hand. I have managed to locate what I guess is my name on a driver's license, but it's ancient. I'm really glad you're here, because I'm pretty much freaking out."

"Understandable. Ya made quite a trip."

"From where?"

"Ah, well, lass, I'll be explainin', but I gotta warn ya, yer about to be freaked out more than yer already freaked. And, if we're going to be precise and factual, the operative word isn't so much 'where' as 'when.' "

I groaned. "Seriously? Thank you for adding to the confusion and angst. Fine. But, please, end the suspense. Go ahead and hit me with whatever."

Instead of verbally responding, she reached into a bag bigger than the duffel at my side. She pulled out a huge, silver-plated hand mirror and held it in front of my face.

I stared at my reflection and tried not to pass out. "I'm going to pass out."

"No, yer not. Breathe. Deep. Again. Slower."

I took a deep breath, then another before hoarsely saying, "Fiona Belle, the trip you mentioned must have been to one amazing plastic surgeon, because unless this is a trick mirror, the image I'm seeing is me, but the way I looked when I was about twenty."

"No surgery involved and I'm aft ta be provin' it to ya. Lift yer leg in a whachacallit, a *develope*. Other folks in the park seem to be focusing on other things, but ya should hold onto yer skirt anyway, to keep it modest."

I did as commanded, robotically at first, then in amazement as I stretched my right leg up to my ear. A feat last accomplished when I was about forty-five. I slowly returned my foot to the ground.

"What's happening?" I paused. "No, hang on. I'm getting a full tidal wave of images. You and I were at the Final Destination Flea Market in Oak Cliff. Eating awesome cranberry-orange scones and drinking iced coffee, which I'd wager had a large dollop of booze in it. You were, heaven help me, offering me the opportunity to time travel." I shook my head. "And did those words just exit my mouth?"

"It's true. All of it. And, brave, wise lass that ya are, ya took it. The opportunity."

Chapter 2

August 21, 1975

I stared at this bizarrely dressed woman who was trying to convince me she'd, uh, 'youthened' me. "Excuse me, but…how? Not the time travel, which is nutty enough and we'll get back to it. I'm talkin' about the age thing. How did I become twenty again?"

She reached into her bag and this time presented me with what looked like one of her delicious scones. "Eat. Don't worry. They're vegan. Yer blood sugar's low. Eat."

I ate. "You're avoiding the question."

Fiona Belle growled, "Not avoidin'. Not answerin'. Two different things. Yer a mite bit of a different case, Shiloh Meridien. The whole reverse-age trick is not somethin' I normally do. But ya best be believin' it's done. You turned twenty two months ago. Of course, in twenty-twenty-five you turned seventy."

I munched on the scone. (How did she get these to be so rich and perfect without butter?)

"Calmer?"

I nodded, my mouth still full. I swallowed and said, "Sort of. I'm not in a state of panic anymore. I've switched to disoriented and befuddled."

She pulled a cell phone out of an enormous pocket in her bee costume and glanced at it. "Ah. Speakin' of time and travelin', I must be off soon. You can keep eatin' while I explain a few minor details to you."

"You're leaving me?" My terror returned, rising a hundred percent.

"You'll be fine. Now listen. Today is August twenty-first, nineteen-seventy-five. And for the rest of this day, but this day only, you can also be recallin' yerself as you were a few hours ago in twenty-twenty-five. Age seventy. You'll have all the memories of yer entire past, includin' the time ya spent in Manhattan when you were in yer early twenties. When ya get to yer apartment, though, I'd advise ya to lie yer head off to yer roommates. Tell 'em yer not feelin' well and don't want ta talk. Ya don't want to be spillin' somethin' about the future."

I groaned. "Jim and Wyatt? I have to face them?"

"Well, unless ya want to sleep on this bench, you'd be wise to go on home." She paused, then literally smacked her head. "Wait up a sec. This was the week the lads flew down to Texas for some stupid fraternity reunion. You're safe. To be honest, I didn't check. Had some other things on my mind." She scowled at me. "Now hush. Ya got me off track. Where was I?"

"Spilling the future. As in, don't do it."

"Yep. For the rest of this day ya stay quiet and try ta avoid discussin' controversial topics or current affairs. With anyone. Shiloh, now ya'd best listen up, girl. Startin' tomorrow, well, ta be more accurate, beginnin' right at the stroke of midnight tonight, ya won't remember anything from today on, includin' havin' this conversation with me. You'll be startin' fresh, except in yer mind you'll have this constant notion buggin' ya to save Marcus Kennedy from dyin' on December sixteenth."

"You're saying I won't remember my life in the alternate timeline I came from? What if I recall something from the future about Marcus and his death? No offense, but a lack of memory doesn't seem helpful in this particular quest of lifesaving."

"Don't be overthinkin'. Ya don't want fifty years of junk floating around in yer mind while yer tryin' to sort out what ya can say to folks. Ya don't want ta end up in a mental ward. I do have ta warn ya, there might be a time or two when events in the world that happened before, events you witnessed, were so strong you might be reliving them. If anyone's around, ya can tell them yer aft to be bein' clairvoyant."

"Well, dang. Finally. The revelation of how all the psychics do it. Time travel. Duh!"

Fiona Belle winked at me. "No comment."

"Okay. I need to ask, what's to keep me from doing a repeat of my old life in this time period, where nothing changes and Marcus Kennedy still ends up dead?"

"Focus."

"Beg pardon?"

"Yer focus will be different. But, more importantly, I'm aft ta be makin' certain ya get the chance to meet Marcus at the age you were first time around in nineteen-seventy-five. Yer not flyin' totally solo here. Otherwise there'd be no point to travelin' back."

I brightened. "I actually get to meet Marcus? Whoa. Total bonus. Of course, I'll probably come off as a blithering idiot and not be able to say a word." I paused before adding, "May I ask, why the, uh, youthening? By the way, whatever the reasoning, it's a cool perk. Thanks."

"Ya earned it. You came back in time not expectin' you'd be young again. You thought you'd be seventy and tryin' to help Marcus Kennedy like you were his grandma or somethin'." She tossed her bag over her shoulder. "I'm aft ta be takin' Marcus' ghost train album with me. Hand it over."

"Why?"

"Ya don't need ta see it once yer memory goes poof. Ya'll be confused and bewildered and start wonderin' why and how, and it'll take yer focus off what ya need to be doin'."

"Well, I don't need to be any more bewildered than I already am, so fine. And it's depressing anyway. Take it." I gave her the record.

"As I said, I'll be poppin' by now and again. But ya won't remember me from when we met in Texas. I'll reintroduce myself to ya, but not engage in any talk about time travel or de-aging. Got it?" She paused. "Ah. One more, tiny thing, before I forget. You have a date tonight."

"I have a what!"

"A date. Double date. Blind date for you. Arranged by Sandra. Remember her? She's in yer favorite ballet class. Her latest boyfriend's brother from Ohio is coming to visit and she didn't want him to be a third wheel. Enter you."

"You have got to be kidding."

"Guess where you're goin' on the date? Yer gonna love this."

"Let me take a wild stab and say the Bellevue Hospital psychiatric ward?"

She snorted. "Cute. Nope. You're goin' to a concert at the Monroe Theater. Folk and protest singers joining together to help Vietnam veterans. It's sure the government didn't. At least not back then."

"Wait. I did this before, didn't I?"

She nodded. "Ya did. But the original tickets were in the nosebleed section and this time you'll be right down in front."

I paused for a moment before commenting, trying not to sound ungrateful. "I hope this isn't how you've arranged for me to meet Marcus Kennedy. There's no way I can handle an intro with the man I've lov-…uh, admired, from the time I was twelve, if I've got my blind date in tow. I'm not comfortable with strangers during times when life is normal, much less when attempting to get my bearings in time and place."

"Nah. Ya won't be meetin' Marcus tonight. But it'll give ya a chance to see him fairly up close. Like I said, you've got fabulous tickets this time around. Third row center."

"I do remember going to the concert to see Marcus fifty years ago. Tonight. Oh man, I'm confusing myself again. Anyway, the night is hazy as to where we went after. Will it come back before I'm with Sandra and the guys? My memory?"

Fiona Belle shook her head. "Nope. Take my word, 'tis best if ya don't recall anything from yer first time around in nineteen-seventy-five. Plus, it'll all be different tonight. Look, take a few minutes ta sit here and do some mulling over all we've said, then head on home. Take a long shower. You're meetin' Sandra and the lads at the one-hundred-and-third-street subway station at seven p.m."

I felt terrified again. "I feel terrified again." I scowled at Fiona Belle. "How am I going to do this?"

"Because you must. Because you're strong. Because you've loved Marcus Kennedy for the last eight years—oops, sorry, I'm aft ta forgettin' yer mind is still seventy, so it's more like the last fifty-eight years. Either way, there's no sense denyin' it. Now, check yer bag to make sure yer apartment keys are in there. I'm outta here."

I leaned down and dug inside the giant bag. The keys were neatly tucked into a front pocket. I grabbed them like a lifeline, then looked up to tell the strange, tiny, fierce, funny *deus ex machina* of time that all was in order. But Fiona Belle Donovan was gone.

Chapter 3

August 21, 1975

Fiona Belle had suggested I stay put for a few minutes and take stock of what life had thrown at me, which sounded like an excellent idea. I hadn't yet come to terms with the way this impossible time travel/youthening/seventy-becomes-twenty trip and transformation had come about, or was offered in the first place. I looked down at the sheet music and somehow, seamlessly, my mind cleared. I remembered.

****

August 21, 2025, Oak Cliff, Texas

"Ooh! Nice. *Remake the Song*. Marcus Kennedy. Definitely his best. I've never understood why some of the stupid critics were less than kind when it first came out."

I waved to get the attention of the impish vendor manning the counter of the Retro Records stall at the Final Destination Flea Market, a tiny but plump woman, whose age I'd put somewhere between fifty and a hundred. Her short frame was swallowed by her striped yellow-and-black bumblebee costume, complete with yellow wings on the shoulders and little yellow antennae balls popping up behind her head.

She winked at me. Her eyelid was covered in cobalt blue eyeshadow and her eyes were hiding behind absurdly long false eyelashes. The woman personified "retro." Possibly in more than one era.

She stated, in a pronounced Irish dialect, "So, lass, are ya interested in buyin'? Three dollars."

"You're kidding. Of course I am. But I feel like I'm cheating you."

"Yer not. Trust me."

I handed the record back to her to bag and ring up the price on a cash register so old it could have been the prototype. "Are you sure about this? I mean, wow! Three dollars for Marcus Kennedy's *Remake* album with the ghost train cover? There's maybe about ten copies floating around the universe at this point. And no CDs were ever made using the alternate cover. I've looked for this more years than I can count."

"I picked this record and specially selected it with you in mind, because of yer love of Mister Kennedy, so don't ya be worryin' yer head about the price."

"Oh-kay." I blinked, and paused a beat before saying, "Hang on. Can we back it up for a moment? I'm sorry, but did I hear right? What do you mean 'specially selected'? How did you know how much I lov-...uh, admired Marcus Kennedy all these years? Like since I was twelve and first heard 'Chasm of Darkness' on an AM radio station." I shook my head. "Dang. I'm old. Turned seventy back in June. It's so weird. I don't feel old. Not mentally. Not physically. Still lean and mean. I was able to fit into this really saucy, vintage, tiered skirt and peasant top I found at another booth... Isn't it cute and weren't they nice to let me change into it? Boots to match. Pretty awesome!"

She looked up into the heavens as if telling herself to be patient, but I continued with barely a pause for a breath. "I can still dance up a storm. Outlast kids in the college where I teach. I choreographed a six-minute number for a show back in May, and half of them pooped out halfway through the first three minutes during rehearsals. I had energy left for days." I stopped and took a breath before asking, "I'm rambling, aren't I? I'm never, ever, this chatty."

She snorted. "Shiloh Meridien, yeah, yer ramblin', all right, but yer nervous. Ya need ta get back on track."

She was right. I was nervous. *Why* I was nervous was a mystery. "What exactly is the track, how do I climb back on board, and while I'm at it, how do you know my name? Either you have spies all around Dallas and Oak Cliff or you're clairvoyant?"

She whispered in a mysterious voice, laced with that curious, on again-off again accent, "I'm the holder of much wisdom, but, darlin', best if ya don't ask." She finished tapping the price of the album into the ancient cash register, then stated, "The sheet music to Marcus's arrangement of an old spiritual, 'Didn't My Lord Deliver Daniel?'—complete with his notes in his handwriting— goes with the vinyl album. Want it?"

"Seriously? You bet." I was about to hand over the bills but stopped. "Oh, wait. *Now* I get it. The bonus sheet music is the catch, right? The record is three dollars but these pages are three hundred, yet you've already suckered me into buying it and I'd feel like a heel if I said no?"

She snickered. "Ach, Faith and Saint Bridget, but yer not a trustin' lass. Nah. The total price is three dollars and about ten minutes of yer time."

"Done."

I gave her the money. She expertly slid the bills into

the register, then slammed it shut, bagged the album into a sturdy cardboard holder, then tucked both the album and the sheet music inside an enormous tote bag, emblazoned with a logo for Retro Records stamped on the front. She pointed at a group of tables set up as a makeshift cafe for weary shoppers.

"I'm aft ta be seein' ya there in five minutes. Would you be wantin' iced coffee or prefer a soda? Mind, choose whichever ya like best with cranberry-orange scones. Everything's on the house."

"Iced coffee if it's decaf," I responded somewhat absently. "Not a soda drinker. But…"

"See ya in five," she interrupted before whirling around and leaving.

I plopped down onto a round, surprisingly comfortable wrought-iron chair, pulled the record out of the case, and took a long moment to study the cover of *Remake the Song,* the last album Marcus Kennedy ever recorded. But this was the outrageously rare cover. A sad and haunting cover. Instead of a photo of Marcus, casually dressed in jeans and T-shirt, smiling and playing a guitar, as there'd been both on the original *Remake* from late 1975, and a compilation album entitled *Marcus Kennedy-1948-1975* released shortly after his death, this alternate cover was created when *Remake the Song* was re-released in 1983. It was downright spooky, showing a train car filled with riders representing musicians who passed away at age twenty-seven from whatever death curse conspiracy theorists had created, starting in the early Eighties. A mere five hundred copies had been distributed and prices jacked up to where the record was only affordable to serious collectors, a decision made by Marcus Kennedy's business manager, doubtless to boost sales, which wasn't really needed because eight years after he died his records continued to fly off the shelves.

Less than two weeks following its release, record stores had swiftly removed any *Remake the Song* albums featuring the ghost train cover, due to a lawsuit brought by the family of one of the other artists, whose likeness was shown riding along with the other dead musicians, most of whom had overdosed on drugs or alcohol. Many were suicides.

Marcus Kennedy. As I'd mentioned to the strange vendor—who'd already known, and yes, her knowing was even spookier than the cover—I'd been a huge fan of his from the moment I heard the song "Chasm of Darkness," a haunting, beautiful, anti-war piece composed by Kennedy when he was in his teens. His voice was rich and filled with emotion and, in my opinion, had a unique quality no other singer possessed. From everything I read about him, which wasn't much, since he never garnered the fame many folk singers enjoyed in the sixties and seventies, he didn't sing about causes to make money. He sang in the hopes of ending discrimination and war and bringing justice and peace to the world. He was a huge proponent of veterans' rights. When I heard of his death on December 16, 1975, I made a total fool of myself, according to my roommates at the time, Jim McLean and Wyatt Paxton, by sobbing hysterically and replaying his albums nonstop for a month until they threatened to evict me.

Marcus Kennedy died on his birthday at the age of twenty-seven. Was he another victim of the legendary curse? No one really could pin down the "why" although the "how" was pretty clear. Theories at the time were that his death, via a needle filled with heroin, was either accidental, although his friends vehemently stated Kennedy had always been opposed to drugs, suicide for no good reason, or murder for no good reason. Fifty years later his death was still a mystery.

An article written in the 1990s in a top music magazine brought up the suicide angle again, stating that Kennedy began experiencing Parkinson's-like symptoms attributed to exposure to Agent Orange in Vietnam, where he'd sung numerous times for the troops in the late nineteen-sixties. But the reporter then went on to discuss motives for murder, mentioning more than one possible suspect, starting with the U.S. government trying to shut down his investigation into the aforementioned spraying of Agent Orange, corrupt and bigoted cops practicing racial profiling in Manhattan before the term was widely used, and a greedy real estate tycoon messing with New York landmarks, including one of Marcus's pet projects, a veterans' center which had once been a famous ballroom dance hall. The journalist claimed that Marcus had nailed all the "bad guys" in a song he'd planned to release as a single. Then he died. If there had ever been such a song, it died with him.

Marcus Kennedy. Born and raised in the midtown West Side area of Manhattan called Hell's Kitchen. He could play nearly any instrument set in front of him and possessed an incredible vocal range. He snagged a record deal when he was sixteen and began releasing folk songs he'd composed himself. He was granted a full scholarship and early admission to Julliard and then, following his graduation, toured for about six months with a professional opera company throughout Europe. After witnessing America's struggles with Civil Rights, war, poverty, pollution, and political corruption from an ocean away, he returned home to New York City. He stuck with the same record label and sang primarily for small audiences in small clubs in Greenwich Village. None of his albums hit gold or platinum while he was alive, which was mind-boggling considering how talented he was.

I'd been a twenty-year-old dancer living on the Upper West Side of Manhattan when I heard the news over the radio on a bright, sunny, December sixteenth in 1975. I'd gotten to see him about four months earlier, in August, in a small theater, also in midtown. It had been a benefit concert for the Am-Vets center, which was the very space the greedy real estate tycoon wanted demolished, and coincidently, the place where Marcus's body was found.

After hearing of his death, I became angry, devastated, and grief-stricken. I was also confused and frightened by my own reaction to the news. How could someone I'd never met impact my emotions for such an absurdly long time? Days, weeks, months, and, yes, years after his death I continued to mourn his loss.

I now stared down at the vinyl album and the liner notes. He'd included quirky new takes on old spirituals like "Didn't My Lord Deliver Daniel?" and "Wayfaring Stranger," an ancient Irish anti-war ballad, "Johnny Has Gone for a Soldier" (made popular during America's Revolutionary and Civil Wars), one or two vaudeville-era tunes like "Any Time" and "A Pretty Girl is Like a Melody" and a beautiful French version of "Always" (*Toujours*) which Marcus had discovered on an album recorded in 1941 at a Paris nightclub called Café Violette.

Years later, music critics finally heaped praise on the work, lauding his courage in not following the trend of other folk and protest singers to merge into rock or pop or disco, and instead provide old songs with a fresh sound. When Marcus was asked in an interview with a major magazine why he'd chosen such a mix of "odd" musical genres, he responded, "Blame an obscure piece of poetry for the inspiration. Let me quote: *The friends that have it I do wrong, whenever I remake a song, should know what issue is at stake, it is myself that I remake.*"

But Marcus Kennedy never got the chance to remake.

Chapter 4

August 21, 2025

"Here ya go." The Irish vendor had returned with a tall glass of iced coffee and a basket of pastries. She placed everything on the table, removed the album from my hands, and encouraged me to chow down.

"Almond creamer in the coffee and no dairy or eggs in the scones. Totally compliant for vegans. I should be goin' that route myself fer me health and to save the earth's critters, but faith, an' I'd be missin' corned beef with my cabbage on St. Paddy's Day somethin' fierce."

"How did you …?" I paused. "Never mind."

She sank down in a chair across from me. "Drink yer coffee, lass, and eat a scone or two. I promise, they're the best you'll ever taste. Homemade from scratch by me."

I took a bite and immediately agreed with her true if somewhat egotistical comment. "You weren't kidding. These are fabulous. You shouldn't be selling retro records, you should set up a pastry shop."

"I've done both." She rose. "Forgot napkins. Be right back. Don't go anywhere."

"Wait. Before you run off, who are you? I mean, your name. Turnabout being fair and all."

"Fiona Belle Donovan Winthorp." She glared at me as though I was in the process of committing a homicide. "But do not—I repeat, do not—call me Winthorp. I despised that man."

There was no sane response other than to nod and watch her toddle off toward the Retro Records stall, the bee antennae bobbing merrily over her head, while I attempted to tamp down my growing anxiety about why she wanted to chat.

Fiona Belle Donovan Winthorp—oops, scratch the Winthorp—had an agenda and I was part of it. Nothing to do but wait for her to get back and fill me in on whatever plot she was, er, plotting. I sat and tried to push down the butterflies in my stomach as they were engaging in some vigorous cardio activity, and wondered how and why I was sitting on a rickety chair, staring at a vinyl album, waiting for a possible lunatic.

And now, a pause for a warning. I'm diving into backstory territory.

Starting with my name. Shiloh Meridien. Given to me because my paternal grandmother died a week before I was born and my parents wanted to honor her memory, but thankfully didn't want to saddle the new baby with "Mildred Ethel Imogene Meridien" so settled for Grandma's place of residence, i.e., Shiloh. Yep. The durn town where the famous battle was fought and songs were later composed about sad women wandering looking for lost loves. Cheery.

My parents, Jason and Valerie Meridien, weren't really sure what to do with a second girl. Mainly because my sister, Lacey, older by six years, was already perfect. Jason and Valerie knew perfect didn't happen twice in the same household. Lacey had blonde hair and blue eyes and reached her all-time height of five-one at age fifteen. Again, thanks to Grandma, I was red-haired, with green eyes, and, at five-ten, way too tall. Lacey was chatty and personable and surrounded herself with friends. I was quiet, a bit shy, and definitely more comfortable in the company of one person at a time. Lacey was smart and business savvy. Family legend had it her first words were "portfolio" and "market shares." As for me? Well, I knew how much allowance I got and how many books or records I could buy before it ran out. End of math skills. The closest I came to the world of business was my ability to type more than ninety words per minute. Lacey won every political office in school, beginning in kindergarten...don't ask. Lacey was royalty. Prom Queen, Homecoming Queen, Winter Festival Queen, Summer Solstice Queen, Fall Harvest Queen.

Oddly, the single area where I excelled over Lacey was in dance. I loved to dance. I danced before I could walk. Because Lacey had been enrolled in classes at Miss Vanda's Academy, starting at age three—in preparation for those beauty pageants—I followed in her toe shoes...literally. I got her hand-me-down pair of pointe shoes before I ever set foot in Miss Vanda's. My technique was spotless. I could whip off quadruple pirouettes with ease and complete the thirty-two *fouettes* required for the evil Black Swan Odille in *Swan Lake* without losing a beat or balance. But, the year I turned eleven and reached a height of five-ten and Miss Vanda discovered she was unable to find princes tall enough to lift this swan, I was used as live scenery in recitals and as assistant teacher in the studio.

Once I came to terms with the realization I'd never be a professional ballerina, I shifted my focus to contemporary dance. Perks: Less *pas de deux* with short guys, more emotion allowed in choreography, and a big bonus of bare feet instead of pointe shoes. I set my sights on getting into the Emma Andersen Dance Theater, a company based in Manhattan who performed an eclectic repertoire of works outside of modern/contemporary including jazz, tap, African, and South Asian…as in Bollywood before Bollywood was a word.

Fast forward. After cramming four years of college into three, I headed for New York at age twenty. It was August of nineteen seventy-five. Emma Andersen's company was out of the country touring for several months, so I went to a few musical theater auditions. I got cast in a Follies-style revue for about ten weeks, performed in an ancient midtown hotel, which sounds seedy but was actually one of the best jobs I had as a performer.

I took an occasional temp secretarial job, those ninety-plus words per minute coming in handy, and taught exercise classes at a gym in midtown Manhattan, enabling me to pay a third of the rent on the three-bedroom apartment I shared with two guys I'd met during college. Jim McLean and I became acquainted the summer before sophomore year when we both had the misfortune of working at a German restaurant in Dallas. I was an incompetent waitress and he was an incompetent busboy. Jim and I bonded one night while cleaning up, when we discovered we were both attending University of Texas in Austin, loved music, dogs and cats and bunnies, and hated injustice. I'd always wanted a brother. He'd always wanted a sister. We'd take breaks at the Bavarian Barn restaurant and fantasize about becoming the next great Olympic ice skating pair champions. Given that neither of us had ever laced up a skate, we agreed our chances of winning (or making it around a rink once without falling) were less than slim.

Wyatt Paxton, a sensationally talented jazz musician, had been one of Jim's frat buddies at U. of T. but he and I met when he came out to play for an event at a veterans' hospital where I was volunteering as a dance teacher. He was two years ahead of Jim and me and had already been accepted to New York University's graduate music program. After Jim and I graduated and were ready to move to New York City, we got in touch with Wyatt. He had a large apartment in the city and was financially desperate and eager to have two friends share the space. Jim managed to snag a job with one of Manhattan's smaller, independent, more "investigative" newspapers and was out hunting stories half the time. Wyatt was gone playing gigs and doing research for his thesis. I was in class or auditioning. We didn't trip over each other at home. Win/win for all.

When, after an extended tour, the Emma Andersen Dance Theater returned to New York, I auditioned. I got in. I happily stayed with the company for twenty years, until financial considerations forced them to fold.

I loved Manhattan, but by 1995 the city had become so expensive I couldn't afford to stay there unless there was a major shift in employment, so I moved back to Texas, where I earned a Master's degree in dance, then taught at a community college in the Austin area. I have to admit I avoided Dallas, Lacey, her perfect husband, their two perfect children, and my parents who spent their days adoring Lacey and her two perfect children.

I performed at various theaters in town. Then I met Gerard Bradley.

Chapter 5

Gerard Bradley. Six-three to my five-ten. As blonde and blue-eyed as my sister Lacey and with the same easy ability to sashay through life convincing others he was generous, kind, and a genuinely good person. And oddly, sister Lacey actually *was* generous, kind, and a genuinely good person, albeit packaged as a financially astute beauty queen. It wasn't her fault she was perfect. Gerard and I met when he came to see the musical *Pippin,* where I was playing the role of Fastrada, Pippin's stepmother, who gets to do one of the best dances in the show, and is basically a strong, determined, sassy, seductive, super-sharp woman. Turns out, my acting was *too* spot on. I often wondered if Gerard originally credited me with being that strong, that determined, that sexy, that audacious, and that smart. And whether he viewed "wooing" me as a challenge to see if he could undo the strength, the determination, the sex appeal, and the boldness, while additionally turning my brain into a puddle of mush. A challenge which was successful, because at the end of seven years of marriage with him, I was pretty much everything Fastrada was not.

In addition to the blonde, sexy looks and charisma, Gerard shared another quality with sister Lacey, which was a phenomenal business sense. Five months after we were married, we moved to Manhattan so Gerard could partner with a former college classmate in creating a dot.com company. It was the late nineties and the boom was on. I was thrilled to be back in New York. I managed to snag a few performing jobs, both as a dancer and an actress. I taught dance at a few adult recreation centers…

I shook my head. The seven years I was married to the man were not pleasant and I had no desire to revisit them. He'd had no relevance to my life for more than fifteen years.

Fiona Belle returned and handed me another tumbler of coffee along with much-needed napkins.

I took a sip before exclaiming, "Dang! This is yummy."

"Yeah. But, finish yer rememberin' and let's move on with yer life. How's it goin'? Yer life, that is."

"Well, apart from a bad marriage I was thankfully able to get annulled, my life has been pretty durn great. Dancing with Emma Anderson's company was a gift from above. I love still being able to teach dance now. The only thing—It's a bit odd…I always felt something was missing. I have this silly notion I was meant to be with someone special. Have a love that grew in intensity forever. But, no offense, why do you care? You have your three dollars and I have a great record, so what's with the questions?"

"Because I'm aft ta be askin' ya to take a giant risk. Ya have to take a look at your life and decide what you want before ya hear the option. And ya can't do it if you ignore the past." She glared at me.

"Okay. Fine. I've got a wonderful teaching job here in Dallas and I've been happy. But, if you're determined to talk about the past and you want the truth, the best part of living in Manhattan in the nineties and the early two-thousands was becoming friends with Zelda."

"Zelda?"

"Zelda Zimmerman. Don't you love her name? She's an incredible actress, but she never really 'got her due,' possibly because she'd had to deal with a very abusive situation, blackened eyes and broken bones included, with her rotten husband Dwayne whom she married in nineteen-seventy-five and finally managed to divorce in nineteen-eighty-eight. We met at an audition for this cool Manhattan Ghost Tour cable TV show down at the old Trinity Church, not long after Gerard and I moved to the city, and became immediate best friends. We share the same sense of humor and spent the majority of our time with each other laughing." I closed my eyes. "Well, except for…"

"What? Yer not seein' a laughin' memory, are ya?"

"No. The total opposite. Horrific is the best description. Zelda and I were downtown on September eleventh, sharing a late breakfast at some diner. We were blessedly far enough away not to be in danger, but horribly close enough to see more than one person jump. We stood in the street and we saw people dying and then we saw newscasts all throughout the day showing what we'd been witness to. I'm not sure which was worse." I blinked back tears. "I will never forget and I still pray for everyone who died that day and their families and their friends."

Fiona Belle squeezed my hand. "You're not alone in yer prayers, Shiloh Meridien." We lapsed into silence for a long moment, before she sighed. "Okay. Backstory over and done with. Now, let's be aft ta speedin' it up ta today."

I eyed her with suspicion. "Which is where you come in with some wacko scheme, correct?"

She flashed a brief, mildly mischievous, grin at me. "Aye, ya nailed it."

I polished off the last of the tumbler of coffee laced with the flavored liqueur. "Boy, this is good."

"Have another." Fiona Belle shoved a second tumbler across the table. "Then you'll be ready to hear the proposition."

I drank the coffee. Very tasty. Did I mention it was both iced and laced? I determinedly pulled my focus back to Fiona Belle.

"Okay, Miz Fiona Belle Donovan without the Winthorp. I'm feeling kind of lightly toasted here and I'm happily sated with scones. In short, I am rip-roarin' ready to take in your words of wisdom and possibly heed them, although I have a gut feeling what you have to say is—again, no offense—flippin' nuts."

Fiona Belle beamed at me. "Now yer gettin' into the spirit, lass. And 'tis quite straightforward. Well, sort of. How'dja like to go back in time and get the chance to save Marcus Kennedy from dyin' young?"

Chapter 6

August 21, 2025

I was right. Fiona Belle Donovan, with or without Winthorp, was nuts. Cuckoo in a nest crazy. Certifiable. "I beg your pardon?"

"Ya heard me. Don't be pretendin' otherwise. I'm presentin' an opportunity fer ya to travel back in time to nineteen-seventy-five. About four months before Marcus Kennedy was found dead."

I stared at Ms. Donovan. "Is there more in this coffee than a bit of booze? Like, oh, some sort of audio hallucinogen? I swear you used the double-T phrase."

Fiona Belle blinked. "Now yer the one not makin' sense. What are ya sayin'? The double-T phrase?"

"Time travel. As in science fiction. A concept which spawned some dynamite books. Movies, too. None of them anywhere near the realm of reality. I have DVDs of all of them." I rose to my feet. "Okay, then. It's been lovely, but I'll be saying bye-bye now and you can give me my bag with the awesome album and the sheet music and I'll wander around the market until I make certain I'm sober enough to drive and can go home and play *Remake the Song* on the really great turntable I bought at the market last year, and cry. Thank you for letting me buy the album and sheet music for a ridiculous price and for feeding me the most awesome cranberry-orange scones I've ever tasted. Thanks for listening to bits of backstory you already knew and I'd say thanks for the laugh about the whole time-travel bit, but I'm too busy being sad about Marcus Kennedy, so mirth and merriment are not high on my list of emotions—if those are emotions, which grammatically I'm sure they're not, but I don't care."

Fiona Belle growled, "Shiloh Meridien, sit back down. You, lass, are aft to be makin' me crazy."

Her tone brooked no disobedience. I sat. "Me? What did I do?"

"Yer not payin' attention and listenin' with yer heart. Which sounds counter-intuitive but isn't. I gotta admit, it's also who ya are, lass, and it's throwin' me for a bit of a loop. Yer not typical of folks I've guided through trips in time."

I started to ask Fiona Belle about previous double-T participants or victims or whatever, but she wagged her finger at me before I got a single word out.

"Don't ya be buggin' me tryin' to find out about yer predecessors. I'm not tellin'. What I *am* tellin,' and you'd best be listenin,' are yer own special rules. Now hear me before ya go chargin' outta here to wonder in thirty years if ya shoulda taken the chance."

"Thirty? Wow. I'd be dang old. My math stinks, but we're talkin' like around a hundred. Or dead."

She didn't waste a beat. "Shiloh."

"Oh. Right. Shutting up now."

"Finally. Okay. If ya make this trip, ya got four months to keep Marcus Kennedy from dyin'."

"Four months? Jeez. I don't mean to be ornery and argumentative here but it doesn't seem like a lot of time. After all, I've never met the man and have no clue how to wangle an introduction, unless you let me make a delivery of a dozen scones to his apartment or something. Then he'd have to listen to me tell him I've come from the future to try and stop a murderer and then admit I have no clue who was the murderer, although I have some suspicions…"

She glared at me. "Stop. I'm not finished."

"Oops. Of course not. Sorry."

"The next thing is, and ya need to listen hard, is at some point, you'll be given the option as to whether to return to twenty-twenty-five. If ya stay, you'll live out your timeline from nineteen-seventy-five and yer stuck with it fer the rest of yer life. No matter what. It won't be an easy decision."

Silence. She was serious.

"Oh-kay, so going back to my original question about the double-T, without being quite so snarky as I point this out, which is redundant, but you do understand you're talking about traveling through time? Something normal people dismiss as an impossibility?"

She waved her hands in the air as if brushing my words away. "Normal is underrated. And ta be honest, impossible shouldn't be included in any dictionary."

"Hmm. Okay. I must admit, I agree. On both counts." I paused, then asked, "So, say I'm looney enough to buy this back-in-time trip concept, can you explain exactly how you do it? As in mechanics of?"

Fiona Belle grinned, showing nearly every sparkling, white tooth in her enormous mouth. Louisiana swamp gators would be envious. "I'm doin' it quite excellently and, no, darlin', I'm not providin' any details in logistics, mechanics, or working procedures. My role is to get it done. To facilitate."

I groaned. "Yeah, yeah. You're a guardian angel or witch or fairy godmother or some alien being from an undiscovered galaxy, but the main thing is you're the one in control."

She patted my hand. "Yep. Now then, let's get to it because I've got places to be and things ta do."

"I'm getting dizzy." I paused for a moment before asking, "If I'm insane enough to take this leap, which, being kind of a wimp about trying new things at age seventy, is one enormous leap, and also, I've been pretty content with life and risk hasn't been my middle name for many years… Sorry, where was I?"

"Insane."

"Right. You're not providing logistics or operational workings, but I assume there's some actual physical thing you jam me into to propel me back through time? A contraption or machine or car or something?"

"None of the above. It's aft to be bein' fairly simple." Fiona Belle pointed to the sheet music with Marcus Kennedy's signature scrawled across it, along with the date—August 21, 1975. "You sing this song and stare at this date and you'll wake up in New York City without so much as a headache. You might not remember your name for a few hours, but it'll pass fairly quickly and I'll be nearby to be sure you don't end up in too much trouble."

Which seemed to presuppose the single T as in "trouble" was part of the package; but not "too much" of it, whatever that meant to this pixie witch who doubtless thrived on "too much" drama.

"I have to close up Retro Records now," Fiona Belle stated, "and yer gonna be needin' some essentials, includin' some hints about who murdered Marcus Kennedy."

My eyes opened wide. "I'm right, then, about him being murdered?"

"Yes, darlin'. The whole suicide angle was garbage. You never bought into it and you've been right fer fifty years. Anyway, everything you need, and more, is in yer big duffel here." She shoved it at me. "And aren't ya lovin' it? Yer a fan of giant carryalls, and this sucker could hold a Saint Bernard puppy and his mama as well. Now, finish yer coffee, and I'll be back in ten minutes."

I sipped my coffee and let my imaginings lead me back to seeing myself in 1975. The idea was wacked. Absurd. Ridiculous. Foolish and foolhardy. Ludicrous. The thesaurus had a string of further words for what I might be about to do. I agreed with every one of them. Might as well add "miraculous" to the list, because this whole enterprise had supernaturally phenomenal written all over it. Yet…

I stared down at the record album in my hand. I took a very, very long look at the cover photo. Although the depictions of the singers were hazy, I had no problem distinguishing Marcus Kennedy from the other men. His deep-set green/gray eyes, the light reddish-brown curly hair worn about chin length, the style of the late sixties. His nose was a shade too big for the thin face, and he projected a smile with a warmth radiating throughout the decades. Even on this sad and eerie cover it was not the smile of a man preparing to commit suicide, regardless of any frightening diagnosis of illness.

Marcus had been murdered. Fiona Belle had confirmed it. And now I'd been presented with a bizarre opportunity to keep him from dying, although I was clueless as to exactly how to accomplish that particular task once I'd traveled through time and met the man. Bizarre? Forget bizarre. This was flat-out bonkers.

Yet...

Fiona Belle had nailed it. My choice was made. To be honest, it had been made the instant she'd thrown out the chance to go back. I had to take this risk for someone I'd never met yet always felt connected to. I would do everything I could to make certain that, this time around, Marcus Kennedy lived.

Chapter 7

August 21, 1975

My recall session from the future (a paradox if there ever was one) was over. There was no point lingering on the park bench once Fiona Belle had gone, doubtless to torment some other poor time traveler. I had to go prepare for a date with some guy in his twenties when I was still mentally feeling seventy. I slung the absurdly oversized bag over my shoulder and walked up Riverside Drive toward W. 103rd Street, where I turned away from the river and headed east down the block to what had been my apartment, beginning in June of 1975. I decided it might be wise to buy a newspaper and catch up with current events, which were long past—again, paradoxical and downright confusing—so I walked another block to hit the news stand at the corner of W. 103rd and Broadway, then backtracked to my old place.

I was relying on faith that Fiona Belle wasn't some mischievous sprite who flitted around fooling people into believing time travel was real and I'd turn the key (found in a pocket of the carryall) in the front door of the apartment and casually walk inside and not frighten some strange tenant who'd shoot me, making the whole "save Marcus Kennedy and remake what had been his song" enterprise a total wash. I silently apologized to my college English 101 teacher for creating a ridiculously long, run-on sentence, albeit (fortunately) in my head.

The apartment I shared with Jim McLean and Wyatt Paxton was kind of bizarre. Wyatt had found the place through some helpful agency at NYU and started renting in 1973. Jim and I joined him in sharing the apartment in June of '75 a few weeks after our own college graduations.

We called it The Den. (Possibly thinking "of iniquity" but no one would ever own up to the unspoken addition). A three-bedroom apartment with what was euphemistically referred to as a garden, renting in 1975 for (brace yourselves) three hundred and fifty dollars a month. Admittedly, at the time, places this far uptown were not considered ideal, but I always assumed it was the bathroom that put off (or terrified) prospective renters. It was tiny. It was black and red. Everything was either black or red, except for the mirror. The toilet, sink, and tub/shower had been painted. (Toilet in black, sink and shower in red.) Basically, the bathroom décor screamed "early horror movie." Jim, Wyatt, and I loved it. I generally put on my makeup while sitting on the floor in front of the full-length mirror in my bedroom, which got the most natural light from the barren garden, so I didn't care what the bathroom looked like. Apart from days when aches proved too much and I needed to soak in the tub, I've always been a "get in/get clean/get out" shower person, and I definitely did not ponder the ambiance of the bathroom when doing what one normally has to do first thing in the morning.

The rest of the apartment was pretty standard in color. Dull. Kind of a dingy beige, although Jim was haggling with the landlord to allow us to paint, which would have meant blues in the bedrooms and sage green everywhere else. The apartment was huge. Wyatt had been thrilled beyond measure to discover an upright piano in the living room, left there by a tenant years earlier. I was thrilled to have a living room with a space allowing for full-out practicing of dance moves. Jim was thrilled because he had the biggest bedroom of the three with enough space for a desk and typewriter as well as a king-sized bed to accommodate all six feet four inches of the man.

The key to the front door turned with the smoothness of consistent use and I stepped inside the space I hadn't seen after moving to a small studio down on W. 78th and Amsterdam in 1982. The first thing I spotted (hard to miss—it took up a full corner of the room) was Wyatt's "cave" which included his state-of-the-art stereo system, with the gigantic speakers, amplifiers, and receivers, the shelves filled with albums and sheet music, music stands, microphone, and a stack of unusable pens with dried ink. Jim had stolen one shelf for himself. It was filled with camera equipment and tons of small notebooks and a variety of pens with fresh ink.

I stared at the clutter and sighed in satisfaction and relief. For the first time since I'd landed back in 1975, I felt I was home.

I spent the next three hours reading the newspapers and catching up on the events of the week in case the recall thing went haywire tomorrow and my brain remained in 2025 mode. I put away the clothes Fiona Belle had thoughtfully provided me, stuffed the magazine clippings, along with the sheet music, back inside the giant duffel, and then took a long shower.

I surveyed the closet, wondering what to wear for this date, and found a cute skirt and top in varying shades of green. I remembered buying it at a thrift store down on West 14th Street back in July. As in July, 1975. It was quite similar to the circus-fortune-teller-slash-early-rock singer ensemble I'd found at the flea market this morning, fifty years in the future, and worn during my trip through time. It worked great with my boots and the belt. I tried not to freak out as I eyed my dual-aged self in the mirror while applying makeup, then made it to the subway stop a block away in time to meet Sandra, her boyfriend Edward, and his brother Ethan, who apparently was my blind date.

The train stalled for twenty minutes around Seventy-Sixth Street, but we still managed to arrive at Monroe Hall on W. Forty-First Street with about five minutes to spare. Sandra and Edward got the tickets in the lobby and the four of us headed inside, with Sandra and Edward leading the way.

Ethan handed our tickets to the lady standing behind the back row of seats. I bit my lower lip and tried not to laugh. It was Fiona Belle Donovan. Dressed in a cute usherette uniform, circa 1940s, that did nothing for her chubby figure: i.e. black short "tap" pants and white blouse with giant red buttons, complete with a red pillbox hat and white gloves, she glanced at the tickets, announced we were in Row Three, Seats Sixteen and Seventeen, dead-bang center, then winked at me. "Faith and Saint Bridget! 'Tis gonna be a marvelous show!"

"I'm thrilled to be able to see it," I stated. I meant it.

Fiona Belle, as usual, was right. The evening began with a short speech by City Councilman Benjamin McGuire, who provided the objective for the concert.

"We're here to raise money for the Am-Vets Center, but also to ensure its survival. Some of you may have heard about developer Roger Masters angling to buy the building and tear it down to create a residential building which will offer studio-size apartments at exorbitant rates. My office is working with the Manhattan Historical Society to get the Center declared a landmark and keep it preserved for as long as New York City remains in existence, but I'll be honest, we're facing some fierce resistance from other members of the city council. We ask—heck, we're begging—all of you to please sign the petition the ushers will have waiting for you in the lobby at the end of the concert. It should go a long way in helping certain politicians make up their minds." He waved at the audience. "But enough talk...how about a big round of applause for Mister Tommy Phillips!"

Phillips was the first of ten different performers who'd risen to, if not top celebrity status, then a decent level of prominence, for their contributions to folk and protest music during the Sixties. Each singer took the stage and entertained with a mix of old and brand-new tunes. The newer songs incorporated a lot more electric equipment than the earlier works, showing a clear move to more of a soft rock or pop sound. But the voices were still strong and sure, and I forgot I was a senior citizen hiding in a twenty-year-old body. I grooved to the music.

All the singers urged us to take a stand with the veterans and fight for a decent space in the city where they could work on healing.

There was no intermission. I was glad. As noted, I wasn't a great conversationalist with people I'd recently met, apart from short, fierce, senders of folks into time, so being able to listen to nonstop music was a relief. I was also afraid one small, seemingly insignificant topic of conversation would trip me up with my date—if I casually mentioned a future event.

Finally, around nine-forty, the last act was announced. Marcus Kennedy. He strolled onto the stage by himself, took a stance behind a microphone in the center stage, waved, then jumped right in.

"The war is pretty much over, right? It's unofficial but, Hallelujah! The troops are home. No more gut-wrenching scenes played out on the nightly news. No more protests to organize. No more drafts to avoid." Marcus paused. "Well, I hate to break it to everyone, but the war is far from over. It continues daily for too many brave soldiers who came back broken. I apologize. I should be singing, not making speeches, but this is too important to let slide. We're here tonight to try and make a difference. Too many vets deal with having lost a limb. Too many are unable to cope with life on a daily basis. Maybe they're addicted to drugs. Maybe they duck to the floor every time they hear a loud noise. In World War One, emotional trauma was called shell shock. In the second world war, it was referred to as battle fatigue. The latest trendy term is 'gross stress reaction.' But, people, it doesn't matter what you call it, these men are in a world of hurt. We're here tonight to assure them we'll do everything we can to alleviate their pain." He stopped for a long beat. "You've heard all of us talking about trying to keep the center open and out of the hands of developers like Roger Masters. But I'm asking for more. Something on a more personal level. I'm inviting everyone to drop by the midtown Am-Vets Center and say 'hi.' Stay for a few minutes and chat, or an hour or two and watch a basketball game. Please, just show them you care."

His incredible smile shimmered over the audience and my bones turned to mush. "Now then. I specifically picked this old spiritual, because I want everyone to understand that if God can save a man from a lion's den, He can bring the wounded, whether physically or emotionally, back to a place of healing." Marcus then nodded to a young black man who'd joined him onstage carrying a guitar. Marcus lifted his bandaged right hand into the air and announced he'd sprained his wrist. "Which is why I'm getting some help from the extremely talented Mister Benny Roderick, whom I thank with all my heart."

Benny offered a brief wave to the audience before he strummed the opening chords of "Didn't my Lord Deliver Daniel?"

Marcus Kennedy's voice was emotional and solid and beautiful. But I was curious. Did the bandage hide tremors from early onset Parkinson's strong enough to keep him from playing an instrument? Was he aware there was more than an injury at this point? And then my thoughts turned dark as I wondered who could possibly hate this man enough to want to see him dead less than four months from now.

The stage lights bled over the first few rows of the theater. Marcus stared straight at me as he nailed the last chorus of the song. It's trite, but I felt my pulse speed up as if I'd been dancing nonstop for the last hour or so. He continued to stare at me, even when the entire audience stood and cheered. The crowd was effusive and sincere in its adoration.

I understood and accepted the reasons why, much as I wanted it with my whole heart and soul, I wouldn't be meeting Marcus Kennedy tonight. But hearing him, seeing him onstage, made me bless Fiona Belle for giving me the chance to come back and do everything in my power to prevent his life from ending far too soon.

Chapter 8

August 21, 1975

I was trapped. Captured. Stuck in O'Somebody-or-Other's Irish pub with Sandra, Edward, and Ethan for however long they wanted to eat and drink following the show at Monroe Hall. There was no graceful way out. I mean, what could I say? *Hey, y'all, it's been a really long day, like fifty years long, and I'm suffering from a major time-travel haze and I have no idea if I'm going to turn into a slobbering amnesiac come midnight, so could we skip the drinks and the chow and go home?*

I played it as normally as I could and acted upbeat as the trio bugged me about ordering the pub's special fish 'n' chips. I good-naturedly explained I didn't eat meat, poultry, fish, or dairy. "No, I don't take cream in my coffee, and to be honest, I don't normally eat *anything* after five or six. Sandra, my friend, I have no idea how you manage to chow down and sail through without crashing to the floor in the middle of a pirouette." I shrugged. "Clearly, I'm a wimp. And guys, I really am fine with normal coffee, but what the heck, I'll give the decaf with the Irish whisky a try."

I stopped. This was my seventy-year-old self talking. For years, I'd been eating my largest meal in the early afternoon, often skipping dinner. But when I was twenty I could eat at all hours of the day or night with no problems in or out of class. I considered telling the group I was joking but decided it wasn't worth it.

Both Edward and Ethan shifted from discussing my oddities in cuisine preferences to the variety of financial problems New York City was currently facing and any and all possible solutions. My sister Lacey would have loved the discussion but it went over my head, so I sat, sipped coffee, and nodded when it seemed appropriate.

Sandra realized I was zoning out and nudged the boys to quit with the talk of monetary bail-outs. "Shiloh? Did you like the concert?"

I perked up. "I loved it. I mean, I'm furious about this jerk Masters who wants to demolish the center, but the concert was fantastic. The music was inspiring, and the whole idea of helping veterans with PTSD is awesome."

Silence.

Ethan stared at me. "PT-what?"

"PTSD. Post-traumatic stress disorder?"

"Sorry. I'm lost. My residency is in pediatrics, not psychiatry," Ethan replied. "I've never heard of PTSD. What the heck is it?"

Ouch. I'd stepped deep into time-travel doo-doo. I needed to do some fancy tap dancing to stop anyone from asking questions I couldn't answer. "It's what Marcus Kennedy was saying, but he referred to it as 'gross stress reaction.'" I paused before adding, "I'm wondering if this is one of those New-York-versus-Texas phrase differences? Because, I, uh, volunteered one summer during college at a veterans' hospital" (True) "and the doctors said the kids in the mental wards were suffering from what used to be called battle fatigue but now was being called post-traumatic stress disorder." (Not true. I had no idea what the term was in the early seventies, but in 2025 it was called PTSD, although the politically correct phrase some folks had started using was PTSI, meaning Post-Traumatic Stress Injury.) "Apparently, it refers to stress in combat, but also can include tragic occurrences in a person's life."

Three heads nodded sagely. Sandra asked, "What did you do at the hospital?"

"I led the vets through kind of a mix of dance and drama. Silly improvisational stuff across the floor like pretending to walk through peanut butter, or avoid broken glass, or swim through marshmallows. Tons of simple dance movements with a lot of arms. It was quite an experience and one of the best things I've done in my life."

"Sounds interesting," she said.

"It was. Actually, after hearing what Kennedy said, I'm considering asking at the center if they might like to have me do the same kind of program here. I'd imagine it'd be more helpful than merely popping in for coffee or to watch a basketball game."

"I'll bet they'd love it." Ethan said, sounding sincere. He paused, then said, "Maybe I shouldn't bring this up, but there's another big concern involving veterans no one outside of the medical profession seems to have heard about. Doctors are seeing more and more instances of really serious illnesses, like cancer or heart problems normally associated with much older people, or a variety of motor disabilities, cropping up in guys who served in Vietnam. Rumor has it the military was using some kind of very deadly herbicide to kill off crops and no one realized the damage it could cause to humans." He grimaced. "Or worse, they knew and didn't care. After all, it interfered with any strategies to win the war."

Again, my seventy-year-old self kicked in. I knew exactly what he was talking about. Agent Orange. But there'd been hardly any mention of Agent Orange until the nineteen-eighties. Then I recalled reading something, maybe on cover liner notes? About Marcus Kennedy having sung for the troops over in Vietnam. Could he have been exposed to the herbicide? Could it be the cause of what might be Parkinson's? I needed to make a note before midnight when this type of information would vanish from my brain.

Sandra and I both winced. Sandra exclaimed, "How horrible! Those poor soldiers."

Ethan nodded, then stated, "Sadly, there's not enough proof yet to determine whether this stuff was as lethal as suspected. And the military isn't talking. Stay tuned, folks."

I shook my head. "Wow. Add this to Roger Masters actively trying to destroy the Am-Vets Center without a mention of an alternative if he gets his way. Like these poor guys don't have enough to deal with?"

Three voices chimed in with, "Agreed. It stinks."

Sandra decided to change the subject by asking Ethan if he was going to leave Ohio and join his brother in Manhattan once he'd finished his medical residency.

"No way," he responded.

"Why not?" I asked.

"Too dangerous. I almost didn't come here when I ran into some friends back home who'd visited New York over Thanksgiving last year and got mugged." He winked at me. "Then again, the girls in Ohio aren't nearly as pretty as Manhattan dancers. I might have to reconsider."

I blushed as inwardly I thought, *Honey, I'm old enough to be your grandmother. Well, at least for the next ten minutes or so.*

Sandra chuckled. "Tourists. Muggers can spot 'em a mile away. Those of us who actually live here generally have no problem."

I added, "You have to get the New York City vibe going. It's easy, although, since I'm generally not the brazen type, it took me a good month to really get it down. But you basically need to look arrogant and like you'll plow through anybody who tries to interfere with you before you get where you're going. Keep an expression of total determination on your face at all times. Plus, whatever you do, never stare up at tall buildings with your mouth open. Huge tourist tell."

Edward nodded. "She's right."

Sandra stated truthfully, but with more than a trace of humor, "It also doesn't hurt if you're a dancer who carries around a beat-up old bag with a pair of pink tights hanging out the top. Muggers have been told from the time they were toddlers all they'll get out of us is a card for ten dance classes at our favorite studio and if they're really lucky, a couple of subway tokens."

We all laughed, then Ethan asked, "But you're talking about mugging for money. I've been reading how dangerous it is to be on the streets after dark with people being knifed or shot over drug deals going down. And then, although this has nothing to do with muggers but more the overall violence in the city, anyway, I saw on the news the story about some poor black kid who was killed by police last week, apparently over nothing more than being in the wrong neighborhood."

"I'll bet Black Lives Matter will be all over that soon," I said.

Three blank faces. I'd done it again. I had no idea when the Black Lives Matter had taken the name for the movement, but I was quite positive the year hadn't been 1975.

Edward was first to voice his confusion. "What on earth are you talking about?"

"Black Lives Matter." I stopped. "Oops. Sorry. Did it again. I swear Texas is like an entirely different other country with its own language. Anyway, it's a civil rights group. Well, really, more what I'd call a movement. They've been protesting things like police shootings, mainly of young men, some no older than their teens, who are unarmed and pretty much killed for being black."

Sandra grimaced. "It's so sick and sad this kind of stuff is still happening. After all, it's not the sixties anymore. I thought everyone had moved past the stupid racial hate. Unbelievable. Was this kid in Brooklyn last week unarmed?"

Edward shook his head. "Honestly? I haven't seen anything one way or another mentioning guns or knives…or lack of guns or knives." He added, "I was surprised the singers tonight didn't bring up his death. Several of them were involved with protests around the city last week. Then again, if they'd talked about all the different injustices going on in the world, we'd've had a marathon instead of a one-night concert."

I needed to take notes on the shooting as well as memos about Agent Orange and real estate moguls. If singers during this time were protesting police corruption, especially where it concerned racism, and

Marcus Kennedy had been one of those protesting, he might have uncovered facts regarding things certain politicians didn't want to hear, which, in turn, might have led to his murder.

I glanced up at the antique clock behind the bar. It was now five minutes to twelve. Nearly doomsday in terms of my 2025 senior citizen's memory. Thankfully, if Fiona Belle had been telling the truth, my physical appearance would stay the same, so no one would suddenly point at me and begin shrieking, "She's youthening! She's youthening!"

I reached into my bag and found a pen and a small notebook, pulled them out and quickly jotted down some phrases, hoping I'd be able to make sense of what I was trying to tell myself when I read them later.

A huge grandfather clock standing in the corner close to our booth began to chime. Midnight. I prayed the fairy tale wouldn't turn into a nightmare as I deliberately dropped my pen, slid out of my chair, and began searching for it under the table, making certain I wouldn't find it and emerge from my hiding place until the clock finished announcing the time.

I could hear the faint echo of a grandfather clock chiming. Then silence. There was a flicker of something. A vision of myself as a much older woman? Then my world went blank for a long moment.

Strange. I blinked and realized I was under a table, staring at the floor which was in need of some serious cleaning. I spotted a pen rolling around and assumed I'd tried to retrieve it which was why I wasn't sitting on a chair. I scrambled back up and slid into the empty space next to a girl and two men, none of whom I recognized. Panic was setting in. I did not have a clue who I was with and I couldn't remember my own name. One of the guys stared at me. "Shiloh? Are you okay? You look like you're about to faint."

Shiloh. Interesting. Must be me. I managed to breathe again. "I'm okay. I hit my head under the table searching for my pen. Feeling a bit dizzy but I'm okay. No concussion or anything." Sounded plausible.

An absurdly short, plump woman, age somewhere between fifty and a hundred, dressed like a Christmas elf in a green jacket, red tights, a red cap topped with a fuzzy white ball, and green slippers curling at the toes, appeared at our table bearing a basket. She plopped it in front of us and announced in a strong Irish accent, "'Tis cranberry-orange scones I'm aft ta be givin' ya. On the house. I'm Fiona Belle Donovan, fillin' in fer Patrick, who had ta leave ta make it to the airport fer a flight ta Dublin tonight."

The girl sitting beside me was staring at the substitute waitress. "You look familiar. I swear someone who could be you or your twin was ushering at Monroe Hall earlier for the concert. And, no offense and I'm probably rude for asking, but why are you dressed for Christmas when it's August?"

"Ta answer yer first question, aye, lass, I was there. At the concert. I get around. Wearin' many hats, as it were. As ta Christmas? Darlin', there's never a bad time a year ta be festive. Now, enjoy the scones, everyone." She winked at me. "Shiloh, lass, you can dive right in with nary a qualm. No butter, no dairy, no eggs."

Click. Fiona Belle. Last name Donovan. Yet I was sure there was a Winthorp somewhere in the name and she didn't use it because she "despised that man." I'd seen her before. First, at the concert I finally remembered attending a bit less than two hours ago. And perhaps back in Texas, not too long ago? I had this vague, quick image in my head of Fiona Belle selling me a record album at a flea market just outside Dallas. Then it vanished.

I glanced down at the notebook in my hand. I'd written nonsensical words and phrases, yet I kept equating them with the folk singer Marcus Kennedy. Something to figure out later. *Agent Orange? Police corruption*? *Drug deals? Roger Masters and Am-Vets Center*? *Early version of Black Lives Matter*? And a truly scary word…*Murder*?

Seeing the notes brought back my recall of the last few hours, including going to the concert with Sandra, Edward, and Ethan, then discussing some fairly heavy topics here at the pub. But there were gaps and lapses I wasn't sure would ever be filled.

So I sat and ate my vegan scones and drank my coffee with a large dollop of Irish whisky added instead of cream, and made polite conversation and wondered why, even though I'd been living in Manhattan since June, it felt as though I'd arrived just this afternoon.

Chapter 9

August 28, 1975

The daily activity diary I'd found in my bag, the night I came home from the "Benefit Vets" concert at Monroe Hall, lay open to August 28th. A note, written in purple ink, in handwriting I didn't recognize, encouraged, or rather, commanded, me to attend the audition for a Hoboken, New Jersey dinner theater production of *Dames at Sea* being held at the Thirty-Ninth Street Studios at ten a.m. What the heck. Emma Andersen's Dance Theater was on tour in Europe for at least another month, so I might as well try out for other things. If nothing else, it would help me get accustomed to auditioning in a city filled with dancers whose backgrounds were probably a lot better than mine. As for the daily diary book? Well, a little mystery (as in the where, how, and why I'd gotten the durn thing) was good, right? Or not.

I hauled it out of the subway, made it to the corner of Thirty-Ninth and Eighth Avenue at exactly nine a.m. and spotted the eccentric lady who ran a mobile food and souvenirs cart. I'd first seen her when she'd ushered my date and me to our seats at Monroe Hall for the "Benefit Vets" concert a week ago, and soon after at O'Callahan's Pub, where, attired as a Christmas elf, she'd gifted our table with a basket of fabulous cranberry-orange scones and introduced herself as Fiona Belle Donovan.

I took in the full effect of today's outlandish outfit, thoroughly amused. Four days earlier I'd seen her manning her cart, decked out in an ensemble doubtless left over from last year's (well, some year's) Halloween party—the long-established and stereotypical fairy-tale witch's garb, including a peaked hat almost as tall as she was. The second time I'd seen her with the cart, two days ago, the petite vendor appeared to be ready to do some fancy stepping for a Russian Army ballet company, dressed in a brown jacket with gold buttons, dark tan poofy trousers, knee high brown boots, and what I supposed was the traditional military headgear.

Today, Fiona Belle Donovan was attired in a commedia dell'arte Harlequin clown costume and contrasting fuzzy pink bunny slippers. The clown suit did nothing for her plump figure, but she wore it with enthusiasm.

I hadn't yet bought any of the touristy trendy globes of the Chrysler Building, Empire State Building, or the Statue of Liberty she had available, but I did purchase a great black T-shirt depicting a dozen or so court jesters, in a variety of colors, cavorting above the words, *Dance, Fool, Dance!* I was wearing it today.

I waved at her and pointed at my shirt. She yelled, "Looks good on ya, Shiloh! Have fun at the audition, lass." I wasn't sure how she knew my name, but then, scenes and conversations from the night at the pub with Sandra and the two "E's" were still hazy. I assumed somewhere between the boozy coffee I'd been persuaded to imbibe and the best scones I've ever tasted, introductions had been forthcoming.

There was a line outside the building, but those of

us auditioning still made it inside within about ten minutes, leaving me with plenty of time to sign in and warm up. The audition notice in both trade papers specified tap would make up the initial round. I found a spot in a hall near some windows and stretched and jumped up and down and stretched again, then donned my tap shoes with the two-inch heels.

Two hours later, I was back in the hall, lying on the floor, resting up. Callbacks were to be announced by twelve-thirty. I was going over the routine we'd learned in my head, in case I got called back, and softly intoning some vocal warm-ups when I became distracted by the sound of a tap shoe hitting the wall about twelve feet away from me. I glanced over at a cute, short, sandy-blonde-haired girl, who exuded an energetic pixie vibe, and who was clearly frustrated. She was taking out her irritation on the innocent wall, using her shoe as a lethal weapon. I was hit with an odd, but very fun, bout of *déjà vu*. A glimpse of this girl reciting lines with me inside the old Trinity Church downtown while a camera rolled nearby. I say odd because we both appeared to be older by at least twenty years.

I shook off the vision, rose, and joined her, although I generally don't approach others at auditions. But she seemed distressed and I also couldn't shake the strong feeling we were meant to be friends. I asked, "Sorry to bother you, and tell me to go away if I'm being nosy, but why do you seem less than enthused about the next phase of the tap audition? As in panicked. Do you need some help?"

She sighed. "That obvious?"

"Well, you do look a bit, uh, perturbed, and the wall is definitely now worse for wear."

"Heck, maybe if enough paint gets chipped off they'd give it a redo. I'm also an artist, and I'm tellin' ya, this gray is depressing and does not appear on any color wheel I've ever seen." She looked up at me. "Are you serious about helping? Tap is not my strong suit and Mister Maniacal Choreographer was throwing in steps I've never seen before. I'm not sure I'll get a callback after singing, but if so, I'd like to *not* end up falling on my behind in total humiliation."

"Maniacal about covers his whole persona. I'd bet money he was improvising the entire time. Did you notice he never used any terminology?"

"Aha! Should have been the first clue there was something off."

"Listen, I started tapping when I was three, so I've got this. I'll show you what he taught this morning. And, big bonus, I'll give you a future tip for impressing choreographers at almost any dance audition for musical theater."

"Ooh! I'll take it," she replied. "What's the tip?"

"Well, it's ridiculously easy. When in doubt about what your feet are doing, smile big and wave your arms a lot. Mind, I repeat, use the smile and waving arms strictly for musical theater and tap. This does not work for modern or ballet companies and they will toss you out the nearest window if you try it."

She and I spent the next twenty minutes going over the routine the choreographer had shown us when we first arrived at the Thirty-Ninth Street Studios this morning. Finally, she called a halt.

"I'm starving. If I'm going to live through the rest of this afternoon, I need sustenance." She plopped down on the floor, grabbed her bag, pulled out a ham and cheese hoagie along with a bag of potato chips, then glanced over at me and appeared stricken. "Oh, pooh. I've only got one sandwich. I'm sorry. You deserve something for helping me with one amazing tutorial. Bless you. You're one whale of a great teacher. Want half?"

"Thanks. But no need. I came prepared with apples, bananas, and a raw vegan burrito." I reached into my own bag for my lunch as she stared at me.

"What's vegan?"

"Vegetarian on acid." I said.

She raised an eyebrow. "What? I've heard of vegetarian, of course, but not vegan. Where'd you come up with the term?"

I thought for a second. "I'm not sure. I heard someone say it, but couldn't tell you when or where or who. But I looked it up after I heard it and got the full scoop."

She nodded. "Now I'm intrigued. What's the scoop? And what's the difference between vegetarian and vegan?"

"Okay. Scoop and difference. The term 'vegan' was first used in nineteen-forty-four by an animal rights activist in England to refer to vegetarians who take things a step further by not eating dairy or fish or any being who once had a face."

"I like it. Both the concept and the word. How long have you been vegan and what caused the change?"

"I don't really remember exactly when I changed my eating," I told her. "But I did some research online and the instant I discovered how badly animals are treated and how awful meat and dairy is for humans, well, it was bye-bye to burgers and ice cream forever."

"Say again? Research online? What's that?"

I paused and tried to recall where I'd heard the odd phrase. "Actually, I have no idea. I'm fairly certain some scientist somewhere said it. I must have mixed it in with my research for the last paper I did at University of Texas on dance and health. It was about two weeks before I graduated, which means my brains were scrambled more than the eggs I don't eat anymore."

I tried to cover my own growing confusion. "Anyway, the burrito you see before you is kind of a slaw mix of cabbage, peppers, carrots, and zucchini, with some vinegar and ginger thrown in. The vinegar helps keep it together and the ginger makes it mildly spicy. All neatly wrapped in a corn tortilla. I hate to cook, but this is easy, thanks to a musical roommate who likes to release tension by chopping veggies. Wanna bite?"

"Sure."

I tore off a piece and handed it to her on a large napkin I'd wisely stuffed into the bag holding my lunch.

She chewed. "Oh, wow! Awesome. I'm making these as soon as get home. Well, after I hit the grocery store for the ingredients. Unlike you, I'm a very enthusiastic and dang excellent chef, if I do say so myself, but I really should be making healthier dishes. And I do love the idea of saving animals from harm."

I nodded. We ate in a comfortable silence. When we finished, she beamed at me. "I am happy and sated. Thanks again for the help with the tap and the bite of burrito. I promise I'll repay you by having you over and cooking something wonderfully vegan. I'm a wiz at changing up recipes. By the way, what's your name?"

"Shiloh Meridien. You?"

Pause.

"Zelda Zimmerman."

Pause.

We stared at each other, trying not to laugh. We failed.

Finally, I was able to speak. "Oh-kay. Don't tell me…you're named after the wife of a certain superbly talented literary figure, possibly most noted for his works of the nineteen-twenties, although one or two movies snuck in later."

"Nope. Ready for this? My eccentric, film-mad aunt persuaded my mother to name me after the flamboyant flapper girl in the movie *Singin' in the Rain*, which coincidentally came out the week I was born. I gather Mom didn't care. She was exhausted and wanted to rest. I'm never going to hit five feet tall, but word has it I was a very big baby." She took a breath. "Oh-kay. Don't tell me…you're named after the famous battle noted for crushing the Confederate Army."

"Nope."

We both giggled again before I responded with, "You're close, though. I ended up with Shiloh in honor of a grandmother who lived in that town her whole life."

We solemnly shook hands.

"Great to meet you, Shiloh Meridien. I love it. It's very theatrical. Got a cool, sexy, soap opera villainess vibe."

"And you, Zelda Zimmerman. Love both meeting you and the theatricality of your name."

"I hate to ask, but in your opinion is the ZZ alliteration a bit much? It *is* my real name but—"

I interrupted with, "It's perfect. Peppy. Cute. Agents and audiences will remember it. And any edge in this wacky business helps. I say keep it."

"I agree. But my fiancé, who, to be honest, isn't keen on me wanting to be an actress, keeps saying it's 'over the top.' Then he reminds me we're getting married this coming spring and I'll be Mrs. Dwayne Bunyan." She shrugged her shoulders. "I guess Zelda Bunyan isn't a bad name. Although, to me it seems to lack an exotic, dramatic, theatrical zip."

Whatever response I would have given was interrupted when the stage manager arrived in the hall.

My new friend with the two ZZs received a call back. So did I.

Zelda and I made it through the next cuts of dance, singing, and reading some lines from the script. The director, choreographer, and various extras at the casting table called it quits at seven-forty-five p.m. It had been a very long day. But non-union theaters, especially those from out of town who are casting for dinner theater or summer stock, often cram auditions into one day so they don't have to pay rent on studio space for extra time.

According to the stage manager, phone calls would be made by the end of the week, at the latest, to those who were cast. He added that some folks might receive calls tonight. *Dames at Sea* has seven characters, four of whom are male and three of those paired up with the women, and every male I'd seen today was at least three inches shorter than my five feet ten inches. Needless to say, I wasn't terribly optimistic for my chances. But I didn't care. I'd be auditioning for Emma Andersen's dance company sometime in November or December (which was what I really wanted, plus I felt certain my chances were better, career-wise, in aiming for an all-dance company rather than musical theater, as my singing was pleasant but nothing special) but, more importantly, I'd made a good friend today. I somehow knew we'd be friends all our lives.

Zelda echoed my thoughts as we tossed out bags over our shoulders and headed out onto Eighth Avenue. "I have to confess, I'd love to be able to play Ruby. But if I don't get cast, it's fine because this has been the best day I've had since I moved to New York two years ago. I actually had a blast with this audition. All thanks to you."

"Me too."

She glanced at her watch. "Oh, nuts. I told Dwayne I'd meet him at Bennie's Diner at eight. It's about twelve blocks from here. I'm already late. I'd ask you to join us—they have huge salads, so you wouldn't starve—but he'll be in a snit about having to eat so late, and Dwayne's not pleasant when things don't go his way, and—"

I stopped her. "Not a problem. I'm ready to head home and soak in a tub for about an hour. Look, what about meeting up tomorrow at Broadway West Studios? There's a ten o'clock killer tap class, and if you get cast as Ruby, which by the way, you totally deserve, you're gonna need it."

We exchanged a quick hug. She said, "Great! See you in the morning."

I watched her walk west toward the diner as a round of *déjà vu* hit me. This one wasn't fun like the Trinity Church vision I'd had when I first saw Zelda bashing her shoe against the wall. In fact, it was plain nasty. It was nothing more than a wisp, but I could see Zelda Zimmerman, sporting a black eye, sobbing as the sound of an angry male voice filled the air around her. Then the vision was gone, leaving me unsettled and disturbed.

Chapter 10

August 1975

"You weren't kidding, were you."

It was less a question than a statement of fact. "About class?" I asked.

Zelda nodded. "Yep. I swear, five minutes into Bucky Turner's Advanced Tap made yesterday's frenzied, crazy audition sequence feel like a routine from the pre-beginner tots class at Miss Tessa's Twinkle Toes Studios."

I chuckled. "Is there really such a place?"

"Oh, yeah. Smack dab in the middle of a prairie town no one's ever heard of in southern Illinois. Don't ask. But I'm tellin' ya, I'll now be able to nail any combination thrown at me in *Dames at Sea."* Zelda suddenly appeared stricken. "Oh, my gosh, Shiloh, I'm so sorry. Here I am going on and on rambling about the choreographer and the show. I'm in, but you didn't get cast, which is a total miscarriage of any theatrical justice. Shoot, I only got the part because you were kind enough to teach me steps I wasn't able to figure out on my own."

"Not true. I heard you when you were reading with…what's-his-name? Jake?"

"Yeah. Jake Reynolds. Wasn't he great? He called me this morning to tell me he was really excited we'd be working together and wanted to meet before the first rehearsal and maybe go through the script. Which I thought was a sweet thing to do. And it was nice of the casting folks for *Dames* to give him my name and number."

I nodded. "Jake. Right. He was great. And cute. Y'all are the perfect match for Ruby and Dick. I could immediately envision you singing duets and making an audience fall in love with you both. As for me? Do not worry about this. If I'm being honest, I knew the minute I walked into the room for the readings I didn't stand a chance. Did you see the males who'd been called back? Not a one over five-six. I could feel the director staring at me, then at my two-inch heeled shoes, and then inwardly groaning. I'm fine. I am. It's kind of strange, but I have this sense the whole reason I was at the audition wasn't to do dinner theater in Hoboken, New Jersey but to meet you. I mean, this may sound silly, but you're the first person I've ever met I immediately felt a bond with. Definitely here in the city, but, to be honest, in my entire life."

"Not silly at all. Try living in Manhattan for two years feeling pretty much alone, and all of a sudden in walks someone and next thing you're chatting and absolutely confident you can say anything and won't be judged. It may sound sappy or maybe too serious, but if a friendship doesn't start with trust, I'd say it was doomed to dissolve."

"We're already BFFs." I blinked. I knew what the initials stood for but not where I'd heard them.

"BFFs? What's that?"

"Best friends forever. Also referred to as besties."

"Cool. I like it. So, best friend forever and bestie, changing the subject, whatcha gonna order?"

"Spaghetti with plain marinara sauce and a salad with vinegar and oil on the side. I've had it here before. The cook prides himself on only using fresh tomatoes."

"I'll have the same. And a lot of garlic bread. I'm not yet in your league of veganism, if that's a word, so forgive me and don't hate me, but I'm smearing butter all over mine."

The next two hours flew by as we exchanged life stories and talked about our dreams for performing careers and the possibility of one day finding someone to share our lives with. Zelda admitted she had doubts Dwayne was really her Mister Right, but she couldn't yet see a way around getting married. They'd been engaged for three years and both families were thrilled and would be livid if the marriage didn't come off sometime next spring.

I dipped a piece of bread into the tiny bowl of olive oil the waiter had provided along with my vinegar. "Can I share something with you? I have to warn you, it's sort of weird."

"Sure. I'm open. Unless it's kinky or immoral, weird generally makes for a more interesting life. What's up?"

"Well, I haven't quite grasped the whys or hows of what I'm about to tell you, which is the reason I say 'weird' but…" I inhaled. "Diving in now."

Zelda's eyebrows both raised. "Care to elaborate? Maybe it's the glass of wine I'm downing with this meal, but I'm already confused."

I sighed. "Join the club. Okay. It's been a mix of strangeness and a kind of eerie thing happening, all starting about a week ago. To begin with, I keep getting these sort of *déjà vu* flashes, and popping up with words or phrases I swear I've heard, but no one else has, and everyone is clueless as to what they mean, and they stare at me as if I'd announced I was the missing link or something. And I include myself among the totally puzzled when the words or phrases come bouncing out of my mouth as if I'd been saying them every day."

"Could it be explained by the differences in Texas slang as compared to New York?"

"Ah. Logical. Sensible. Rational. Sane. The problem is I've used strange words or phrases when talking to Jim and Wyatt, my very Texan roommates, who then ask me what in blazes I'm nattering on about. I did it tonight, a few minutes ago, here with you when I threw out the terms 'BFFs' and 'besties.' I did it when I met you at the audition and popped out with 'vegan.' And 'online research' too." None of those things has to do with Texas. And, Zelda, that's not all. It goes from strange to dead-bang bonkers."

"In what way?"

"I've known, or maybe I should say I've had a sense, about things happening before they actually did. Visions, but nothing more than a glimpse."

Zelda took a sip of her wine before stating, "People do get psychic images and premonitions. It's not totally unheard of. You're not crazy. E.S.P. is a real thing. As for your odd use of words and visions, which we can call *psychic-isms* although I'm not sure I'd want to come out with the term if I was schnockered. But, let's shelve the *déjà vu*…ooh! let's change it from *psychic-isms* to *déjà-vu-isms*…much easier to say, but for the time being, let's scrap them along with any possible clairvoyance stuff for now. You said there's more? What else is going on?"

"Well, how about me wondering if I've acquired a poltergeist?"

"Could be entertaining, although I'm not sure I'd want one as roommate."

We both grinned, then Zelda continued, "Back to the poltergeist. What happened?"

"August twenty-first, I discovered a huge bag in my closet. One I'd never seen before. I'd been to a concert and then a pub, and this big old duffel was there when I came back. I have no clue where it came from. I've lived in this apartment since June, and I would have noticed it if the tenant before us left it behind. Plus, there were clothes inside and they were all my size. There was also a very, um, eclectic, mix of things."

"Okay. This is getting spooky. Intriguing though. What did you find?"

"Well, some of the stuff wasn't really weird in terms of what they were, but in how they got there. Hang on. That made zero sense. I'll try and get to this logically. Back to the clothes. Nothing unusual, a few pairs of jeans, some T-shirts, and dance gear. As noted, my size. Finally, there was this really knock-out sexy black dance dress, as in 'going out to a club dancing' and not a rehearsal skirt. I do not recall buying any of these things. I do not recall trying them on. Or stealing them."

Zelda waved her hand at me in cheerful dismissal. "I wasn't going to suggest you had, but I'm relieved to hear my new bestie BFF isn't a thief. Go on. What else?"

"Next up on the 'How did this get here?' train was a daily diary. To be honest, reading a note in it for August Twenty-Eighth was how I ended up at the audition for *Dames at Sea* and got to meet you. But it was the only entry written in the durn thing. Anyway, moving on— and, you nailed it, this is spooky—there were two pieces of sheet music in the bag, one with some handwriting on it."

"What did it say?" Zelda asked. "And what was the song?""

" 'The Yellow Rose of Texas.' Not exactly a piece I'd use for an audition unless it was for some kind of throwback singing cowboy movie. The copyright was dated August…wait for it…twenty-twenty-five. Honest. Whoever the printer was must have been on some serious drugs, or blind. The note said something about 'for December' and choosing to 'go back.' Written in purple ink. Made no sense at all."

"Well, you have now veered from spooky right into mind-blowing and super scary. 'Go back?' What was the other sheet music? Not 'Yellow Rose 'with the bizarre date. The one without the note."

"An arrangement of 'Didn't My Lord Deliver Daniel?' by Marcus Kennedy, dated August twenty-first of this year. There are handwritten notations throughout the music, and I assume they're his. I mean, this sucker was not bought at Midtown Records."

"You've got to be kidding."

"I am totally serious. Wait. There's more. Clippings from magazines I've never seen before, with crucial info scratched out, like ads and dates and the names of the publications. Scratches all in purple ink, like the December note. But I do mean clippings. There's not a full story in the bunch. There was one about a cop who should have faced charges for shooting an unarmed black former Marine named Jeremiah Henry. No name for the cop. And there was a story about Roger Masters, the same Manhattan developer who keeps tearing down landmark buildings and putting up luxury hotels and high-rise apartments. He's the guy who wants to destroy the Am-Vets Center, according to all the singers at the concert I went to. Then there was a tiny piece in a newsletter claiming some herbicide used in Vietnam was harming veterans. Interesting because the blind date I had for the Benefit Vets concert mentioned a lethal pesticide. I don't remember much of what he said. Conversations at the pub were a bit of a blur. The creepiest article was about various singers who died when they were all twenty-seven and how it's like a cult or club or something. Again, no clue as to dates or who wrote it or anything. Finally, not spooky or creepy or scary, but interesting, I found a paragraph cut from a magazine called *Vegan Health News.*"

"What's it about?"

"Health."

Zelda chuckled. "Well, at least it's consistent with the name of the magazine. Come on, bet you can be more specific."

I shook my head. "It really was short, with tons of material scratched out, so I didn't want to do much more than skim it. Seemed to be about how following a totally raw vegan diet could help ward off various diseases, including cancer, diabetes, heart ailments, and a variety of motor disabilities. I tried to track down the magazine to see if I could find the entire article, but the vendors I've talked to at the places where I buy newspapers had never heard of *Vegan Health News.*"

"Sounds like someone managed to sneak into your place while you were out and left you all this deliberately just to make you crazy." Zelda's eyebrows lifted. "Or maybe you've got a full-on ghost with an interest in music, politics, and medicine."

"Oh, lovely. I'm being haunted by a maniacal

shopping spook with access to nonexistent magazines but great taste in clothes and music," I said, but couldn't help chuckling. Then I sobered up again. "Back to the weirdness of visions. I've been dealing with some pretty freaky mind stuff. Mental images. Premonitions. Odd flashes."

"Ah, gee. Here I was getting comfy with *déjà vu* and mischievous otherworldly spirits. What else? There's something big, isn't there? Something truly important?"

I took a deep breath before flatly stating, "I have this intense, very real, totally stamped into my brain and my heart, feeling that I'm supposed to meet Marcus Kennedy and somehow keep him from dying. Within the next four months."

Chapter 11

August 1975

Zelda's bread dropped onto her plate as she stared at me. "I'm about to be speechless. But before I go into full radio silence, do you have any idea why it's specifically Marcus Kennedy you're supposed to save? Wait. The sheet music was his. Could that be why you're focused on him? And are you certain he's the one in need of saving?"

"I am. Zelda, it's nuts, but when I was twelve I heard 'Chasm of Darkness' and I fell in love with the man and his music. I was never one of those teenage girls who shrieked and tore their hair and wrote fan letters professing their undying devotion to British pop stars, so this was very unlike me. I felt an honest connection to Marcus Kennedy. Unexplainable. And now I have this 'save from dying' mantra pounding in my mind and I don't understand why, except I'm sure it's true. Of course, I'm not sure how all this is going to come about. Forget saving, what about even meeting him? I did see him at the Benefit Vets concert August twenty-first and could swear he noticed me. Anyway, that was, coincidentally—or not—the same night I got home and discovered the bag with all the weird stuff including his arrangement of the same song he sang at said concert." I paused and thought back. "There was one other odd thing

I found. Not in the big duffel, but in the normal bag I carried with me to the concert."

"Go on."

"I'd jotted down some notes when I was at a pub with my friend Sandra and our dates after the show. Marcus Kennedy's name. Words and phrases, including police, political corruption, murder, Black Lives Matter, and, like I told you, lethal herbicide."

"Wait. Back it up a second. Black Lives Matter? I'm not familiar with the term. Is it another of those odd phrases no one else has heard but you?"

"Yeah. The note is in my handwriting. I'm clueless, although it's an amazing, stirring phrase and it seems pretty obvious what it's supposed to convey. Somehow, it sounds a lot more meaningful and powerful than 'civil rights movement.' "

Zelda nodded. "It is. You're bound to have heard it somewhere and clicked on it in your head as being important. Then again, why include a phrase about a movement designed to end racial inequality in your notes about Marcus Kennedy?"

"Going with Shakespeare, 'Aye, there's the rub.' My one thought was if I did find a way to meet him— Marcus, that is, 'cause I'd say meeting the Bard is a nonstarter anyway—I could suggest he write about some of these ideas in his songs. But Marcus has already touched on police corruption more than once. He's definitely sung about the evils of racism, but maybe 'Black Lives Matter' struck me as a phrase he could use for a lyric in the future?"

"Sounds reasonable."

I shook my head. "To you and me maybe. Not sure a psychiatrist would agree. Another thing. I've been trying to wrap my head around is why I'm sure what I jotted down about December is about Marcus Kennedy. Does any of this make any sense?" I rushed on before letting Zelda answer. "And how exactly am I supposed to keep him from dying? Assuming I find a way to meet him. I am so confused. And I'm also sorry, because I'm totally monopolizing the conversation. I'm never, ever, this talkative."

Zelda didn't laugh. She grew quiet and thought and waved me into silence when I was about to backtrack and expound on the *déjà vu* and supernatural events. "Breathe. Have another sip of wine."

I did both.

"First, cut the apologies. It's obvious you're going through some kind of major crisis and you need to vent and none of this is trivial garbage, and we are, as you pointed out, besties, and neither of us should ever feel obligated to stay quiet about anything! Moving on. I am stymied and bewildered as to why you're getting flashes and strange feelings and *déjà-vu-isms* and how a bag shows up in your apartment from nowhere, but if I can drag Shakespeare back into the conversation, well, I hold his 'more things in heaven and earth' philosophy in high regard, so I say, quit worrying about the details of 'how' or 'why' and go with the feelings and see where they take you. Maybe Marcus Kennedy has a guardian angel somewhere who's decided the pair of you need to be together and is pounding the thought into your head so you won't run away if you ever do get the chance to meet him and somehow, oh, push him out of the way of a speeding taxi? Maybe the angel figured out a way to sneak into your apartment and leave you a few hints? Eventually one or more will make sense?" She paused, seeming to consider something, then stated, "After all, the diary entry did lead you to the audition where two incredible things happened. We met, and you helped me with my tapping skills, which I am convinced got me cast as Ruby."

"Well, you've just laid out a pretty bizarre theory, but it's neat you've come up with a reason for what we're *not* calling *psychic-isms* because I'm not sure the word exists and if it does, it's extremely hard to pronounce after a large glass of wine."

Zelda snickered. "The other option is you *are* clairvoyant but you pass out during clairvoyancy sessions and roam around finding articles and sheet music tucked away wherever other clairvoyants have stashed them, and you sneak them home. Oh, by the way, I've made an executive decision. We're going with *déjà-vu-isms* from here on out. It's got a softer sound to it."

I couldn't stop laughing. "Clearly a well-thought-out theory, Miss Zimmerman. Not to mention an interesting take on many ways to mangle the word 'clairvoyant' and create another word while you're at it. Thanks…maybe."

We lifted our wine glasses and toasted each other.

"So, Zelda. Subject change. When do rehearsals start for *Dames at Sea*?"

"Next week. It's non-union, so they'll be mostly at nights. And of course, some killer long weekend days. I can't wait."

"You'll be loving it. I am having a premonition. But this is a nice one. You playing Ruby will lead to bigger and better shows, or maybe some TV work. There's not a lot going on in the city now. There aren't any new Broadway openings set until December. You guys are in

Hoboken, which is an easy commute to Manhattan. I'll bet y'all will be getting some of the better critics to come review. Oh, man! You're gonna be famous."

"Thanks a lot. Go ahead. Make me nervous. Hey, can I count on you to run lines with me, plus help me out with any dance sequences far beyond my capabilities?"

I waved a piece of bread at her. "Don't be nervous. You'll be awesome. As to running lines and dancing, of course I'll help, although if you keep taking Bucky's class you're going to end up a better tapper than your choreographer and definitely better than me. I. Whatever. The wine is getting to what's left of my brain. Anyway, I'm positive you're going to land something truly amazing as soon as some agent or casting director sees the show."

"Really? Is this more *déjà vu* ESP psychicism?"

I chuckled. "Nah. This is down-to-earth reality. Let's face it. In this city, one show can lead to another show and another and on into infinity."

Zelda suddenly looked glum. "You're now describing precisely what bothers Dwayne."

"Your boyfriend?"

"Fiancé. We haven't set a date, it's been kind of assumed it'll be spring after he finds out what his bonus will be. But, Shiloh, he wasn't exactly what I'd call a hundred percent thrilled when I told him I'd gotten cast as Ruby. Shoot, he wasn't ten percent thrilled. When I mentioned my rehearsal schedule, possibly with too much joy, his response was, and I quote, "You've been avoiding making decisions about venues and caterers and florists and everything else important for months. Doing some stupid show won't help you being wishy-washy.' Unquote." She took another large sip (more of a gulp) of her wine. "Dwayne's made it clear he doesn't want me to have a career in theater. The man is an investment trader. Very successful. He loves it. Numbers are to him what a great piece of choreography or a brilliant script is to you or me. But he sees actors as a bunch of kids playing dress-up. For some reason, he has this notion I'll wash the desire to be on stage out of my system once we're married, and settle down and teach third grade arithmetic. Before you ask, I do have the degree for it, and always considered it as a backup for the future, but it's not what I want to do, although I love children. I want my own someday. I don't really want to be teaching someone else's."

I felt an odd twinge. Again, I could see Zelda, crying and nursing a black eye. Was this a premonition based in reality? Or was my imagination heading into melodrama overdrive? I didn't want to upset Zelda, so for the time being I said, "Promise me you won't let Dwayne mess up your mind about what a great opportunity this is. Don't let him intimidate you."

She nodded. "I won't." She straightened her shoulders. "And if he does, well, my new BFF, Shiloh Meridien, will be there to keep me on the right path."

"She will."

Chapter 12

September 1975

I loved living in Manhattan. Loved the sights, the sounds, the option to walk forty blocks down from my apartment and see a dinosaur exhibit, or head over to the East Side and spend an afternoon at a museum admiring works of art dating from 5000 years ago to the present. Loved being able to sit outside on a bench or retaining wall, people-watching, for free. Loved the mix of old, young, suit-wearing executives, ex-hippies, Broadway stars, and too-skinny ballerinas teeming down the street dreaming of accomplishing great deeds. There were, however, days I was flabbergasted, aghast, and downright embarrassed for my adopted city when I became witness to the demolition of common courtesy.

Today, for instance, I was so disgusted I wanted to exit the subway, run into the nearest toy store, buy a plastic dart gun, fill it full of rubber darts, somehow get back into the same car, and then aim those darts at the five riders who shared train space with me but were either being rude or sublimely oblivious. All five well-dressed commuters were comfortably seated. All five were studiously avoiding looking at a man, clearly in his eighties, who was standing two people down from me, gripping a cane in one hand, valiantly trying to maintain his balance by hanging on to the overhead strap with the other hand. He was too far away for me to be able to help keep him upright and too close for me not to notice what others wanted to ignore because heaven help their legs and feet if they had to stand for longer than five minutes.

Sometimes, no matter how much one wants to open up a can of Texas whup-ass, prevailing wisdom tells you a big dollop of honey and downhome sweetness might be the better option. I glanced down at the occupant of the seat nearest my position hanging on to my own post. He appeared to be in his early twenties, was wearing an expensive suit, had a pricey-looking briefcase on his lap, and perked up when I beamed my biggest and best smile his way.

"Hi there, mister! Ah's so sorry ta ask, but Ah wonder if y'all wouldn't mind lettin' ma poor granddad take yor seat fer a spell?" I drawled in a broad, thoroughly fake, Texas accent. "Ah'm afraid he maght jest keel raght over if we hit a bump on this here speedin' train."

The young man rose, albeit with reluctance. I was delighted and honestly amazed my Texas Honey routine had worked. I raised my voice and got the elderly rider's attention. "Grandpa? This sweet young feller is givin' ya his seat."

The man stifled a laugh, winked back at me, limped away from the over-hanging straps, settled onto the newly-vacant seat, then said, with his own fake accent, "Thanks, li'l darlin'. Ain't New York jest the best?"

The now-standing rider quickly moved to another section of the train. I didn't watch him, so I had no idea whether he'd snagged another place to plop his butt down onto or not. I didn't care. The train slid to a stop a few seconds later and the woman who'd been seated next to the recalcitrant commuter (ignoring the byplay, while firmly but silently refusing to give up her own coveted spot) now stood and raccd out through the sliding doors.

The old man gestured to me to take her place. "You're a good soul," he said. "I've lived in New York my entire life, and it's fascinating, albeit often disheartening, to see who's going to be selfless as opposed to who's not. I'm always able to tell before any actual rudeness is manifested. By the way, my body thanks you. You were quite right when you suggested I might keel over, especially during a less-than-smooth stop. But, changing the subject, where are you off to, if you don't mind me being nosy? I noticed you're not wearing a suit."

"I've got an audition," I replied.

"Dancer?"

I nodded.

"Again, I'm nosy but what's it for? This part of downtown isn't normally associated with cultural activities."

"Have you heard of Guthrie's Gym?"

"Word is they have excellent racquetball courts. Not my favorite sport, especially at my age, but it does seem to keep the young executives in shape. Please, go on."

"Well, they're opening a branch down here in the North Tower, and I'm auditioning to teach an exercise class, along with half the unemployed dancers in the city. It's five classes a week at an absurdly early hour, six-thirty a.m., but it pays well. I'm in a holding pattern waiting to audition for a dance company I've dreamed about getting into practically my whole life, which puts me into a bit of a quandary as to whether I even want the job, but I figure Guthrie's would be a nice back-up in case the company stays on tour, so I might as well go to the audition. Now then, turnabout being fair play, what about *you*? Why the subway ride during the morning rush?"

"Ah. I'm going to meet my *actual* granddaughter for brunch, but I wanted to wander downtown a bit first. She's a lawyer with an absurdly large corporation and I doubt they could tell you her name, but she's a sweetheart to me. This is a treat for the old gent."

"Nice," I said and I meant it.

The conductor announced the next stop, Chambers Street. I stood and shook hands with "Grandpa."

"I'm getting off here. I want to walk a couple of blocks before I get to the audition. I moved to Manhattan in June, but I haven't been this far south except to hit the Ferry to see the Statue of Liberty. I'd like to get a feel for the neighborhood, especially if I end up working for the gym."

"Best of luck to you, young lady. Whatever you decide."

"You, too. I enjoyed chatting with you. Tell your granddaughter she's got a peach for a granddad."

We waved as I slung my dance bag over my shoulder and exited the train.

Like the granddaughter's firm, the neighborhood itself was what I'd call business-oriented, although juxtaposed between the men and women dressed in tailored suits, clutching neat briefcases, were quite a few homeless people pushing ancient shopping carts through the street on feet shod with slippers stuffed with papers. I wondered how many of them were veterans and whether this might be another issue for Marcus Kennedy or other protest singers to take up. Someone, somewhere, needed to care.

I spotted about six very high-end boutiques, more than one place to get a pizza slice, a large assortment of vendors hawking bagels, donuts and coffee, and at least seven small banking establishments. A vacant storefront—its windows plastered with posters left over from the late 1960s urging politicians not to accept the proposal to build the Twin Towers of the World Trade Center—stuck out among the other, thriving, businesses. Their suggestion to quash the idea of the trade center had obviously been ignored. Both towers had been in use ever since they were officially declared open for business in 1973.

Perhaps it was the odors from the pizza stands, already baking before nine in the morning, mixed with burnt coffee from vending carts, or the scent of bacon and eggs wafting through vents from an ancient diner out of place in the neighborhood, but I started feeling queasy. I began walking toward the North Tower, thankfully noting the absence of smelly food carts, pizza stands and all diners, but oddly, felt worse the closer I got.

I reached the outside plaza in front of the building. I looked up (way up) at the massive structure, wondering how I was going to handle an elevator ride to the gym somewhere above the 90th floor, much less teach exercise, with waves of dizziness and nausea sweeping over me. I checked my watch to see how much time I had before I needed to sign up. Eight forty-six a.m.

I stopped. My legs and feet literally refused to move.

I sank to my knees as horrific, unbelievable, terrifying visions flooded into my mind. I saw this same building engulfed in flames, with thick, greasy smoke billowing up and out for what had to be miles. Then came nearly identical images of the South Tower. I was physically dodging chunks from parts of an airplane as the pieces fell from the skies, followed by desks and chairs and reams and reams of paper. The nightmare grew worse. I watched as men and women, frantic to escape the blistering inferno, began to jump from the windows of the highest floors. From *every* floor. Then the building itself collapsed in slow motion. And suddenly there was silence. A silence as terrible in its own way as the screams I'd heard from the dying.

I was shouting and sobbing and flailing my arms around me, trying to dispel the visions. Part of me seemed to be watching what was happening as though it was being shown like a newsreel on a TV screen, while another part was witnessing events in real time and place. I was *there.* Live and in person and helpless to stop any of it.

The last vision was barely more than a glimpse, but it was long enough for me to see a photo in a special, late-night edition of a New York newspaper, showing nothing but rubble where once two, tall, proud buildings stood. I read the headline, which was short and simple. *Terrorists Attack! Towers Fall!* Directly above it was the date. *September 11, 2001.*

Chapter 13

September 1975

A gentle hand touched my shoulder. I was incapable of lifting my head to ascertain if this was real or part of the swirling, horrible images and sounds. They'd faded but refused to completely dissipate.

"It's okay. Hang in there. You're going to be all right. Breathe. You've got to breathe. Listen, please listen to me. Take my hand. You need to get up and off the ground. Please. Let me help you. Whatever it is you're seeing and hearing isn't there. I promise you, you're safe."

The voice was familiar. The visions finally vanished, but the panic and the horror they'd evoked remained. I looked up. For a brief second I thought I was experiencing another hallucination because it appeared as though Marcus Kennedy was standing above me with his hand outstretched. I grabbed it and held on tight as he helped me rise to my feet. My head stayed down as I stared at the pavement. He guided me over to a short retaining wall at the edge of the plaza and eased me into a sitting position.

"Keep focusing on your breath," he said. "Nothing but your breath. In. Out. Slow. Deep. Don't try to speak. There's no need to say a word. Not yet."

I shut my eyes but did as asked. He also remained

silent for a very long moment.

"Better?"

I nodded.

"Can you look at me and work on getting those breaths a bit deeper?" he asked.

I tried to breathe deeply but couldn't seem to get enough air into my lungs. I still smelled smoke. Oily, solid, very noxious smoke. After a lifetime, an eternity, I was finally able to take a big inhale and then speak, even managing to open my eyes. "Dear heaven. What's happening?"

"Look at me. Only me. Nowhere else."

I gazed into gentle, green-gray eyes, allowing the care and concern I saw in them to take me to a healing place. No hallucination. Marcus Kennedy was the person saving my sanity.

He reached out, again taking my hand in his, and softly said, "It appears you've been reliving something truly, incredibly devastating. I work with veterans who suffer from combat stress disorders, and what I saw with you was surprisingly similar to what I've witnessed happening with them. The sights and sounds, often the scents, are vivid and real and you can't escape them, and it feels like your very essence is being squeezed out of you."

I nodded. "I can't...I can't comprehend it. Can't understand it. I'm trying to push it all away but...I need...I have to focus on something else. Anything. Something innocuous."

He smiled. "Will it help you to hear I came very close to dedicating a song to the beautiful red-haired girl in the third row at the Benefit Vets concert last month? Yes, I'm talking about you."

I was right. He *had* noticed me while he was singing. The fact he remembered seeing me helped penetrate the fog and despair suffocating me. He added in a light tone, "Listen, just be glad *I'm* the one who saw you were in distress a moment ago and *not* my business manager. Tough as nails is Miss Angela Dane. She'd've yelled at you for being hysterical, probably slapped you, and definitely told you to snap out of it."

I tried to smile back. "Which would have either snapped me out of it or sent me cowering further into a fetal position, never to venture onto my feet again."

"Do you recall anything of what you saw and heard? It's pretty obvious it was horrific. From where I was standing and watching, you appeared to be reliving the exact moments of an event as if they were happening in the present."

I shivered. "Yes. I was. I mean, I did," I replied. "Except, oh, jeez, you're going start calling to bring on the men in white coats, but I wasn't relieving a past event. Much crazier. It was as if I was seeing something happening in the future, yet I felt I was there in real time. I actually saw a date at the top of a newspaper and it was in the next century. I'm not making the tiniest smidgeon of sense. How does one have a flashback when there's no, um, *back*?"

"Do you want to tell me? Describe what you saw? Sometimes it helps lessen the impact if another person is able to share."

I wanted to tell him. To describe the events I'd witnessed, in the order I'd seen or heard or smelled them, but I stopped. It wasn't a lack of trust. It was a curious need to shelter him from something so incomprehensible and horrible no one should have to experience it.

It wouldn't have mattered anyway if I'd decided to spill the story, because about three seconds after he asked me to tell him, a woman wearing a very smart, very tailored navy-blue three-piece suit rushed over to where Marcus and I were sitting. Her perfume, an expensive gardenia blend, began battling the scent of smoke still in my nostrils, without completely dispelling it. I wasn't sure which odor was worse.

"Marcus! What is wrong with you? We were due in Grant's office five minutes ago. Why are you sitting here hobnobbing with some groupie? He's the best P.R. man in the city and he's not patient and you need him if your career is going to survive. Here, I got coffee for you. With sugar, as requested."

She handed a lidded paper cup to Marcus. He took it, glanced down at it, then turned and gave it to me. I couldn't help but notice his hand shaking a bit and wondered if the wrist sprain he'd suffered before the concert back a few weeks ago hadn't quite healed yet.

The woman spat out in sheer fury, "What in blazes are you doing? I buy you pricey coffee and you give it to some homeless nobody? You and your stinking charitable projects. Enough already. You're such a bloody, arrogant, stubborn cuss. Get it in gear and let's move it. Now!"

"Angela, quit acting like the wicked witch of Manhattan. The young lady has had a bad shock. She needs the coffee a lot more than I do."

"Great," was the clipped response. She shot me a look of irritation, mixed with anger, before yanking his arm in an attempt to pull him away. "Enjoy it, sweetie. It's all you're getting from him."

"Wait." Marcus didn't budge. "Angela, honestly,

there's no need for rudeness."

"Marcus, I'm not saying this again. There's not time for this."

He stopped. "There's always time." He gently squeezed my hand before letting go. "Angela's right about one thing. We are late, but are you going to be okay? I can stay with you and deal with Grant later." He shrugged his shoulders. "Everyone is used to me ignoring what I call the absurdities of the business world. Heck, I'm not sure I even want to work with him."

I had no desire to be the cause of more friction between Marcus and his agent. "I'll be fine," I replied. "But thank you. So very much. I might have ended up in the nearest mental ward if you hadn't been here."

"Well, you owe me two seconds more, then. What's your name?"

"Shiloh Meridien."

His eyes widened. "I love it. It's got a great musical flow to it. It's exactly like you. Unique and beautiful. I hope we meet again."

Marcus let himself be led off by the incensed Angela, "led" meaning she forcefully dragged him away. I sipped the coffee he'd given me without tasting it. I hadn't lied when I said I'd be okay, but I have to admit I was thinking in future tense as opposed to present. It was vital I stay put for a few more minutes and give myself a chance to calm down before descending into a subway station again and going home. It occurred to me the bus would be a better option, as I wasn't anxious to be trapped anywhere.

Auditioning to teach exercise was no longer a viable course of action for my day. The more I considered the whole enterprise, teaching anywhere near the Twin

Towers was no longer a viable means of employment for my future. From somewhere in the fog of my mind came the recollection of a magazine article I'd read featuring an interview with one of the architects for the World Trade Center. He'd enthusiastically described details of a unique, revolving restaurant on a top floor of one of the towers, offering patrons a spectacular view to the entire city of Manhattan, which was slated to be opened sometime in mid-1976. It sounded amazing and I'd been really excited by the prospect of eating there next year. Now I thought about the article and knew I never would. Not to be repetitive, but it bears repeating, I would never enter either tower ever again. I'd be terrified of ghastly visions reaching out, from wherever they lay hidden, to overwhelm and consume me. I was also terrified no one would be there beside me telling me to breathe and helping me to forget.

Chapter 14

September 1975

I swallowed the last drop of the coffee Marcus Kennedy had so kindly given me, grateful for the warmth, then dove into my bag for some tissues to wipe my face. Because of the audition, I'd applied full makeup today, but both the blush and foundation had disappeared. Somehow—thanks to whatever nameless chemist invented waterproof mascara—the tears coursing down my cheeks hadn't left black streaks. So, good news…Marcus Kennedy hadn't gone off to his meeting with the image of a red-haired, hysterical, somewhat maniacal, skunk stuck in his head.

I was suddenly ravenous. I spotted a small cart about a block down the street and figured it might provide a variety of food options, hopefully including something vegan. I rose, slung my bag back over my shoulder, and didn't look back.

I reached the food cart in less than two minutes and blinked three times in case I was having a different kind of hallucination. The woman serving customers looked suspiciously like Fiona Belle Donovan. She was wearing a striped yellow-and-black bumblebee costume, complete with yellow wings on the shoulders and little yellow antennae balls popping up behind her head. I had yet to see another vendor in the city who was quite so eccentric in her choice of wardrobe.

A shimmer of something from the past, or future, hit me. Fortunately, this was not another nightmare of sounds, images, smells and horror. This was shorter and definitely sweeter. I could see Fiona Belle, dressed as this bumblebee, handing me what appeared to be a record album.

She winked at me. Yep. Definitely Fiona Belle Donovan. I had nothing to base this on, but I sensed she was aware I'd been through a traumatic ordeal this past hour.

"Shiloh, lass. How ya doin' and don't bother to answer. What'll ya have?" She continued without waiting for me to peruse the sign with chalked specials behind her. "I'm aft ta be suggestin' a spicy bean, veggie, and rice burrito fer ya. T'would be just the ticket fer the kind of day you've been havin', but I'll be aft ta makin' it two burritos. Ya need the energy boost."

"I'm aft ta agreein' ya might be right," I said.

She immediately handed me two hot burritos in a paper bowl, along with napkins. She motioned to a small, empty table a few yards away. I hadn't noticed it was there. "Take yer food, lass, and I'll be joinin ya. I need a break and folks'll have to lump it fer now."

I did as she requested, and within a minute a chubby black-and-yellow bee was sitting across from me.

"So, ya finally met Marcus Kennedy fer real, then, didja." She asked without including a question mark at the end of the sentence.

"I did. I won't bother to ask how you know. Either you have spies everywhere, are clairvoyant, or you have the sharpest eyes in the city. In which case, you probably also saw or heard *how* I met him. I'm sure I came off as nuttier than a holiday fruitcake. That being said, he was wonderfully kind and sensitive and had an almost uncanny ability to understand what I was going through and what to do and say to help."

She waved her hand to brush away my words and dropped the accent. "He's well aware that you're not crazy. Trust me. And Shiloh, while you can't change what you saw…no one can…it's too big…but the important thing is you met the man. He met you."

"Why? What the heck is it about Marcus Kennedy? Or me? Wait. How do you know what I saw? And why it can't be changed?" I rushed on without stopping for a response I somehow knew she wouldn't give. "Fiona Belle, this was an image of hell. Truly. And it was a vision of the future, yet I saw the news headline and it was as real as this burrito. I don't understand. Why can't it be changed?"

"Can't say."

"You mean won't say," I grumbled.

She ignored my comment and took us back to Ireland with her next words. "Lass, it's not yer place in life to attempt to alter a future event so huge. No one in this world can change it. Yer objective is ta try and save Marcus Kennedy."

I didn't bother to pause. "When?"

"In a couple of months. December. When it goes down, there'll be choices ya have ta make before it all ends. Shiloh, it won't be easy. You'll be lookin' at some hard decisions. Good and bad choices."

A customer yelled from the food cart. "Yo! Fiona Belle! I'm starving here. When are you coming back?"

"Now!" she called back. She rose, then shoved a bag at me across the table. "Scones. Ya need the sugar after all the stress. Take 'em home. Fer now, finish up the burritos while they're hot."

"Wait. Please. You can't drop miniature bombs like 'save Marcus Kennedy' as if he's some slogan on a poster and tell me I have hard decisions and good and bad choices to make and then casually walk off."

She winked at me, then vigorously nodded her head, setting the bee's antennae to bouncing, before smugly declaring, "Ah, Shiloh, lass, but I can."

Chapter 15

September 1975

Following the events of yesterday, if I'd had my druthers, I'd've spent the next week holed up in the apartment, wallowing in exhaustion, confusion, and misery, watching soap operas, and devouring massive amounts of tortilla chips loaded with guacamole, hot peppers, and pinto beans covered in my favorite brand of spicy chili powder sent from Texas by my sister Lacey.

I also have to confess, embarrassing as it was, I was feeling mopey and depressed because, absurdly, I kept waiting for Marcus Kennedy to call me. Totally irrational, yes, beginning with how would he get my number? I wasn't exactly listed in the Manhattan white pages. Secondly, if he found my number, why on earth would he want to get in touch with a lunatic? Then again, the look in his eyes had been clear. Inane and silly as it sounds, I knew he felt as I did. We shared a love so strong it defied logic and time and place and would last forever. Words and sentiments as sappy and overdramatic as the soap operas I deliberately avoided tuning in to because it was time to go to class.

This is what dancers do. The End of Days might be tomorrow, but dancers go to class. The day following my less-than-elegant meeting of Marcus Kennedy, I hit four of them. Five, if one counts Terry Travers' early morning martial arts lesson. The others were ballet, modern, jazz, and tap, all at the same studio, each allowing for a ten-minute break in between. No time to think. No time to allow myself to get weepy or to relive in my head everything I'd seen and heard the day before.

By three-thirty in the afternoon, I was back home. I intended to eat a huge late lunch, soak in the black bathtub while staring at the red and black tiles, then see what evil doin's were being done on my favorite soap (*Exit to Eternity*) or curl up with a new mystery novel I'd bought at a bookstore on W. 90th Street on my way back to the apartment. My plans disintegrated shortly after I arrived home. After dumping my dance bag in the living room, I trotted off to the kitchen to fix a salad and discovered a message tacked up on the bulletin board from Jim telling me to call Zelda, *Pronto!!!* With three exclamation points. A fist punched, then twisted inside my stomach. Something was wrong.

I called Zelda, who answered on the first ring as if she'd been sitting by the phone, waiting.

"Something's wrong," I stated the instant she answered with a hesitant, "Hello."

"Yes, but how can you tell?"

"Jim wrote *pronto* with three exclamation points on the message board. Jim is a reporter who sees more disturbing things going on in the world than should be allowed to any human. Jim is not into melodrama either in word or deed. Ergo, something is wrong. Plus, your voice is…off. Added to all the above is that I'm feeling my gut churning, and not from a spicy bean burrito. Especially because I haven't eaten yet."

"Can we meet at Gentry's?"

"Sure, um, thirty minutes if the train doesn't stall?"

"Yeah. Thanks."

She hung up. This was not the chatty, bouncy, lively Zelda Zimmerman I'd met up with for the last couple of weeks to hit dance classes. Not the Zelda who'd gone with me after those classes to hang out at this strange, educational, wonderful attraction called The New York Subway Experience which was located less than two blocks from our favorite dance studio in midtown. The space was meant to be a tourist attraction, providing new Manhattan residents and visitors with a history of the underground train system. But it was also a welcome sanctuary for dancers and actors and singers who needed a place to chill between classes and auditions, a place where one could grab a cheap coffee or soda from a vending machine, then sit at a bistro-style table and converse with a friend. Avoid the millions of people going about their business in the street above. Avoid the noise in the street above. Zelda loved the place as much as I did, and we'd shared gossip and sodas any day we'd taken classes together at the nearby studio. However, this was not the right venue to talk to a friend when something was "off" and Zelda clearly wanted to meet somewhere far more private. Hence, Gentry's.

Gentry's Diner was one of those stereotypically Manhattan diners found all over the city, featuring faded and cracked vinyl seats in booths, absurdly cheap breakfast specials (including as many free coffee refills as one's bladder would allow) and lunches with Greek dishes (generally sprinkled with nutmeg) prominently featured on the menu. I'd eaten there so often (ordering the giant salad while asking to "cut the hard-boiled egg and the cheese and double the tomatoes, chick peas, cucumbers, and peppers") the owner told me he'd decided to create something similar and call it The Shiloh. I wasn't sure if he was kidding or not.

Zelda was already seated in our favorite booth in the back near the kitchen but next to a window. She was eyeing her coffee as if it were a dead snake in a blender, but managed a feeble wave as soon as she spotted me.

I slid in across from her and asked without preamble, "What did Dwayne do?"

"Why do you think Dwayne did anything?"

"Because since the day you got cast in *Dames at Sea*, the man has been bugging you to drop the show and spend your waking hours coming up with wedding plans. Something tells me the ante got upped today." I gently added, "Not to mention, you still have some mascara smeared on your cheeks and I seriously doubt you applied it this morning to anywhere but your lashes. So, what happened?"

Zelda swallowed before responding in a hoarse whisper, "He slapped me."

I nearly jumped out of the booth ready to do battle. I forced myself to sit quietly and listen before tearing over to Dwayne's office and beating the living stuffings out of him. I could do it, too. The year I turned twelve, I'd signed up for martial arts classes about five minutes after seeing a classic Chinese movie released in 1928 called *The Burning of the Red Lotus Temple*, which was playing alongside a couple of old silent-era romantic comedies. Somewhere in the midst of watching evil monks battle a military commander (in silence) I'd had the brilliant idea of adding martial arts to dance. Part of this desire stemmed from having been teased from the moment I hit five-nine, at age nine, and, while not bullied to the point of despair, I wanted to achieve the skills and confidence to land a punch on anyone who upped the ante to physical harassment. Since then I had amassed an arsenal of moves with which I could defend a friend, and I wasn't the least bit afraid to do so should the occasion arise. Add the last four months with Terry Travers and I was one holy Texas terror.

"Tell me."

She nodded. "He invited me over to his place for lunch around noon. I was all excited and I started going on and on, blathering nonstop about what a terrific rehearsal I'd had last night. I'm so stupid. I'm extremely aware Dwayne hates me talking about anything to do with theater, especially if it involves me doing a show."

"You're anything but stupid. Go on."

"Well, suddenly he's telling me—no, wait, he's *yelling* at me, and being very snide and rude, saying he doesn't understand how I was able to get into the show because I'm nowhere near as talented as people he's seen on TV or in the Broadway shows he's gone to." She shook her head. "It's ironic, but one of the perks of his job is that he gets free tickets to shows so his firm can entertain clients. Dwayne has never taken me, even when clients cancel and he can't exchange the tickets. Claims his bosses won't allow it, which is total rot."

"You're stalling."

"True." She took a deep breath, exhaled forcefully, then continued. "Okay. So, there I am, trying not to burst into tears while he's spewing all these painful things about me having no talent, and then, out of nowhere, he grabs my arms and he starts squeezing and shaking me and shouting at me, saying I need to face reality and give up the whole idea of performing. I screamed at him to stop, and he slapped me and told me I was being hysterical. Then he told me to leave until I could control myself." She pointed to her long-sleeved shirt. "I have bruises forming already. I haven't looked in a mirror. I'm afraid to see what's happening with my face."

"What's happening is the beginning of one swollen, and soon to be black, eye. What a stinkin' monster. I'll kill him. Phooey on my principles of nonviolence. He deserves to die."

"Oh, lovely. My best friend not only loses her moral compass but ends up going to jail for me." Her eyes welled up.

I reached into my bag and found several unused tissues, then handed them to her. She dabbed her eyes, blew her nose and stared down at her untouched coffee.

I took a sip of water before calmly stating, "All right. I won't kill him. But can I at least deliver a few fierce karate chops to some tender areas? Turn him into a soprano for a few hours? Or, better, for life?"

Zelda emitted a weak chuckle. "I'm all for it as long as you're not arrested." She sighed. "I've just been wandering around midtown like your mysterious ghost. What should I do?"

"Can you report him to the cops? I mean, good grief, the jerk assaulted you."

"What! I couldn't turn him in to the cops. The man's my fiancé."

"Who gives a rap? I don't care if you've been married for twenty years. Someone hurts you, you press charges."

Zelda sighed. "Well, let's get real here. Suppose I did report him. The cops wouldn't do anything about it. Heck, look at what goes on in this city every day with muggings and stabbings and stuff. Not to mention normal murders."

I raised both brows. "Normal murders? What precisely constitutes a normal murder?"

Zelda's eyes twinkled with a hint of amusement. "Oh. The usual. Drug dealers shooting each other over stashes of heroin. Robbers shooting bodega owners when they don't open the cash register fast enough. Um, jealous lovers killing one another."

"Got it. I don't like it, but I see your point. Turning Dwayne in is not an option because of the overworked guys in the NYPD dealing with real live street crime. I suppose kung-fu-ing him into the next century is probably not a crackerjack idea either?"

"Kung-fu-ing? Is that a real word?"

"Nope."

"Very descriptive, though. I like it." She finally picked up her coffee and took a sip. "Ugh. It's cold. Well, more like just past tepid. I must have forgotten I ordered it. Yeah, I'm in a fog."

I flagged down our waiter, a sweet elderly man who'd probably served folks at Gentry's when it opened in the nineteen-thirties. "Teddy? Could we get some fresh hot coffee for Zelda? And a cup for me as well. And food. I'll have my usual salad." I nodded at Zelda. "What about you? You need to eat before you pass out."

"Oh. I did kind of skip the lunch after the slap. Honestly, if it doesn't bother your vegan sensibilities too much, I'd really like a Western omelette."

"I love you, my friend. And today, you could order a triple cheeseburger with bacon and I wouldn't hassle you." I reached across the table and squeezed her hand.

This almost set her off again crying, but she took a big inhale, then asked Teddy for extra mushrooms in the omelette.

Teddy shot her a look, wrote down the order, then said, "Miss Zelda, whatever it is, don't be sad. Miss Shiloh loves you and so do we. You'll feel better after I bring hot coffee." He added, "And I'll add very fresh mushrooms plus many peppers in the omelette."

"Teddy, you are a saint and you will go to heaven," I told him.

He grinned, bowed, then turned and headed back to the kitchen.

I inhaled, then came out with it. "Zelda, you can call me a nosy bi…uh, witch, but you need to tell Dwayne where to stick it and give him back the ring and be done with him. Forever."

"But…"

"No buts. Any spawn of Satan, which he is, who'll shake and slap a girl, won't hesitate to hit and punch a girl and escalate to inflicting severe injuries. You don't deserve it. You're incredibly talented and smart and wonderful and kind and I would say this even if I wasn't your best friend." I took a breath, then added, "Okay, shifting to our beloved *déjà-vu-isms*, can you remember back to when I was telling you about the premonitions and images?"

"Sure."

"Well, I've got one. It's tiny, it's not exactly spelling everything out but what it *is* doing is screaming at me to make sure you stay safe and get away from Dwayne because you've got one amazing future ahead of you. Now, forget about Mister Bunyan and tell me about last night's terrific rehearsal."

Chapter 16

September 1975

I didn't tell Zelda about my psychic experience from yesterday. The last thing she needed, while reeling from the discovery her boyfriend was an abusive s.o.b. would be to learn her best buddy was a raving lunatic who had conjured up images of horror no one should ever see or live through. I wanted to tell her I'd met Marcus Kennedy, but I couldn't yet find a way to describe the meeting because he was part of the whole "Shiloh losing it at the North Tower of the World Trade Center" scenario. I sipped my cup of coffee, decided to table anything to do with Marcus and horrific visions, and let her ponder how best to deal with Dwayne. So, for a few minutes, we sat in silence.

Zelda chugged her own coffee without appearing to notice the hot steam rising, then shook her head. "Shiloh, this is tricky. To my folks, Dwayne is perfect and we're perfect together. I will get a ton of grief for this. Putting it mildly, my parents are not going to be happy when they hear I've broken off the engagement. Livid might best describe their feelings."

"Well, if they do get snippy, point out they'd be far less happy the year you fail to show up for Thanksgiving dinner and you call to say you're in the hospital, laid up with a couple of broken ribs, two black eyes and a busted nose, all because Mister Perfect got ticked you didn't use his mother's recipe for cranberry sauce." I suddenly had a new vision—Zelda living through that exact scenario. I took another sip of hot coffee, keeping my hands around the cup to savor the warmth and dispel the cold waves creeping over my body.

"Ouch. Could things really get that bad?" Zelda asked, then put up her hand before I could say a word. "Nah. Don't bother to answer. I'm having my own flashes here and they're not psychic like yours. They're very real and they all revolve around the look in Dwayne's eyes when he's putting me down. Sometimes it's for wanting to be an actress. Sometimes it's as ludicrous as being five minutes late to meet him. The put-downs have been occurring more and more often over the last few weeks. Especially after rehearsals started for *Dames*. And, of course, today, the look ramped up a few notches right before he began shaking me as if I were a martini mix."

"Vivid if painful analogy. He truly is one greasy slimeball."

"Thank you for liking the analogy. And thank you for pointing out the not-so-great possibilities for violence in a future I'd prefer not to live through." She took another gulp of coffee. "So, my wise friend, how do I do this? Should I call him? Um, break up over the phone? No preamble, just launch into 'it's over, go away, now'?"

"Yep. This is why phones were invented. I see no reason to tell him to his face."

Zelda nodded, but then grimaced. "Oh, nuts. I can't. I was so upset I totally forgot until now. When I went tearing out of his apartment earlier, I left my other bag. My big canvas bag with a ton of essentials. I have to get them back, and I'll bet once Dwayne gets a break-up message he won't be inclined to pack anything up and send it to me. Besides…"

"Besides?"

A look of grim defiance crossed the cute, impish face. "Besides, I have to give him the ring back."

"You could mail it. Maybe insure it first. Or not. But, in the interest of keeping him away from you, how essential are these essentials?"

"Essential. Driver's license from Illinois. Bank checkbook. A check to be deposited if I want to eat this week. Oh, man. It's worse I stuffed this week's trade papers in there as well."

"Ah. Yep. Essentials. Although, I did buy both papers back on Thursday, so you're welcome to them. The newsstand down my block seems to get them before the rest of the city. Night before, actually. Which is cool, albeit not relevant to the discussion. Okay. We can handle this. What time does Dwayne get off work today?"

"Seven. We're supposed to meet outside at his favorite pub on Ninth Avenue at seven-thirty so he can go home first and change into something casual. I can't begin to tell you how much I hate that place. Dwayne is making more money than anyone has a right to at his age, but he'll chug down the most ghastly, unappetizing appetizers, all because they're free during Happy Hour."

"If you're talkin' about Leland O' Toole's, I totally agree. Gross. I went there once, back in July, and tried chewing down on something they advertised as a bean-and-guacamole nacho and tasted more like…well, I can't say. Or won't. My parents brought me up not to use bad language."

Zelda laughed. "Thank you. I needed a bit of humor, but also it's satisfying to have one's opinion reinforced about the culinary arts."

"Hey, girl, you're talkin' to a nacho connoisseur, here. I'm tellin' ya, don't mess with Texas."

"Cute. Saucy and sassy. I like it."

I groaned. "It *is* cute. And, yes, saucy and sassy. I like it, too. Unfortunately, I don't have a clue as to where I first heard it. Okay, back to you and your essentials, you can call Dwayne and remind him you left your bag and to please bring it. You don't have to say anything else. Better, you could call his office as soon as we finish eating and tell the receptionist to convey the message so you won't have to personally speak to him. And at seven-thirty, on the dot, we will meet Dwayne together, and all five-foot-ten inches of your bestie BFF will stand by your side when you retrieve your bag and hand him back the ring." I batted my lashes. "I promise not to injure his future prospects for fathering children unless he gets rowdy or rude, in which case I will open up a can of whup-ass so big he'll be knocked six ways to Sunday."

Zelda's eyes widened. "Other *déjà-vu-ism* phrases?"

"Nah. Just good Texas phrases. No clairvoyance involved."

I closed my eyes for a moment, trying not to shake as I briefly relived what I'd experienced at the World Trade Center. Was I clairvoyant? It didn't matter. I'd already sworn to myself I would never reveal what I'd seen, felt, heard, and smelled to another soul. If I absolutely had to talk about it, I'd hunt down Fiona Belle Donovan.

"Shiloh?"

I opened my eyes.

"What's wrong? It's more than my mess with Dwayne. I can see it. I can feel it. Something happened to you yesterday. I may not have your *déjà-vu-isms*, but I've got nearly empathic feelings when it comes to a close friend, and you're giving off some painful vibes."

I was saved from answering by the arrival of Teddy with our order. As even a die-hard vegan is aware, omelettes are close to number one on the list of foods one does not want to eat cold, and Zelda needed a protein jolt fast, so I muttered, "Let's table it for now and chow down."

We ate. We discussed which auditions we should choose from about four being held on the same day next week, which would work for Zelda. We talked about Zelda's dream job, which was to play any character she might be offered on the soap we were both addicted to, *Exit to Eternity*, but she'd gratefully accept a role on the equally sudsy *Destiny's Chances*. We talked about politics and whether there was any truth to the embezzlement rumors about City Councilman Gregory Campbell, who was running for mayor, and if so, would New Yorkers care, as it was assumed all politicians were corrupt anyway. We talked about whether or not the protests being staged by folk singers, such as Marcus Kennedy, against Roger Masters to keep him from buying the building where the Am-Vets Center stood, would really work and whether Masters was bribing the aforementioned Gregory Campbell, a possibility we agreed was highly probable.

We did not talk about Dwayne.

We spent what was left of the afternoon window shopping along Madison Avenue, looking at clothes we couldn't afford and were way too conservative in style for our tastes anyway, then hit Midtown Records, hunting for sheet music and albums.

At six thirty, we stopped at a bakery for some bagels to put something in our stomachs before meeting Zelda's soon-to-be-ex fiancé, headed to a nearby plaza, and found a retaining wall where we could sit and eat.

At seven-twenty-five, we were standing outside Leland O'Toole's pub, waiting for Dwayne to arrive with Zelda's bag, when I spotted my friend Sandra standing under the entrance arch outside an Italian restaurant across the street.

I glanced over at Zelda. "Is Dwayne an 'arrive early' type of guy or does he get to places late?"

"On time. Swiss watchmakers should be so precise."

"Ah. Will you be okay for four minutes? Sandra told me a few days ago she'd met with someone in the company who had the latest scoop regarding Emma Andersen and possible auditions and she'd pass the word, but I haven't seen her to ask what's up…however, if you're worried he'll show up sooner, I'm sticking with you and I'll grab her tomorrow in class."

"I'm fine. As long as you keep me in your sightline and haul it back if you see him approaching."

Chapter 17

September 1975

I ran across the street and chatted with Sandra for about two minutes. She did have news, but it wasn't what I wanted to hear.

"The company's extending the tour," Sandra said. "Ready for this? They're off to Japan next month."

"Wow. Color me jealous," I said.

"Add me to the mix."

We both sighed. "Were you able to find out when they're coming back?" I asked.

"December. Sounds definite. With auditions slated for either the end of the month or early January." Sandra appeared mildly concerned. "Of course, we're all assuming they're taking on new company members. But, if they are, you'll get in, Shiloh. You're way too amazing a dancer for Emma A. not to hire you."

"Well, thanks. So are you, like I'm telling you something new."

"Aww, thanks back atcha. But, honestly? I've about decided to dump the idea of getting into a professional company and set my sights on musical theater instead," Sandra said.

"Why? Your dance technique is superb," I told her.

"Longer shelf life and more opportunities. Plus, I have more voice training than dance. But again, thank you for the compliment."

Sandra's date arrived as Sandra was telling me why she was switching to musical theater. She provided a quick introduction to a good-looking guy wearing jeans along with a tuxedo shirt and jacket (and I admit I barely listened, partially because I was keeping a sharp eye on Zelda to make sure she was okay and partially because Sandra dates about five different guys a week so there's no point in catching their names.) I gave Sandra a quick hug, and then she and Whoever went inside the restaurant. I stood at the curb, impatiently waiting for a taxi to finish driving down the street before I could cross back over to Leland O'Toole's.

Zelda had shown me Dwayne's photo when we were at Gentry's and I recognized him the instant I spotted the man, dressed in jeans and a navy-blue pullover sweater I'd bet money was cashmere, sauntering down Ninth Avenue. Dark brown, wavy hair, cut and styled in corporate length, chiseled jawline, straight nose. Movie-star dashingly dreamy looks. What Zelda had failed to mention was how tall he was. Dwayne appeared to be around six-feet-one and all muscle, in comparison to Zelda's barely five feet in heels. He did not look happy. To be honest, he looked ticked beyond measure. My protective instincts went into overdrive.

I ran across the street, nearly hitting the back end of the cab, but Dwayne still reached Zelda about ten seconds before I did. It was time enough for him to thrust her bag at her chest, hard enough to cause her to sway backward and nearly fall to the ground. He then grabbed her arm at the same spot where I'd seen the bruise forming earlier this afternoon. She winced as he hissed at her like some villain in an old-time melodrama,

"You're such a stupid, silly girl. How could you leave behind the one bag you need with all your important papers and money?"

Zelda's eyes welled up with tears.

I hadn't had the best couple of days. Witnessing the horrors at the Towers yesterday. Making a fool of myself in front of Marcus Kennedy. I hadn't mentioned it before because I'd been consumed with anguish and despair from the abovementioned trauma, but this morning I'd dealt with the annoyance of no hot water in the apartment, riding in a way-too-crowded car on the train, and taking a ballet class with a new teacher who proved to be nasty and derisive. At Gentry's, as I listened to Zelda telling me about Dwayne's abusive behavior, I'd grown progressively more furious. Barely sixty seconds earlier I'd learned I'd have to wait another two to three months, maybe more, before getting the opportunity to audition for the dance company I'd set my sights on from the moment I saw them perform on a television variety show when I was ten.

All of which probably doesn't justify scrapping every nonviolent principle I'd held dear after taking on the label of "pacifist." I marched over to Dwayne Bunyan, yanked his hand off Zelda's arm and spun him around to face me—not that anyone needs reminding, but I'm five-ten, and I'd worn a pair of high-heeled black boots today, bringing me literally face to face with him. I assumed a fighting stance, and, without hesitating, delivered an elegant, but efficient, uppercut to Dwayne's perfect nose.

He howled in pain, then began yelling at me, "Get away from me! You broke my nose! Who are you?" He yelled a few more phrases at me, but as they were all unsuitable for the ears of anyone not engaged in armed combat in foreign climes or the porn business, I'll skip them. Before I had a chance to answer, he pulled his fist back, clearly preparing to retaliate with a punch.

I shifted my stance and prevented his arm from moving any closer. Then I quietly stated, "My name is Shiloh Meridien. I repeat, Shiloh, as in 'Battle of.' Now hear me loud and hear me good, Dwayne Bunyan. You touch Zelda again and I promise I will do more than tap your nose, which, by the way, is not broken, or bruise a rib or two. I will go for an area more tender and doubtless more important to your so-called manhood."

He stood quietly, staring at me, holding his hand over his nose as blood dripped down his face.

I added in pleasant tones, as if we were about to order tea, "Zelda is now giving you the ring back. You will take it and you will say, 'Thank you.'" I glanced over at Zelda, who was calmly removing the ring from her finger. She winked at me and I breathed again.

Zelda cleared her throat, then stated, "Goodbye, Dwayne. I'd say it's been a blast, but it wouldn't be the truth and I've never been a liar. I wish you luck and I hope you treat your next girlfriend a lot better than you treated me. No, wait. Truth telling. I hope you never have another girlfriend. Or at least, not until you've learned the basic concepts of respect and kindness."

She handed the ring to the stunned Mr. Bunyan, then hoisted the canvas bag with the "essentials" over her shoulder before saying, "Shiloh? I can't stand Leland O'Toole's. Lousy food, lousy music blaring, and lousier patrons." She glanced at her watch. "It's seven-thirty-five. We're about three blocks from where *The Wiz* is playing. What say we haul it over there and see if they have any tickets left for tonight's performance? I'm in the mood for some superb singing, dancing and acting by all those artists who haven't yet grasped the idea there are financial jerks in this world who perceive them to be children playing dress up…just like me."

Zelda and I sauntered down to Forty-Fourth Street Avenue, fighting the urge to laugh. We weren't certain if the urge came from hysterics, shock, or genuine amusement. Halfway down the block I stopped the progress.

"What?"

"A gift for you."

"You already gave me a gift. It's called my life and self-respect and future," Zelda said in a cracked voice.

"Well, this is more immediate."

She stared at me as I reached inside my dance bag and pulled out a sheet of paper, then handed it to her.

"What is this?"

"Next month's schedule at the Forty-Sixth Street Studios. Check out the highlighted blocks, Monday through Friday at seven in the morning, when most theater people are sleeping off last night's performance."

Zelda glanced down at the paper, then did break out in laughter. "Karate classes for dancers taught by Black Belt Master Terry Travers. This is perfect. Sign me up."

Chapter 18

September 1975

Less than a week after having landed the immensely satisfying punch to Dwayne Bunyan's nose, and following up the bout by pushing myself to take as many classes as I was financially able to swing, I'd convinced myself I was emotionally back to normal. No frightening visions haunting my waking hours. No words or phrases spoken I hadn't already spoken a million times before, along with the rest of the planet.

Admittedly, I kept wishing Marcus Kennedy would figure out a way to track me down. Today, after finishing an energy-ramping jazz class, I managed to refrain from phoning Wyatt at home for the fifth time (he was trying to get some composing done but not succeeding as long as his neurotic roommate, i.e., me, was bugging him) to ask if I'd gotten any calls from any protest singers. Instead, I found an empty step in front of the New York Library at 42nd Street, plopped down, opened my dance bag, and pulled out the slightly crumpled copies of the show biz trade newspapers I'd bought to check out possible job opportunities. Becoming part of Emma Andersen's troupe was on hold while they toured Tokyo and Okinawa and Kyoto, but I needed to work.

There were some open calls for chorus for a couple of shows way out of town. I skipped checking the casting breakdowns for anything out of the tri-state area. I tried not to delve too deeply into the reasons why, because, if I was being honest, there was only one—I felt compelled to be in the same city as Marcus Kennedy, regardless of how slim were the chances of running into him again. Plus, how could I save him if I was in another city?

I perked up when I spotted a sparse notice for an audition for a musical revue to be performed in midtown. This was unusual. The majority of "Off-Off Broadway" shows had venues in tacky fifty-to-eighty-seat theaters off Fifteenth Street near Greenwich Village.

The audition for *The Golden Age Revue* was scheduled for seven tonight. A perk for theater people with "day jobs" in offices, usually working as temps. Something I'd done more than once since moving to the city in June (grateful I was a ridiculously fast typist and could take my pick of employers) but something I intended to avoid in the future if at all possible. Anyway, according to the audition notice, this job paid. Many Off-Off Broadway shows don't…performers take them in hopes a casting agent or director pops in and notices how wonderful they are and whisks said performer away from Fifteenth Street. The salary mentioned wasn't huge, but if I got in, it was large enough to keep me from having to worry about helping with rent for the next three months, which again meant not having to resort to typing legal briefs for midtown law firms during the better-paying night shifts.

I checked my watch. I had two-and-a-half hours of free time before the audition. Well, two hours, if I made sure I got there thirty minutes ahead of schedule to do a warm-up. Enough time to cruise the surrounding streets and grab a salad at a diner. Maybe check out the neighborhood to see how many drug dealers were hanging out on corners so, if I got the job, I could avoid those corners and make it safely to work.

I probably sound either crazy or paranoid, but I was neither. I loved New York, but it had its drawbacks. Crime in the city was a major problem, along with the huge economic crisis threatening to shut down a variety of businesses, and of course, the ever-popular electrical power outages, very often leading to looting and vandalism. I'd never been mugged but, as Sandra and I had explained to Ethan, my date from Ohio the night we saw Marcus Kennedy in concert, carrying a cheap bag with a pair of worn tights hanging out was a decent indicator to a prospective attacker to ignore the target, who was undoubtedly a dancer, which generally meant a victim with zero cash or jewelry. Smart muggers went after tourists. I had dealt with the July blackouts, thankful I didn't live in one of the neighborhoods ravaged by rioters, and almost embarrassed to admit the power outage hadn't had a major impact on my life apart from the annoyance of trying to stay cool without the benefit of an electric fan. I'd seen some drug deals going down but wasn't stupid enough to walk by the small traffic island near W. 72nd Street, often referred to as Needle Park.

As to economics? I was clueless and would remain so. I'm sure my sister Lacey would have understood every nuance of the fiscal disasters facing the city (and probably been able to solve them) but as long as dance companies and Broadway remained standing, even reading in the news about the city's mayor begging for help from the rest of the country didn't mean a lot in my daily doings. If I sound callous, I'm not. I couldn't personally arrest muggers and drug dealers, restart electricity, or figure out how to bail out America's largest city, so it was more important to focus on things I could actually control, such as which auditions to hit.

I found a cheap diner around the corner from West Thirty-Sixth Street and ordered a small dinner salad and a large glass of iced tea. I stared out the window, enjoying the nonstop parade of New Yorkers in suits who were either hurrying home or meeting other New Yorkers in suits at much classier, pricier restaurants than the one I was in, perhaps before catching a show.

I didn't have time to scour the neighborhood for other restaurants, delis, bagel bars, or avant-garde thrift shops. I remembered the location of the Am-Vets Center Marcus Kennedy talked about during his concert in August was in this area. I was ashamed because I'd been meaning to pop into the center and take a look around. Be brave and offer my services as a volunteer to teach. For now, I needed to prove to the casting folks for *The Golden Age Revue* I was worthy of consideration.

After I finished eating, I headed over to the Henske Hotel, mildly curious as to who Henske might have been to get a hotel named after him. I gave my name and headshot to a cute dark-haired guy with a moustache, wearing a white shirt possibly last seen draped over the chest of one of the Romantic poets, tight jeans (doubtless found on sale at one of the trendier thrift shops I hadn't had time to wander through) and sporting granny glasses and a ponytail. Stage manager? I was tempted to ask him whether the "golden age" referred to in the show's title was the Twenties or the Sixties, given his "look" was very last-decade, but I decided it could be regarded as a rude question if it turned out he didn't have a sense of humor.

The theater was inside a now somewhat rundown hotel on W. Thirty-Sixth Street, which had been built back in the last century, but it boasted a 300-seat house and a stage nearly the size of many Broadway theaters, complete with proscenium, real curtains for lowering and raising, and enough wing space to hide performers before they made an entrance.

It turned out to be the easiest and most enjoyable audition I'd ever attended.

I'd been right in my original assumption—"golden age" meant the jazzy era of prohibition, tall chorus girls, wisecracking comics, short, corny but hilarious, skits, along with new tunes composed by first-generation immigrants brought up on the Lower East Side for New Yorkers to play on battered upright pianos after buying sheet music for about a penny.

The director/choreographer for *The Golden Age Revue* was Mr. Frank Kaufman, who, in his seventies, still stood straight as the proverbial arrow at six feet tall and boasted a full head of white hair along with clear, sparkling blue eyes. I felt certain he'd escorted more than one beautiful chorus girl to wild parties out in the Hamptons during the nineteen-teens and twenties, to those ladies' great delight. He taught us a dance combination designed for an audience's entertainment rather than to show off technical skills. And, bless the man, he took the time to hunt for someone taller than I for a waltz routine. When no one could be found, Frank partnered me himself, while his assistant, a petite white-haired lady, also in her seventies, beamed at us as though we were father and bride at a wedding, while she made notes for casting. I soon learned she was his wife of fifty-odd years, Fredda Kaufman, who'd danced in more than one *Ziegfeld Follies* and *George White Scandals* revue alongside her husband.

The audition took three hours. At ten p.m. Mr. Kaufman lined up those of us who'd made it through, thanked everyone, and announced the results, telling us this was the second call they'd had in the last week, so four other performers had already been cast.

I barely heard him. I was in.

Chapter 19

Early October 1975

The Henske Hotel was shabby and faded and I was fairly confident had been in need of repairs from its basement to the top floor for the last forty years. The cast referred to *The Golden Age Revue* as "Tea Time Theater" because, instead of watching a show on a tiny stage, while eating a fancy and expensive dinner, folks could pop into the Henske at four in the afternoon, devour cucumber sandwiches or other finger foods, scones with clotted cream, *petit fours* and a variety of fruits, real English tea, and watch us do our thing for about an hour on the surprisingly large stage, and then go on their merry way. We did one show a day, five days a week, two on Saturday. Sunday was a bit later in the day, at six p.m. Mondays were dark.

I loved it. There were eight of us, nine if you counted Frank Kaufman, who donned a tux and came onstage for each show to twirl me around in the waltz, even though he'd cast two male dancers over six feet who could have managed quite well. Ridiculously talented, Frank and Fredda also were two of the kindest people I'd met in my life. They'd lived at the hotel for thirty years, after being hired to create the kind of short musical revue New York tourists—or even New Yorkers—on a budget could bring their kids to see. The hotel provided the couple with a small apartment on the top floor, the sixth, and Frank confided it helped keep them in superb shape. They never took the elevator.

The performers and the routines changed every ten weeks, but the name remained *The Golden Age Revue* and usually consisted of twelve numbers, all song and dance. There were no comic sketches. The music was diverse, with the majority of songs being up-tempo dance tunes like "Ain't We Got Fun," "Alexander's Ragtime Band," and the less-familiar "Perdido Street Blues." We performed three ballads: "Let Me Call You Sweetheart," "Always," and "Danny Boy" (for the Irish in all of us). Frank and I danced our waltz to "The Band Played On" while Dave Felix, the hippie-looking guy who'd originally helped out collecting headshots and resumes at the audition, sang, with his moustache shaved off and a wig better suited for a 1920s revue fitting snugly over his ponytail. The cast was accompanied by a small band consisting of a percussionist, pianist, violinist, and a reed player who shifted from clarinet to saxophone depending on the tune.

Following a Wednesday show my second week in, I was sitting in the lobby, resting, when I was joined by Frank and Fredda Kaufman. Fredda grabbed my arm and then pointed in the general direction of the hotel's entranceway. "Shiloh, who's the short vendor in the far-right corner near the door wearing kind of a fairy godmother costume? All pink. I've seen you chatting with her, and it's driving me crazy because she looks familiar."

"Her? She's a hoot, isn't she? Fiona Belle Donovan Winthorp is her name but she never uses Winthorp. He must have been one nasty dude because, whoever he was, she told me she despised him. I've never seen her when she hasn't been dressed in some kind of wacky outfit. But, in addition to all the touristy souvenir stuff, she bakes the most delicious cranberry-orange scones on the planet. The hotel chef needs to get her recipe or hire her to bake a few dozen or so here as an addition to the tea mix. Anyway, she has this wonderful knack for showing up when I'm in crisis or in need of cheering up."

Fredda squinted and then shook her head. "I could swear I've seen her before. She's a dead ringer for the concierge of the boarding house where I used to live when I was performing with the *Follies*. But it's impossible she's the same person because she had to have been at least fifty years old back then." A wicked grin flashed across her face. "Admittedly, I was very young at the time, barely fifteen, and I wasn't paying a lot of attention to older landladies. I was too busy hoping they wouldn't notice me sneaking in after hours. I did love those nearly-all-night parties! But, if memory serves, her name was Mrs. Donovan, so maybe Fiona Belle is her daughter? Mrs. Donovan was an interesting lady. She somehow got involved in trying to rescue a girl who went missing. I'm not sure exactly what happened. The girl either ran away or was kidnapped. I once considered writing a silent movie script using what little I knew of the story, but I never could come up with a spiffy title."

"Ooh. I like the idea of a movie. You've definitely got me intrigued. Let's see, titles…um, *Fleeing the Follies*? *Running from the Revue*? *High Kicks and Kidnappings*?"

Fredda chuckled. "They're all pretty terrible. Good thing you're a dancer, not a script writer. It's curious, while I'm talking about familiarity and dance, but you remind me of a different girl who was in the show we did in nineteen-nineteen. Not thc one who went missing. This girl was a tall redhead."

"Really? In what way? I mean, is the resemblance in personality, or dancing style, or simply the red hair and the height?" I asked.

"A bit of everything. There's this air of something rather otherworldly about you both. Almost as if you belong in a different era. In her case, I'm adding mysterious, because what became of her is a mystery. Melody was in the show for just a few months before she left."

"Melody. Pretty name."

"I agree. I can't recall her last name. She was a few inches taller than you, not the dancer you are in technique, but she had a great presence on stage. She was quite likeable. Best friends with another girl in the show, Saree. Her last name is also a blank right now. Saree moved to Memphis at some point after she finished working with the revue. Melody was originally from there as well, and word was she moved back too."

"Maybe you *should* ask Fiona Belle," I said. "If your old landlady was actually her mother, she might have heard some details about what happened to those folks. If nothing else, make friends with the pink fairy godmother and order a couple of scones. They are past delicious."

Frank had joined us and overheard this part of the conversation. His eyes widened. "You ladies have me intrigued about this woman. It's curious. She looks like someone I met during the war. Before America got involved. This was in Paris during the Occupation. I flew as a navigator with the RAF and our plane was shot down in France in March of nineteen-forty-one." He flashed a wicked grin. "I probably shouldn't say this because it gives Fredda nightmares, but I had an absolute blast parachuting to the ground. It was like being on an out-of-control roller coaster. You're terrified and exhilarated all at the same time. Anyway, the pilot and I were rescued by a Resistance group based in Paris. We stayed at a nightclub for less than twenty-four hours, and then we managed to sneak into an old theater for a couple of nights. But I remember this short Irish lady, always dressed in black, who used to come popping into the dressing room where we were hiding. She'd treat us to cranberry-orange scones. She never told us her name, but Pierre Simon, who ran the club and was the Resistance leader, mentioned she was the wardrobe mistress for both the club and the theater."

"Now I'm totally intrigued. Do you suppose there might be a grandmom, daughter, and now granddaughter, all named Fiona Belle?" I asked. Then I groaned. "We shouldn't have brought up eating those scones. I have no business eating them—they're probably hundreds of calories in each bite, but they are irresistible. Y'all wanna come with and see if you can ferret out some info on her ancestry?"

Frank and Fredda both nodded. Frank politely helped me up out of my far-too-comfy-and-way-too-deep chair, and the three of us headed across the lobby.

But when we reached the spot where we'd last seen Fiona Belle Donovan hawking her wares and waving a pink fairy wand at potential customers, she was gone.

Chapter 20

Early October 1975

When it became clear that tracking down Fiona
Belle Donovan would be a fruitless enterprise, I decided,
even though it was early evening and not exactly office
hours, it might be the perfect time to head over to the
place I'd wanted to visit since landing the gig at the
Henske. I was due to meet Zelda for a drink but I had a
good hour until then, so I gathered up my courage and
walked down the street to the Am-Vets Center, which
was around the corner from the hotel and theater. I felt
moderately schizophrenic and completely nervous
because it occurred to me, on the trek over, there was a
strong possibility Marcus Kennedy might be at the
Center. Half of me was almost desperate to see him
again. The other half worried he'd view me as the
deranged girl who'd caused a scene down at the World
Trade Center revisiting a nonexistent traumatic event
live and in color, and he'd haul it over to Broadway
where he could disappear into the nearest, darkest pub
until he was certain I was gone from Manhattan. Possibly
from the universe. I wasn't sure I had the confidence to
croak out a faint "hello" if I did run into him.

I had no idea what to expect in terms of space at the
Am-Vets Center. When I'd been in college in Texas I'd
volunteered at a V.A. hospital outside of Austin, which

had been a huge complex. There were separate wards slated for use for a variety of issues, including burn treatments, physical therapy units, and a large auditorium which seated something like 500 people. I'd taught dance/drama classes on the stage of the auditorium. I hadn't been able to do much to stop the war (I was never sure the petitions and protests helped at all) but teaching movement gave me the sense I was at least doing something tangible that might heal some emotional wounds in these soldiers once they were out of the hellhole.

The Manhattan Am-Vets lobby was huge. A young man in a wheelchair, stationed behind one of the tables, waved enthusiastically at me the moment I opened the door. His black T-shirt sported a white name tag identifying him as one Billy Don Browne.

He beamed at me before exclaiming, "Wow! Finally, someone pretty coming through those doors instead of a lot of scowling, ugly ex-soldiers." He chortled. "I really lucked out on welcome duty. So, what can I do for you, miss?"

I blushed, but his cheerful reception banished most of my natural shyness and I was able to respond with, "Well, first, thanks for the compliment. You're very kind. Um, I came by this evening because I used to volunteer at a V.A. hospital in Texas when I was in college—I taught dance—and I wondered if there might be something similar I could do here at the Center? I'm kind of embarrassed because, honestly, apart from basketball games, I have no idea what else y'all do here."

"Oh, hey, we've got a lot more going on than just B-ball—a variety of classes, but we're always looking for volunteers for new and exciting things. Dance is definitely new. I need to introduce you to Toby, who directs the day-by-day activities. But would you like a tour of the facility?"

I nodded. "Absolutely. Thanks."

He turned and clicked the "on" switch attached to what appeared to be an ancient intercom system set into the wall. "Hello? Toby? You there? Or Sid? I've got a gorgeous lady out here who wants to see the place and hopefully end up doin' some volunteering. Can y'all come out, or are you still messin' with the projector for the film?"

Someone mumbled what sounded like a "yes" through the outdated speakers, and the young man chuckled. "I'm not sure who, but it appears someone human will be out in a second. We need a new intercom system purty darn bad."

I hid a smile as I asked, "So, Billy Don Browne, you're from—where? Nacogdoches? Tyler? Lufkin?"

"Whoa! Durn close. I'm from Henderson. It's like the other towns in looks, including the obligatory courthouse in the middle of town, we're just not as famous. How'd you guess?"

"I grew up in Dallas, but during college, I dated a guy from San Augustine. When you said 'film' you gave it away the instant it turned into 'fim.' Nobody from East Texas ever pronounces the L."

He laughed. "True. Then there's the other bad habit of chopping up certain three-syllable words into two."

"Oh, yeah. Trinity River was the biggie. I recall it always ended up as "trin'ty."

"Also true. Well, you obviously read my name tag, but what's your name, Dallas lady?"

Before I had a chance to answer, the doors to the

facility were flung open and a voice called out, "Her name is Shiloh Meridien."

Marcus Kennedy.

I felt my face flushing. "You remembered my name."

"I remembered *you*," he said. "Emphasis on 'you.' Admittedly, you've got a beautiful, unique name, to match your beautiful face. I can't stop singing the folk song about the sad Civil War lady roaming the hills and valleys of Shiloh looking for her lost love." He smiled at me. "Miss Meridien, seeing you in the audience at Monroe Hall was a pleasure. Third row, if memory serves. Making you breathe through what was clearly a hellish experience at the World Trade Center was also clearly unpleasant on your end, but it gave me a chance to show you my gallant side and meet you. You coming here today is fate. Kismet. Destiny." His left eyebrow lifted as I struggled between laughing or fainting. He added, greenish-gray eyes twinkling, "What? Over the top?"

I chose laughter. "No more than your average Victorian-era melodrama. But, hey. You're a performer, Mister Kennedy. You're allowed to go over the top." I paused before softly adding, "Especially when you're saying very lovely things."

We stood in silence for a long moment, staring into each other's eyes until the young veteran from East Texas coughed. "'Excuse me. If the gazing portion of the evening is done, um, Marcus, Miss Shiloh here said she's interested in volunteering. Um, unless Toby suddenly pops up in the next few minutes, would you mind showing her around before the guys come in to watch the movie?"

"Love to." He turned to me. "And if they arrive in the middle of the tour, perhaps you'd like to stay and watch? It's Audie Murphy's first Western, *The Boy from Texas*."

"Where Murphy was really from," Billy Don added with much satisfaction.

"Sounds fun, guys, but sadly, I'm meeting my friend Zelda for a drink in about forty minutes, so I won't have time."

"We show old films twice a week," Marcus said, "And you're welcome to come watch them with us. Sometimes, Toby even manages to rustle up popcorn. Meantime, let me show you the vets home away from home."

Marcus pressed a button on the wall and the panels behind the reception table became sliding doors, opening onto a huge space.

My eyes widened. "Oh, wow! This is gorgeous. What's the history of the place? I recall y'all saying at the Benefit Vets concert it was a city landmark..." That evening's memories, including all the intros and pleas to help the veterans by the singers, had been oddly hazy, apart from Marcus's performance, but until I had a clue as to why my recall was foggy, there was no need to bring up the fact the only words I remembered had been those said by Marcus.

Marcus replied, "It was originally a ballroom called The Rhythm Palace. Built in nineteen-twelve by Mister Cyrus Seeger, who rivaled the other giants of industry in the late eighteen-hundreds and early twentieth century. One thing that differentiates Cyrus from his contemporary millionaires was his passion for dance. He hated tiny venues and decided to create a space where folks could cut the proverbial rug without worrying about crashing into each other."

I held my hand up. "Wait."

"What?"

"I shouldn't interrupt you because I am truly entranced and want to hear all about Mister Seeger and his original Rhythm Palace, really I do, but before I get the full lowdown, may I ask you something? It's horribly personal, but I've been wondering about this for years and never saw the answer in any liner notes on your albums."

"Unless my answer would end up being embarrassing, sure." He lifted both eyebrows, waiting.

"Well, it's really kind of two questions, depending on the answer to the first one, and I'm probably not making any sense."

"Not much, but I'm intrigued. Go ahead. Ask away."

"Okay. How did you manage to avoid getting drafted into some branch of the military during the whole Vietnam mess?"

"Ah. That's actually a good question. It was tough, but I claimed, and, after some major haggling, was granted, conscientious objector status. My parish priest, Father Joe, went to bat for me and told the board he'd counseled me and would swear on the proverbial stack of Bibles I was sincere. And I shall forever be grateful to my dad, who was a proponent of the war but still went with me to the hearing and said he vehemently disagreed with my beliefs but he knew I wasn't lying about being a pacifist. Plus, my older brother, Colin, had already served in Vietnam and maybe some of the gentlemen on the draft board didn't like the idea of having two kids from the same family over there, especially when they heard Colin's helicopter was shot down and he was killed. I guess they felt sending the younger son into battle would be a bit too much. The Manhattan branch of the draft board was also slightly more amenable to my position than many of the boards from other parts of the country. I've met more than a few guys from the Deep South or Midwest who told me trying to claim C.O. status when the government is determined to cram you onto a plane to kill people in a hellhole thousands of miles away is practically impossible. You were just introduced to one of them."

"Billy Don Browne from East Texas. He seems like a great guy."

"He is. Smart too. Organized and super-efficient. The center couldn't do without him." Marcus paused. "But something tells me you still have that second question?"

"Yep. And possibly a third. Then I'd love to hear about the ballroom and its history. Honest."

"Go ahead, Miss Meridien. Second question…and third if needed."

"How did you get involved with the vets and, the iffy third, how did they react when you started working with them?" I couldn't tell him the reason I was asking was due to an annoying poltergeist who'd left intriguing notes in my bag about Marcus, the most disturbing including the word "murder," forcing me to search for any and all possible motives.

I plowed on. "I can't help but wonder if they resented someone who hadn't been in the war coming in after the fact. And whether anyone still feels that way."

For a long moment there was silence.

Chapter 21

Early October 1975

When Marcus remained quiet for a very long minute, I prayed I hadn't overstepped and offended him.

"Am I being too nosy?" I asked.

"No. Absolutely not. I'm just reliving life a few years back. Um, the answers are sort of a reversal of the questions."

"How so?"

"Because I did take part in the war. I just didn't fight. I toured with a couple of different groups and sang to the troops. I was careful and I was respectful. I had no desire to start riots or disputes among soldiers risking their lives for a cause they may or may not have believed in by belting out a variety of protest tunes, so I sang old folk songs and spirituals and a few old jazz standards from the days of the big bands." He paused. "Jumping ahead, and way off the subject again, I got the idea to do the *Remake the Song* album when I was in Vietnam, where I realized I wanted to use music to soothe and inspire instead of incite."

"Well, staying on the subject of your album for a second, I can't wait to hear it. I'd read in some magazine you were bucking the trend of folk singers switching to pop or rock with this record, and I'm all for it. I plan to be first in line to buy it."

"Kind of you to say but there's no need. Save your money. I'll get you a copy right off the press." He sighed. "I wish you'd tell Angela Dane, my business manager, you like the idea of me going against the grain. She keeps griping, 'It's not commercial enough and the critics are going to hate it.' She wants me to go with electric guitars and heavy metal next. I'm not kidding, although, if I'm being truthful, let me moan and groan and wail my distress…it's far worse. Angela has been touting the benefits of doing a disco album." He shook his head. "Don't get me wrong. I enjoy taking a turn around a dance floor doing a variation of the Hustle now and then. But singing disco is not me, will never be me, and I'm not selling my soul in order to make money." He flashed a grin, making him look like a mischievous boy of six caught in the act of opening the forbidden cookie jar in his gran's kitchen. "You should have heard Angela when I suggested doing a full gospel album. She nearly had a heart attack when I included three spirituals in *Remake the Song*. But I'm leaning more toward singing songs people relate to and can sing along with, which is what I do in my sessions with veterans here."

"I love it. No offense, and tell me to mind my own business, but if this Angela person won't get on board with what you need to do to feed your creative soul, you might consider getting a new manager."

He nodded. "I have. But apart from the loyalty issue because she's the person who landed me my first recording contract, it's a pain to go looking for someone else. And these days, the majority of singers are going the same direction anyway. As in, what sells. Most managers and agents agree with Angela Dane's point of view." He took a short beat before adding, "By the way,

I'd never tell you to mind your own business. You're not being nosy or pushy. You're sensitive and caring and…and I've gotten us far afield from Vietnam. Sorry."

I was still blushing after hearing him call me sensitive and caring. "No apologies necessary. I started it by asking how you managed not to be enlisted. And it's really interesting to hear about other singers and where they're headed with their music. It's bad news for those of us who want all of y'all to keep on fighting and protesting, but it is understandable they're going commercial. After all, one does have to eat and pay bills and can't always follow the heart." I paused, then added, "I'm sounding sappy and naive."

"You're sounding honest, and it's great."

I continued to feel the heat rushing over my face. I determinedly pushed on. "Okay. Back to you being in Vietnam. You were singing to the troops."

"Yep. All over the stinking jungle and in some very seedy dives in Saigon. I wasn't on the front lines with a gun but felt very much a part of the action and barely escaped serious injury when a bomb went off at one venue." He grimaced. "Shiloh, it was beyond horrible. Two musicians I toured with were killed in two different explosions a few days later. And sadly, I was at the bedside of more than one soldier who died in a MASH unit or in one of the larger hospitals."

"I am truly sorry. How awful for you, losing your friends, and really, for everyone who was put through sheer agony over there—for nothing. I felt so helpless every night when I watched the news, because there was nothing I could do to stop it."

"I guess this leads to your other question as to why I do what I do now? I saw up close what these soldiers…the majority of them kids of nineteen or twenty…were going through. Like you, I felt helpless. But I was determined to do whatever I could to help these veterans recover. I marched into the Am-Vets Center two and a half years ago and told them I'd like to help any way I could."

"Did everyone here freak out about you being the protest singer who'd fought against the war for years?"

"Not as much as you'd imagine. The reaction and reception was surprisingly warm. My first day at the Center I invited everyone to join me in a sing-along. There were about twenty-five guys sitting in a circle on the stage and one of them yells out, 'Yo, Marcus! Sing 'Chasm of Darkness' for us. The others echoed the request. I sang it. Word had gotten around I'd been over there performing for the troops and ducking as bombs went off around me, and they took me in as one of their own." He paused for a brief moment, then lifted an eyebrow. "Any other questions about the life and times of Marcus Kennedy in regard to Vietnam? I promise to answer everything with total honesty."

"Nope. Curiosity satisfied…at least for now." I had nothing to back up my feelings but I was positive no one at the Am-Vets center would be behind any attempt of murder. Which meant I needed to continue to look elsewhere for motives. But it was time to shove speculation to a corner and stay in the present. "I'm eager to hear about the Rhythm Palace."

"Well, as I said before, it started life as a ballroom for big social dances. Very popular with the high society set of New Yorkers at the turn of the century and up until the thirties. They managed to stay open during the Jazz Age. Officially, no booze was served, although there are rumors of tunnels underneath leading to small rooms where one could purchase shots of scotch or bourbon in a coffee cup. The place remained a dance hall throughout the Depression. There are photos in the main office"—he pointed all the way to the end of the space—"showing couples involved in marathon dances. It was all very *They Shoot Horses, Don't They?*"

"Good movie, although it was painful to watch. Especially for anyone who regards dance as something to enjoy, not endure."

"Well, now this same ballroom works beautifully for guys in wheelchairs playing basketball, and they do more than endure. They enjoy."

"Aha." I grinned at him. "This explains why, and trying not to be too offensive, it smells like my old high school gym. Are there dressing rooms...oops, I mean locker rooms, anywhere?"

"Yep." He pointed behind the huge makeshift bleachers. "With real showers and soap dispensers, although, now that you mention it, it is a bit gamey in here. There was a practice earlier this afternoon and, you're right, Eau de Sweat is definitely lingering in the air."

"I have to say, it's better than some dressing rooms I've been in with divas reeking of supposedly high-quality perfume. It's bad enough after a show, but before or during intermission...? Trying not to inhale kind of makes performing tough. Be it dancing, singing, or acting."

"I was right."

"About?" I asked.

"You being a dancer. The day I met you, even watching all the emotional turmoil you were going through, I couldn't help noticing you still moved with grace. And by the way, I've been kicking myself I didn't get your number, thanks to Angela tugging at me, so I had a hunch the best way to track you down would be to start combing the studios in the city. I've visited about five places so far." He flashed one of those wicked grins my way. "I admit, I avoided the ballet companies. I've never seen a ballerina in this city who was taller than five-two, and I grew up here. And Shiloh, if you hadn't walked in here today, I was considering hiring a hot-air balloon and flying over the city with a banner reading, *"Beautiful Redhead from Twin Towers...Where Are You? Meet Me at Am-Vets!"* There are a lot more dance studios in Manhattan than I imagined. Going all over New York has been taking up a lot of my time."

I nearly went into shock. "You tried to find me?"

"I did."

"Why?"

Marcus took a beat before saying, "Maybe to do this." Then he reached over, gently touched my chin, and tilted my face up to join his lips to mine.

"Hey, Kennedy. Not fair," came from the left side of the gym. "Kissing a beautiful woman nobody's had a chance to meet yet?"

Talk about grace...Marcus let me go without thrusting me away, and then turned to greet a tall, bald-headed, muscular man dressed in sweats, with the words *Black Veterans Got the Power!* emblazoned on the front of the shirt. He looked very familiar, except the person he reminded me of had two arms. This man was missing one. I couldn't stop staring at his handsome face.

Before he could say a word, I blurted out, "Do you have a doppelganger? Or a twin?"

He laughed. "The latter. You must have met my brother, Terry Travers."

I beamed at him. "I take martial arts classes from him. He's wonderful. Does he also teach here?" I stopped. "Oh, heck. I apologize. I'm being rude, diving right in and asking nosy questions before introductions have been made. I'm Shiloh Meridien."

"Toby Travers," he responded. "And, yeah, Terry occasionally teaches here, but it's mainly me. Like my brother, I'm a black belt, and surprisingly unhampered by the loss of the arm. In a way, it's much better for me to be the one teaching, because no matter what kind of injury these vets are dealing with, it helps them to watch…and learn…from someone with physical challenges who can still kick butt quite well."

"You and Terry trained in Japan, right?" I asked.

"Yep. We were born in Harlem, but then our parents became missionaries and did the majority of their work in Okinawa, which was home for about ten years. We trained in martial arts over there. Of course, as soon as we were eighteen and back in America, we were both called up by Uncle Sam to serve. We ended up in different units, much as we tried to get them to take us together." He shook his head. "Terry just happened to be faster than I was in avoiding booby traps in the Mekong Delta."

Marcus was following all this with genuine interest. I determinedly stayed focused on the conversation to keep from swooning like some Southern Belle after our kiss, which, I freely admit, had been more than faint-worthy but way too brief.

"Shiloh's a dancer, Toby," Marcus said. "And she wants to volunteer her services here at the Center."

Toby gave me a warm look of appreciation. "Awesome. Marcus does sing-a-longs and gives guitar lessons to a couple of the guys, but teaching dance would be amazing. Have you done anything like this before?"

I told the pair about teaching at the veterans' hospital in Texas during college. Both Toby and Marcus seemed impressed.

"Tell you what," said Toby. "Let me work out when the space is free and get back to you with some days and times." He paused for a second. "Wait. Am I rushing ahead? You haven't had a chance to decide if you want to work with us. But, assuming you do, what's your schedule?"

We spent the next few minutes discussing work conflicts and were pretty satisfied we'd avoided sneaking me in to teach during short spurts of basketball breaks when the doors burst open and about ten guys in wheelchairs and twenty-five more walking with or without canes or crutches came barreling into the gym. It seemed the movie was about to begin.

Chapter 22

Early October 1975

I had about twenty minutes left before I was due to meet Zelda. Toby Travers assured me he'd call later tonight so we could iron out the details of having me teach some classes, including what I needed in terms of music. He said he'd check with Billy Don Browne, who, according to Toby, was a talented deejay, to see if he'd like to do some "platter spinning" for the class. The Center had recently been gifted with a huge turntable system which rivaled some of the best discos in the city, and Toby was sure Billy Don would be delighted to help out.

Marcus offered to escort me back to the Henske where I'd left my overly large, overstuffed dance bag, and I accepted with more pleasure than a two-block walk should warrant.

"So, Miss Meridien, you're up on the life and times of Marcus Kennedy," said Marcus. "Although, and I don't mean to continue a discussion about me, but earlier you sounded pretty adamant about me sticking to my guns and not going commercial, so I'm curious as to when you started listening to my stuff."

"Oh. Not to boost your ego, but I have to confess I fell like the proverbial ton of bricks for you—for your music—the first time I heard you on the radio. And, yes, the song was 'Chasm of Darkness.' "

"Oh, man, I'm afraid to ask, but how old were you?"

"Twelve."

"Ouch! A baby, but clearly already a discerning woman of taste," he teased.

"Well, before you grant me any brilliant critical status when it comes to music, you might want to hear the sad, seamy, shameful truth." I allowed a far-too-gleeful tone to emerge. "My grandmother on my mom's side, the one who did *not* provide me with my first name, adored all the operettas of the early twentieth century, and she used to sing them to me when I was a baby. I learned to appreciate more than a few tunes some folks might consider to be somewhat less than highbrow. I don't spread it around, especially to other performers, but I can sing the entire score of the stage version of *Rose Marie*. Granny and I used to do duets to the 'Indian Love Call' whenever she'd come to visit. My parents and sister were not amused."

Marcus struggled not to laugh…and failed. "Also not for public consumption, but while we're confessing our musical sins, I'm personally a big fan of all the sappy, schmaltzy songs composed by Rudolf Friml, whose melodies made Sigmund Romberg's stuff sound positively funky."

I shook my head. "No wonder your manager is worried about you crossing over to the dark side. Doubtless she's afraid that after singing spirituals, a few cabaret tunes, and a classical aria or two, you'll head right into fake cowboy songs made popular in the early talkie movies from the thirties."

Marcus eyes lit up. "You may have something there. It's just wacky enough to sell. I'm getting this wicked idea of doing an album of lonesome, bluesy melodies from the range. It would open up a whole new audience. Or I'd be deported. Okay. Definitely enough about me. I know nothing about you. So, Spill, Shiloh. Backstory."

"Oh. It's not terribly exciting." I gave him a brief lowdown. "Born and raised in Dallas, Texas. One sister who was a beauty queen and financial genius, making me feel like a slug. Neither she nor my parents ever acknowledged a career as a dancer to be anything but useless. A semi-pacifist, because I wouldn't hesitate to use martial arts training for self-defense, although I would do my best to only fell or cripple an opponent— wound, not kill. I moved to New York back in June and my biggest career desire is to dance with the Emma Andersen troupe, but I'm having a great time at the Henske with *The Golden Age Revue* while waiting for Andersen's company to return to the city so I can audition. End of life and times of Shiloh Meridien."

"Any current boyfriends?"

I ducked my head down, not sure where this was leading. "Nope."

"Want one?" He winked at me.

What the heck. The man had kissed me. He was interested. Time to be bold. Be cheeky. Be totally unlike me. I looked right into his eyes before asking, "Are you applying?"

"Absolutely."

We stopped walking in the middle of the block in front of an Irish pub, forcing more than one pedestrian to swivel to the side to avoid crashing into us.

Bold and cheeky disappeared. I became speechless. While I was desperately trying to frame a brilliant, witty, cute response, Marcus kindly rescued me. "Well, as we're both used to auditioning for things we want, which I guess could include my achieving boyfriend status, what would you say to a real live date?"

"Do you have something in mind?" I asked, trying to breathe.

"I do. Although it depends on how you feel about engaging in more dancing after all the performances you do in a week."

"As long as I'm not in pointe shoes, I'm pretty much game for any and all dancing, especially if it's social and I don't have to worry about impressing anyone with my technical prowess."

"Perfect," Marcus said. "There's this very cool Latin club in Spanish Harlem, and they have one amazing house band. The flute player, Manuel Perez, lives in my apartment building right across the hall from me. Manny and I have been friends for years, so I've gone to *Club Roja Rosa* to hear them play more times than I've had my own concerts in the city."

"Do you ever sit in with Manny, et al?" I inquired.

"Now and then. But, I promise, as a polite and attentive escort, I would never abandon my date, which would be you, to play a set." He chuckled. "I may be just a clumsy folk singer, but I can execute a mean tango, although rumba is more my speed. Of course, this assumes my partner, which also happens to be you, can follow my lead."

"Challenging me? Fine. You're on. Being tall, I always ended up as the leader in ballroom dance classes I took at my old dance studio in Dallas when I was a teenager, but I did manage to learn the follower's steps as well. I always played nice and did not push or tug my partners around."

We smiled at each other, then continued our short trek to the theater. Very short. Too short. We were at the entrance of the Henske Hotel less than a minute after our discussion of dancing at the club.

"I'm sure you'll want to get home and change after your show Friday," Marcus stated. "How about I come by around nine-thirty? Will you have enough time? Oh, yeah—I need your address and phone number before I have to go hunting you down again."

"Nine-thirty is great. More than enough time. I learned the concept of quick change when I was about three. Let's see. Phone and address. Do you have a pen and paper? If not, I do." I started to open my bag to grab the small notebook I carried with me everywhere.

He shook his head. "No need for pen or paper. I have an amazing memory."

I gave him my address and number. "My memory isn't as wonderful as yours, so if it's okay, I'm writing your info down in case the worst happens and I'm going to be late or something."

Marcus provided his home number, his phone service, and his address, before saying, "This will work perfectly. I live not far from here in Hell's Kitchen, so we can head right up to the club from your place. No backtracking."

"You do? Live around here, I mean?"

"Yep. Same apartment where I grew up." His expression reflected sadness for a moment. "Maybe I suffer from sloppy sentimentality, but I like being in the space and having my folks' and Colin's things around."

"All your family is gone?" I asked.

He nodded. "My mom died during my last year of high school. Colin was killed in Vietnam. And my dad

140

had a heart attack, then pneumonia, about six months after we got word of Colin's death. It was as though he missed them both so much he finally decided he had to join them. I sort of understood, but it was rough losing everyone within the space of about six years."

"I am so very sorry," I said.

"Thank you. I miss them all, but living in the old apartment somehow keeps everyone close. I swear I feel my mom's presence when I'm composing. Like she's still there, listening. If I don't feel her approval, I start over."

"I like that," I told him.

We reached the entrance to the Henske and stopped.

Marcus took my hand in his, then leaned down and kissed the top of my palm. "Till Friday, then, Shiloh Meridien. It can't come soon enough."

It was strange. I'd been a bit shy at first about talking to Marcus and trying not to respond too eagerly to his charm and charisma and end up appearing silly. I suppose I should have been intimidated after meeting him, but I was as comfortable talking to him as I was with Zelda. Yet, at the same time, I could feel the racing pulse and flippy butterfly flutters inside which often accompany a new relationship.

He turned and went back toward the Am-Vets Center. I stood for a moment, trying to compose myself, before I stepped inside the Henske hotel.

Either Marcus had flirting down to a fine art or we were in sync and somehow had crashed right into a romance in full speed.

Didn't matter. I agreed with him. Friday couldn't arrive fast enough.

Chapter 23

Early October 1975

Over the last few months I'd attended a variety of dance classes in New York taught by excellent instructors, many of whom were famous in the dance world. All of them had started their careers as performers but now used their considerable skills to pass on what they hoped would be a legacy of greatness to the next generation. A few were still performing and/or doing choreography. My teachers included Marina Ivanov, a former Russian prima ballerina who danced with one of the premiere Russian ballet companies and defected from the Soviet Union in the early nineteen-sixties. Ivanov offered her services to a newly formed troupe based in Harlem, who were thrilled to work with her, even as they struggled to understand her heavy accent, courtesy of Moscow. There was the eighty-year-old vaudeville tapper Bucky Turner, who'd learned his craft on the streets of Philadelphia, and had students of all ages sweating proverbial buckets two minutes into his killer warm-up. Possibly the hardest teacher, in terms of insisting on precise, pristine technique, was Vashti Banik, a choreographer who'd worked with Emma Andersen's company. Banik was originally from New Delhi, India but moved to New York at age sixteen to become a dancer, against the wishes of his parents.

My absolute favorite, both as instructor and person, was my lyrical jazz teacher, Dario Bernardi, whose name was synonymous with inspiration. I always left his class feeling refreshed, light, and loose-limbed, ready to face challenges and overcome obstacles with grace and determination instead of fear and indecisiveness. He preached continuous movement, which embedded itself into one's consciousness throughout class and in daily life. Dario's philosophy of maintaining a positive attitude, refusing to give up, using movement along with grit and resolution in order to heal physically, mentally, and emotionally, was what I hoped to instill in the veterans who'd agreed to take part in what was, admittedly, an experiment with no certain outcome.

Toby Travers turned out to be one heck of an efficient organizer. I'd met him Wednesday evening. He called me late the same night to coordinate schedules and Thursday morning at eleven I was at the Am-Vets Center to teach my first class. The old Rhythm Palace ballroom boasted a large stage, suitable for dances featuring the big bands of the twenties, thirties, and forties. Toby and I decided it'd be best to leave the ballroom floor vacant and I'd teach the class on the stage, where it would be a bit more intimate. Hopefully, it would be reassuring to the participants and less intimidating than pushing them to feel they had to fill a giant empty space.

I'd been very honest with Toby about never having taught movements for guys in wheelchairs. We agreed that, much as we hated to exclude anyone, we didn't want a single vet physically hurt if I was the slightest bit unsure about what I was teaching. I promised I'd figure out how best to add some wheelchair moves in the future if these initial dance classes were well received. In turn,

Toby gave me the number of one of the physical therapists employed by the Center, assuring me he'd be able to steer me in the right direction.

So there I was, Thursday morning, being introduced to seven veterans, starting with Dave, who, like Toby, was missing an arm (his left), and Rocky, who was working to overcome PTSD symptoms of violent outbursts and whose wife had left him out of fear he might harm her. There was Andrew, healing from severe leg injuries, Sid, who'd been experiencing some respiratory issues and a ton of headaches, Rick, who'd suffered a back injury that made it painful for him to walk more than a few steps at a time, and Calvin, who had to sleep with the lights on and ducked every time he heard a loud noise. And finally, there was Jonah, who looked like he wasn't much older than sixteen, and who, according to Toby, hadn't spoken a single word in the three years he'd been back in the States. Word had it Jonah hadn't talked for a total of four and half years. I maintained as much of an objective, professional presence as I was able, determined not to break down and burst into tears upon meeting each of these brave men who were acting as guinea pigs in this experiment of healing.

Toby acted as my assistant and, true to his word, brought in Billy Don Browne, the paralyzed vet from Texas I'd met the day before when he was acting as receptionist and greeter in the lobby, to work his magic as deejay with the giant turntable. Both Toby and I hoped to eventually include live music for upcoming classes, but we wanted to ease into the dance-as-therapy concept before adding another layer to the mix.

I designed the class to follow the structure of classes

I'd taken (or taught) throughout my life. My intent was not to turn a bunch of Navy seamen, Marine infantrymen, or Army Rangers into a Broadway chorus line or a corps de ballet of elegantly lithesome swans, but I knew if there was one thing the military was great at instilling in its troops, it was discipline. The vets I'd taught in Austin had responded favorably to the strict routine of a dance class. I would not be teaching technique, but I did follow the established pattern of warm-up, center and/or "across the floor" movements, plus a cool-down stretch sequence made up of simple balletic or yoga positions and a ton of deep breathing.

I somewhat nervously faced seven tough ex-members of teams who'd fought in unimaginably terrifying and gruesome conditions, men who wouldn't suffer fools or wimps gladly. They could have made a mockery of the class, but these guys were solidly with me from the moment Billy Don Browne placed the needle on the eight-minute long track of an R & B album from the mid-sixties and we began a warm-up intended to hit body areas from top to bottom and back up again.

When it was time for center work, I had the guys do some silly improvisations to the sounds of current disco music I'd heard in clubs around Manhattan. They seemed to enjoy pretending to "dance" their way through imaginary sticky marshmallow whip (accompanied by lots of laughter) splash through nonexistent puddles as if they were doing a scene from *Singin' in the Rain*, or spin like a small tornado winding up before taking off and destroying a town. I finished the center portion by putting everyone (including me) into a circle and swaying to the sounds of a British rock group, which, like the opening warm-up music, had hit top popularity in the mid-sixties.

Marcus popped his head inside the ballroom as we were finishing up and proved himself to be a man of sensitivity and perception. He didn't stay more than a minute, at most, clearly not wishing to interrupt the flow. He waved at me and gave me a thumbs-up while I was gently placing a hand on Rocky's lower chest area to show him the correct position for diaphragmatic breathing.

Marcus was waiting for me in the lobby outside the ballroom. He appeared angry and distressed, totally unlike his demeanor when he'd looked in on the class.

"What's wrong?"

"It shows?"

"Well, Marcus, let me say if there was a punching bag anywhere near by, I wouldn't give two pennies for its survival."

"You'd be right. Wow. I meant to greet you with a big hug after your class, and I will, but I need to calm down."

I waited.

Marcu inhaled. "I've just been meeting with the parents of Jeremiah Henry, Junior, former PFC, late of Brooklyn. I use the term late because Jeremiah was shot and killed by a cop two months ago. A cop who continues to earn a paycheck from the city of New York. No disciplinary charges were filed. No censure given. His parents are trying to find someone who'll speak up for their son and other sons who are dying in the street for the crime of being black."

I didn't mention Black Lives Matter. I didn't know how I'd heard of it, and if, as I suspected, it was another clairvoyant *déjà-vu-ism*, it wouldn't be helpful.

"I'm so sorry. Is there anything anyone here can do?" I asked.

"Well, not really. We've already mounted a few protests, but tangling with the current NYPD administration is synonymous with beating one's head against the proverbial brick wall. Don't get me wrong. Not all the cops are bad, by any means, but it seems there are a few who remain on the force without any consequences. I did tell the Henrys I'd talk to Sid, who's a heartbeat away from being a licensed member of the New York State Bar, and see if there's a way to file charges against the cop who murdered their child. Or sue him in civil court? Private Henry was a veteran, but he was only twenty-two." He tried to laugh. "Where's the punching bag you mentioned?"

"Hey, you're more than welcome to use my dance bag. There are a couple of peanut butter and jelly sandwiches that should have been thrown out yesterday. This could be one way of getting rid of them."

"Might take you up on it." He physically shook off the anger and took a huge breath. "Okay. I'm better. Since you brought up dance, um, I didn't want to disturb the class and barge in, but from what I saw, you seemed to be performing a miracle or two."

"Miracle? What? How do you mean?"

"Heck. Strips of leather left out in the sun for decades are softer than these guys. Yet each and every man was listening to you. I could feel this astonishing calm descend over everyone even from where I stood. It was amazing and impressive."

"Wow! Thank you. I hope it's true. If anything, I'm guessing I act as a kind of conduit for their own abilities to get to a better place both physically and emotionally.

Which has got to be rough. I'm not sure there are enough synonyms for 'horrible' to begin to describe their experiences. I had to force myself to stay upbeat and not break down and sob. All of them have such gut-wrenching stories." My voice caught for a second. "Marcus, the kid who really got to me, as in the 'break my heart' department?"

"Let me guess. Jonah."

"Jonah. What kind of hell he must have been through to literally not be able to communicate with words and speech for more than three years."

Marcus grimaced. "Yeah. I can't imagine being so traumatized I wouldn't be able to sing." He paused, then continued. "I read his file when I originally started doing the sing-a-longs, because I was trying to find some way to encourage him to participate, even if it was just to sit in the back and listen. He never did. I learned that after watching his entire squad, of which he was the youngest, wiped out during a battle in an area they never should have been sent to, he was shot, captured, and held prisoner. No one's ever revealed which POW camp he was in…although, if there's one saving grace, it was *not* the infamous Hanoi Hilton. I'm not sure how he came to be released. The military gets testy and close-mouthed about those kinds of details, and I have this gut sense it was not a sanctioned release, but an escape. Anyway, there were five others who were at the same camp with him who returned to the States at the same time, and they were pretty clear about the use of torture being common. Geneva Convention prohibitions and laws? No such animal in Hanoi. Rumor has it Jonah stopped talking after his second month in prison. He has no family, so he relies on the guys at the Center to give him all the support he can get."

I was fighting back tears at hearing more of Jonah's story. "They've all been to and through hell and are still clawing their way out, aren't they?"

He nodded. "It's one reason I'm so passionate about wanting to keep this particular center open. Where else can these guys go where they can play sports and gripe to each other about things no one else understands?" He smiled. "And where else will they find beautiful, passionate, caring dancers attempting to bring some peace and harmony back to their wrecked lives?"

I was starting to compliment him on his own contributions to the Center when he smacked his hand to his head.

"I almost forgot to ask."

"What?"

"Sunday. We're having a protest demonstration in front of Roger Masters' offices in midtown. Which I plan to expand in scope to include some speeches about racial inequalities when it comes to policing in parts of my hometown. Do you want to come? I'm aware you've got two shows Saturday and you'll be exhausted, and of course on Friday you'll have done your show and then have been out dancing the night away with a certain singer," he flashed a grin, "but you're young and healthy and I'd love to have you with us, so whaddya say?"

"Are you kidding? Sign me up and give me a placard, bullhorn, lectern with microphone, or whatever it takes. Honestly? If I need to do a marathon dance for a week in pointe shoes to save the Center, and now to focus attention on racial issues, I'll do it."

Marcus hugged me. "This, Shiloh Meridien, is just one more reason I adore you."

Chapter 24

Early October 1975

My closet held exactly one dress I'd call suitable for a night of Latin dancing in Spanish Harlem. The rest of my meager wardrobe consisted of jeans, tees, a ton of leotards, jazz pants, sweats, and two outfits suitable for temp jobs in business offices. I hadn't a clue as to how the sexy black, lacy, tiered number with the handkerchief hem had made its way into my suitcase when I packed last summer (since, as I'd told Zelda when discussing a possible poltergeist, I also couldn't recall buying it) but there it was, hanging neatly from a plastic hanger. It had been shoved into the back of the small closet, hiding behind a charcoal-colored pants-and-blazer set purchased with those temp jobs in mind.

I'd pulled the dress out Wednesday when I got home from performing at the Henske, the day Marcus invited me to go dancing, hung it in front of my closet, and spent way too much time staring at it during the few hours I was home Thursday.

Friday night after showering, applying non-stage makeup and attempting to do something to tame my overly curly hair, I donned the dress and twirled around a few times for Wyatt and Jim. Both guys whistled their approval. Wyatt's girlfriend Cathy was a model, and he somehow had acquired her knowledge regarding what was fashionable and trendy. Jim, as well as being a sharp reporter, painted watercolors and had an artist's eye for design and line. I was thrilled when both of them proclaimed Miss Shiloh Meridien to be one hot mama. Jim went on to gleefully predict Mister Marcus Kennedy would melt into a quivering mass of jelly the moment he laid eyes on me.

Promptly at nine-thirty, the buzzer rang. Wyatt and Jim answered the door in tandem and immediately assumed the role of nineteenth-century parents inspecting their teenage daughter's prom date. Marcus and I were too busy staring into each other's eyes to notice my nosy roommates standing behind me but far too close. Neither Jim nor Wyatt shifted position or said a word.

Finally, Wyatt nudged me and coughed. "Introductions?"

I made them.

Wyatt then scowled before directing what I guess he hoped was a steely-eyed, take-no-prisoners glare at my date.

"So, Mr. Kennedy, exactly what time does this place close?" came from Wyatt. "And is the neighborhood well lit?"

"Two," Marcus responded. "And it's bright as daylight on a beach."

Jim joined in with a puny attempt to portray a responsible adult put in charge of a demented child. "I must inform you, Marcus, Shiloh's an extremely lousy drinker. Do not let her down more than one glass of whatever every two hours…max. If she comes home intoxicated, there will be serious consequences to your future well-being."

I sighed.

"You *are* bringing her home, correct? Not planning on sticking her inside some miserable cab by herself?" was Wyatt's next contribution.

"If you're not displaying all the traits of a proper Southern gentleman, we'll come up and get her ourselves," Jim added, "long before two a.m."

"No need," Marcus stated, trying gallantly to keep a straight face as the twitching at the corners of his mouth betrayed his amusement, before I had a chance to grab his arm and steer him back outside. "I hired a town car, which is currently waiting outside and will be at the club promptly upon closing. When we get back here, I'll personally escort Miss Shiloh to the door and make sure she locks it behind her." He casually tossed out, "Then again, I can't promise I'll ignore an impulse to head to Elkton, Maryland, home of elopements up and down the East Coast."

Marcus winked at me as my mind and heart shouted—and yes, I realize it's physically impossible—*Don't ignore!*

Neither roommate had a sharp or witty response to this. Neither did I.

I said, "Okey-dokey. Uh, Marcus? Perhaps it's time to go, before my supremely over-protective and ridiculous roommates decide to act as chaperones for the rest of the night?"

Jim and Wyatt came with us to the promised town car. For a moment, I thought the pair of them were going to climb into the back seat, but they stood in silence, watching with a high degree of intensity, as I slid inside, followed by Marcus.

Once we were underway, I turned to Marcus.

"You've heard the Latin term 'in loco parentis'?"

Marcus's eyes twinkled. "Of course. Collegiate dorm monitors make a point of referring to it when they're chastising some kid for breaking curfew. Kids don't care."

"Well, let me say, my dear roommates have shifted from Latin to Spanish and are now officially *loco* guardians. I'm assuming they were trying to make an impression on the big, bad, protest singer, although I'm not exactly sure what it is they wanted to convey, apart from their willingness to make fools of themselves in order to keep safe the girl they consider their baby sister."

"They're both crazy about you." Marcus paused. "Totally understandable. I've been pretty unhinged myself since I first saw you at the concert in August. It took all the control I could muster not to jump off the stage, swoop you into my arms, and whisk you off to some deserted tropical island where we could be together without interference from another human for the next fifty years or so."

"You do realize, Marcus Kennedy, you are a charmer?" I asked. "Capable of enticing a fourth wish out of a grumpy, pig-headed, resistant genie without ever breaking a sweat."

"Is this a good thing or a bad thing?" Marcus asked. "And aren't you mixing your metaphors?"

"Hmm. I'd say the good or bad all depends on your sincerity and honesty when using your charm. As to the metaphors? Undeniably a messy blend, but then, I was a dance major, not an English scholar."

Marcus took my hand in his and gazed into my eyes, holding and locking and captivating me. "Well, Miss

Meridien, rest assured, when it comes to you, I will always be honest and sincere. Will you do the same for me?"

"Yes."

The drive to *Club Roja Rosa* took about fifteen minutes. I'd never been in this area of New York before. I'm usually overly curious about my adopted city, and any other time, I'd've been eagerly drinking in my surroundings, but tonight I didn't care. The best view was the one in the car, the man sitting beside me.

The club was located in the middle of a block of what appeared to be primarily made up of bodegas (still open) and gigantic thrift shops (closed for the night). I made a mental note to check out the stores for later. I'd see if Zelda wanted to join me in an afternoon of bargain hunting. At the opposite end of the block from the nightclub was a vacant lot, set up as a makeshift basketball court, where twelve teenage boys were currently engaged in a fast and furious game of hoops.

I'd gone out dancing about ten times since moving to Manhattan in June. All the venues had been cavernous clubs spotlighting abnormally large spaces, most had a sparkling, brightly lit ball that spun above one's head, and none featured live bands. Every club's decor included long tables set up for folks to grab some liquid refreshment, sit for a minute or two, then haul it back to the floor. Talking was nearly impossible due to the volume of the music. It made for a fabulous and fun night out when one solely wanted to cut loose and dance. No worries about trying to impress a casting director or even fending off a date more interested in drinking and trying to score than gyrating to the latest sounds played on gigantic, fancy turntables controlled by disc jockeys determined to be up on the absolute latest hit tunes.

Club Roja Rosa was the opposite of the big discos. It was intimate and cozy, with tables for two set up around a dance floor barely spacious enough to accommodate eight couples. The antique, wrought-iron, cafe tables faced a stage with a platform providing an adequate, but not huge, space for a live band. Tonight's musicians consisted of a percussionist, a pianist, two guitarists, and one trumpet player.

Marcus and I were ushered to a table on the opposite side of the club from its entrance by a man in his mid-fifties who had the look of a Latin movie star from the silent era. He hugged Marcus before turning back to me, taking my hand, and delivering a very classy, European-style kiss on my palm. Then, in Spanish, he said to Marcus, "Thank you. You've brought a most beautiful lady to my club. I am so honored. Perhaps a pitcher or two of our special *Agua de Valencia* is in order? On the house for you."

I tried not to react. There was no need for anyone to realize the tall Texas girl had been speaking (and understanding) Spanish from childhood. I did smile at the man who'd been introduced as Carlos Martinez before Marcus replied, also in Spanish, "Sounds great, but as always, I'm not accepting freebies. Let's get a tab going." He turned to me and said, in English, "Carlos is going to bring us a pitcher of *Agua de Valencia*, which is a Spanish version of a mimosa. It's made with cava, which is like champagne, plus orange juice—fresh, when one does it right—and gin or vodka. Sometimes both. Pretty strong but very delicious. And, of course, everyone pretends it's healthy because of the extra, citrusy vitamin C."

"Sounds wonderful."

"Perhaps, Señor Marcus, as an exchange for the drinks, you would sing a few songs for us?" was Carlos' response, this time in English.

Marcus glanced at me. "Is that okay with you? Would you mind being left alone while I'm on stage? I won't sing if you'd prefer I didn't. I recall promising you when I invited you to come dancing with me that I wouldn't desert you, and I do try to keep my promises."

"Are you kidding? Fancy drinks and a serenade of tunes by my favorite singer? You're not deserting me; you're sharing your wonderful music. This night keeps getting better."

Marcus turned back to Carlos. "It's on, then. And perhaps some sparkling water? Gulping cocktails generally isn't helpful when trying to impress a lady with one's skill at the tango or rumba."

Carlos bowed slightly, held out a chair for me, then turned and headed off to give our order to a short, chubby guy sporting a huge mustache. I assumed he was either the bartender, our waiter, or both.

I'd barely scooched my chair closer to the table when Marcus was back on his feet, his right (unbandaged) hand extended to me. "*Quieres bailar, Senorita Meridien? La musica es demasiado buena para desperdiciarla.*" (Would you like to dance? The music is too good to waste.)

"*Gracias y si, Señor Kennedy.*" I let him lead me from the table, then stopped before we hit the dance floor. "*Como supiste que hablaba espanol?*" (How did you figure out I spoke Spanish?)

"I'm very observant, especially around you, and I saw your eyes light up when Carlos was suggesting bringing *Agua de Valencia* pitchers to the table. Also, you blushed when he called you beautiful."

Couldn't help it. A flush was spreading across my face again. "Well, um, okay. Mystery solved. *Bailando es!*"

****

Magical and enchanting. Those were the two words best describing four and a half hours of dancing at *Club Roja Rosa,* although both words were inadequate in attempting to cover the night's special moments and emotions.

There was the *Agua de Valencia.* I'm not much of a drinker, but I found I fully appreciated the subtle flavors of the cava, gin, and vodka blending perfectly with orange juice taken from fruit so fresh I was tempted to check outside the club for a handy grove.

There was the atmosphere. Romantic, intimate, yet thoroughly comfortable and devoid of tension. As if all the people enjoying this night at the club were one family sharing music and laughter and love while keeping the rest of the world at bay for a night.

There was the music. The band was small but made up for any lack of size and instrumentation with an unstoppable energy penetrating the senses of the bodies on the dance floor and the folks who chose to sit and listen.

There was the dancing. Marcus led me through rumbas and tangos and cha-chas as if we'd been rehearsing steps for years, leading without forcing, and making it clear this was a partnership, not a domination. The one...glitch? Snag? Problem? Whatever. Twice, Marcus stumbled, almost as if his knees refused to provide enough support. He ignored it, putting the weakness down to too much basketball at the vets' center with guys who spent half their time lifting weights and the other half driving wheelchairs with more force and speed than a professional racer.

Finally, there was Marcus. I'd teased him about being a charmer, and it was true, but there was nothing fake about his charisma and nothing fake about the way he treated me.

When we got back to my apartment at two-forty a.m., he walked me to the door, leaned down, and kissed me without holding me, stepped back, then politely opened the door for me. I turned to say, "Thank you for this magical evening…" Which is when Marcus released the arm he'd been hiding behind his back and handed me one single, perfect, long-stemmed red rose.

Chapter 25

October 1975

Saturday was spent in a dreamy haze of reliving every moment at *Club Roja Rosa*, until I had to head to midtown and perform at the Henske. We did two shows on Saturday, one at brunch and one at the regular tea time hour. Thanks to years of training (and being too young to realize a night out should knock me six ways solid to Sunday), I was able to focus on what I was doing—instead of remembering swaying to the sounds of the rumba tune "Por Fin Te Enconte" with Marcus, I executed technically perfect high kicks in the middle of a chorus of "Alexander's Ragtime Band."

Sunday was the Am-Vets protest demonstration against Roger Masters and his entire corporation or institution or operation or syndicate or whatever one calls a multi-millionaire's business, to be held in front of his offices at the corner of Fifty-Second Street and Sixth Avenue (aka Avenue of the Americas). The weather was perfect: upper sixties with no rain. The turnout was bigger than I expected. I wasn't sure how many guys called the Am-Vets Center "home" but I counted more than thirty-five men, some in wheelchairs, each and every one of them proudly wearing the full-dress uniform of whichever branch of the military they'd served. Five members from my dance class who'd been able to make the demonstration waved at me with great enthusiasm when they spotted me.

The last time I'd attended a rally had been four years ago in Dallas when I was still in high school. The year was nineteen-seventy-one and the theme was a general protest against the Vietnam War. It was one of those "we came, we sang, we waved signs in the air, we signed petitions, and we feel frustrated, empty, helpless, and hopeless because we can't see anything changing regardless of our efforts" events. After I was enrolled in college, watching my friends hit demonstrations on a near-daily basis, I grew disenchanted with the idea of rallies when it became obvious all the protests in the world were doing nothing to stop a war. So, rather than marching, I'd opted for dancing. I'd focused on helping the vets who came home and were feeling…let's say less than whole. I volunteered to teach dance at the hospital, hoping to make a contribution, however slight. Today's demonstration was much like the one in Dallas, apart from the protestors, who, instead of a bunch of rowdy teenagers were primarily guys from the Am-Vets Center determined to do what they could to keep the place open. It was their lifeline to normalcy and, in some cases, to sanity.

Toby Travers had gotten in touch with the president of the historical landmark society and the pair of them conceived the brilliant idea of printing up hundreds of brochures (consisting of five pages) featuring photos displaying a chronological history of the place, starting with the old Rhythm Palace during its first (and possibly best) dancing years. Shots had been added of numerous veterans, taken over the last two years, showing them playing basketball or ping pong, lifting weights, or cycling on stationary bikes. There was a photo of about twenty vets singing as Marcus accompanied them on guitar. One of the most interesting pictures was empty of people. It depicted original artwork created by three very talented veterans, all of whom were being courted by one of the galleries down in Greenwich Village and none of whom had ever picked up a brush before being encouraged to do so after coming to the Center. Each brochure included an address and phone number for both Am-Vets and the landmark society. Toby had somehow managed, following the visit by Jeremiah Henry's parents on Thursday, to insert a sheet of paper urging folks to call local congressmen and members of the city council and ask them to put pressure on the NYPD to ensure that racial justice might actually prevail.

We handed out the brochures to any passersby who'd accept one. Hopefully, people would take the time to read them and not toss them into the nearest trash receptacles. The vets in wheelchairs had a more important task. They were in charge of petitions, and it was gratifying to see such a large number of folks signing in favor of keeping the Center and not allowing it to be destroyed. Billy Don, with his quick wit and sweet personality, was charming everyone within hearing distance and proudly displaying the hundreds of signatures he'd collected.

Around noon, a mobile vendor's cart appeared, with Fiona Belle Donovan (attired in her Christmas elf ensemble) at the wheel. She parked (illegally) in front of the building and waved at me to join her.

"I'm aft ta bringin' everyone coffee," she explained. "Do ya want ta help me distribute?"

I did.

The rally was going quite smoothly for the first ninety minutes or so. The petitions were filling up. Marcus had corralled a few other singers to come to the protest and perform, and he himself started a sing-along, encouraging the veterans and onlookers to join in. He also added some of the civil rights songs made famous in the mid-sixties.

An enthusiastic crowd of about sixty people were in the middle of singing a rousing rendition of the spiritual "I Shall Not Be Moved," which was quite apropos in terms of veterans and landmarks, when we were joined by the bully boys. Five males (I refuse to refer to them as gentlemen), all of whom were at least six-four, made of solid muscle, dressed in black form-fitting shirts and black combat pants tucked inside black knee-high boots. Topping off this exhibit of what the sharply dressed mercenary should wear this season, tucked over hair so blonde it was close to platinum were black, military-style berets with a spiffy overlap on the side, as opposed to the comfy, daily headgear worn by most French citizens.

They looked scary. When the tallest and biggest of them marched over to the low platform and planted himself in front of Marcus, who was adjusting a microphone while he was singing, and began speaking in what sounded like a South African accent, they *looked* scary shifted to they *are* scary.

The song ended. Not by choice.

"Time to push off, mate," the gigantic goon shouted at Marcus, his voice dripping with menace. "Mr. Masters has had enough of you lot."

Marcus looked up, and calmly replied, "I'm not your mate, we have a permit, and we're here for the next two hours. Mr. Masters will have to deal with it."

The guy grabbed the microphone and pulled it away from Marcus. "I don't give one—*expletive! expletive! expletive!*—about your bloody permit. You and your rejects are leaving now!"

"No! We're not. We have a perfect right to be demonstrating in this spot until three this afternoon, and you can't stop us. Now, you and your buddies need to head back into the building or, hey! Here's an idea. You're welcome to stay outside with us and learn what this demonstration is about, or, better still, bring Masters out here where he can discuss issues like a man instead of hiding behind his…employees. We have songs to sing and there are folks waiting to hear them."

That's when things turned blurry, hazy, and downright ugly. Time simultaneously yet impossibly moved in slow motion, even as fists began flying at off-the-chart speeds. The big soldier who'd ordered Marcus to leave grabbed his guitar and smashed it against the edge of the platform, then quickly yanked Marcus himself off his feet and onto the ground. He followed up the first assault with a kick (using his booted foot) in the ribs. If this was the day I was supposed to save Marucs Kennedy, I was doomed to failure because there was no way I could get to him from where I was standing. I had a brief flash remembering Fiona Belle saying something about "December" so when Toby Travers flew out of nowhere, emitting cries of sheer rage as he tackled Marcus's attacker, I breathed again, knowing this wasn't the right date for murder.

Then I looked around in shock and anger, watching these overly large soldiers of fortune punching and kicking veterans with zero regard or respect for the true heroes they were. The crowd who'd gathered to sign

163

petitions and listen to the singing began screaming at the mercenaries. I shouted at Fiona Belle, who was close to the building and engaged in punching some galoot five times her size, to quit fighting and get inside and call the cops.

The tallest thug seemed determined to claim the title of "Worst of the Lot" by showing no mercy or shred of humanity. He jumped in front of Billy Don, reached down, and literally hoisted him out of his wheelchair, throwing him to the pavement. Toby was going toe to toe with Marcus's attacker. It was up to me. I ran to where Billy Don lay and, blessing those years of martial arts training, wasted no time in delivering a solid kick to the stomach of this goon who was so pleased with himself for proving what a cowardly bully he was that he hadn't bothered to notice some silly female moving his way.

He reacted by throwing a punch at me, which I was miraculously able to deflect. He was immediately surrounded by two of the vets I'd taught back on Thursday, and they rained blows on every inch of his body while I tried to get Billy Don back into his chair.

Then came the sound of a very loud gun firing. At first I thought it must be the police, but I hadn't heard sirens and it was too soon after Fiona Belle had run inside to call, so I knew this was someone else. I was right.

The next voice, shouting over the microphone, turned out to be Mr. Roger Masters himself. "Enough! *Expletive! Expletive! Expletive!* Get off my *Expletive!* property now!" He turned to Marcus, who'd managed, with Toby's help, to stand again, but was holding his hands across his ribs and trying to avoid blood dripping down his face. "You! Folk singer! You've had your insipid, ineffectual rally. Go home before I have the cops arrest you. I can and I will do it. I will also not hesitate to fire this rifle at something more substantial than the sky." His tone was nothing less than sheer delight. My bones turned into ice.

Rogers Masters wasn't quite what I'd expected. I'm not sure why I'd thought he was a young man. He wasn't. He was clearly past fifty. He sported a patch of salt-and-pepper curly hair in need of a trim, which matched the color of his suit. He was short, maybe five-five, tops, and overweight by around forty pounds. He should not have been an imposing figure, but the—oh, heck, I'll say it—the *evil* emanating from him was palpable.

Marcus and Toby looked at each other, then surveyed the scene of bloodied veterans, some still on the ground, and a crowd of frustrated and frightened onlookers, all standing in silence. For this day at least, the battle was over.

Chapter 26

October 1975

Five of the vets involved at the demonstration had been taken to the hospital. Six of us regrouped back at the Am-Vets Center. Marcus and two of my dancers, Rocky and Sid, had been injured at the rally but refused to go to an emergency room. Another vet from my class, Calvin, was currently training to become an emergency medical technician and was able to use his skills to see to anyone in need of medical attention. My nursing background consisted of opening new boxes of tissues for my sister whenever she had a cold, but I offered to help Calvin by playing errand girl and grabbing first-aid supplies from a closet I suspected had once been used as the coat room during the center's ballroom dance days. My next task was to get pots of coffee brewing and dig out the mugs and sugar. Toby, who'd been pacing nonstop since we got back to the Center, quelled his desire to toss a few chairs around the room in frustration and rage and helped me carry everything.

No one was in the mood to talk. We were all too discouraged. The violent turn taken at the rally had been unexpected and unwelcome. It had been made clear by his action in casually firing a large rifle in front of a crowd without fear of consequences that Roger Masters had more than one city official in his pocket. Further evidence of his influence were the two cops who showed up (after Masters ordered us off the city sidewalks he didn't own) and threatened all the demonstrators with arrest if we didn't leave immediately, our permit for rights to assembly and free speech be hanged.

I was really worried about Marcus. He was playing super stoic, claiming he was fine. He wasn't. I managed to persuade him to allow Calvin to clean off the blood and slap some tape around his ribs. Once the blood was removed, there was no color in Marcus' face, and he was having so much trouble holding his coffee mug I asked if I could get a straw for him.

"I'm fine, Shiloh. Let it be," was his curt response. "I'm less concerned about my bumps and bruises than how we're going to keep Roger Masters from destroying this place."

Toby stopped marching in circles to chime in. "It's incredible. This jerk has hired foreign mercs to do his bidding. Those guys are lethal and it was pretty obvious they enjoyed hurting people. Between the goons and the cops, I'd say our days of demonstrating are done. Well, at least anywhere near Masters' offices."

"I wish my roommate Jim had been there, along with his paper's photographer," I said. "He's a reporter with *The Manhattan Legend*. A few shots of overly tall, overly muscle-bound, overly nasty soldiers from a whole different country tossing decorated, heroic, uniformed veterans out of wheelchairs on the front page of the paper might have been very helpful to the cause." I nodded at Calvin. "Speaking of heroes, is there some way we can find out how Billy Don and the others are doing? I'd love to know before I have to leave you guys and go do the Sunday show."

"I called a friend from EMT services about ten minutes ago," Calvin replied. "He's going to check on all five of the guys who were taken to the emergency room by ambulance, especially Billy Don, who took a blow to the head. Everyone's at Bellevue. I told him I'd call him back in a half hour for updates." He grinned at me. "By the way, Miss Meridien, I was delighted to witness the awesome kick to the stomach you inflicted on Billy Don's attacker. Who knew our sweet dancing teacher was so tough!"

I groaned. "Maybe it's just as well Jim wasn't there. Or any reporter. I doubt it would further my career prospects to be showing off roundhouse swings with my legs instead of high kicks." I winked at Calvin. "I might incorporate some of those moves into Monday's class, though, assuming we *have* a class. Since two of the guys from last Thursday's session are now undergoing medical treatment, they might not be in the mood for jumping around."

"They'll be there," Sid, also from class, who himself was nursing a banged-up shoulder, stated firmly. "Tough doesn't begin to describe them. It takes more than a bruising or bashing from a stupid mercenary to get a vet to quit. Right, Marcus?"

Marcus laughed, then winced. "Ouch. Yep. They'll show up more determined than ever to heal their wounds." He tried to lighten the mood and said, "Speaking of bruising and bashing, I'm embarrassed to admit I'm mourning the loss of my guitar. If I'd realized the goon was going to destroy a musical instrument, I'd've whapped him over the head with it. Thankfully, it wasn't my best one." He stopped for a beat, then mused, "If I sued Roger Masters for destruction of private property, would I win? Sid?"

Each and every one of us shook our heads "no" before Sid had a chance to answer. When he did, his response wasn't encouraging. "I'm a bar exam away from becoming a practicing attorney. Graduated Columbia Law, where the school started a program to provide free or cheap legal counseling to individuals. We've had a slew of tenants from Masters' residences come to us for help. Yet none of us has yet been able to come up with a strategy to defeat Roger Masters. It's tough and frustrating. The man personifies greed and corruption, but proving it is nearly impossible. After today, I'm going to personally file a suit against the man and his goons for injuries suffered and for destruction of personal property as well." He flashed a hint of a smile. "Including musical instruments." Then he shook his head. "Of course, no chance of winning."

We all lapsed into silence again, not wanting to admit total defeat, yet clueless as to what the next step could be in the fight to keep the center open.

Marcus finally spoke up. "Shiloh did have a good point."

I lifted my eyebrows. "Me? I did? About what? What did I say?"

"Reporters. We need media outlets to cover this story. I'll bet half the folks in Manhattan despise Roger Masters, thanks to his rep as slumlord and his tendency to snatch landmarks and turn them into ugly high-rises. If word got out about the rally and his tough guy tactics against veterans, maybe it would make a difference. Although I do wish we could find proof about his criminal activities. The papers would love a scandal, even if courts might ignore us."

A proverbial light bulb flashed in my head. I sat up very straight.

"Whoa. Okay, guys, I have an idea. A plan. It's probably an insane idea, possibly also illegal, but desperation sometimes calls for, um, unorthodox strategies."

Five men turned and stared at me. Sid chuckled. "As the legal eagle here, do I need to leave the room?"

"The opposite. I might need to hire you on retainer to keep me out of jail," I said, not entirely joking. "I have about a dollar in change in my bag, along with a subway token. Is that enough?"

He laughed. "I'll be your attorney for free, as long it doesn't involve blowing up any buildings or people, although there are a few, who shall remain nameless, who deserve it."

Marcus nodded at me. "I'm now full of painkillers and, consequently, my brain is somewhat worse for wear, but I want to hear your plan. If you've come up with something ingenious, we'll applaud you. If it stinks, which it won't because you're brilliant, we say 'scratch it' and order some Chinese delivery and a case of bourbon, and spend the rest of the night bemoaning where our lives have landed us. And I'm not sure I'm making sense but chalk it up to the meds." He said to the air. "This is why I hate drugs. They zap you out of focus."

I inhaled. "Okay, gents. The plan. To begin with, and this is not common knowledge, but I am a wiz of a typist. Consequently, from the day I moved to Manhattan, I've had my pick of temp agencies who employ typing wizards. Which also means, I can also choose businesses and hours for employment."

Nods but confused expressions. Toby asked, "If you're volunteering to type up more brochures or a legal brief for Sid, sounds great, but not sure how that helps our situation."

"Hang on. I'll be happy to do some typing for y'all but my plan actually involves trying to get some dirt on the sleazy developer himself. If someone can find out which agency Masters uses for his document work, I can almost certainly get myself hired for the night shift. If I'm in his offices, I can do some snooping and hunt for something incriminating enough for my roommate to write about for *The Legend*, or even better, something so egregious it can't be ignored by law enforcement agencies."

There was a mixed chorus of "Wow!" "Cool plan!" "I love it!" and "Shiloh, you can't do this!" The last exclamation was from Marcus.

"Why?" I asked.

"Because it's ridiculously dangerous. You saw what kind of thugs Masters keeps around him. Who's to say they don't prowl the offices at night waiting to find someone to beat up on?"

I shook my head. "I get your concern, and I'm not the bravest person on the planet, but are you telling me you really think mercenaries are going to be interested in a girl typing away, headphones on, listening to the dulcet sounds of Masters dictating whatever garbage he needs for the week, and end up following her when she goes looking for pens or more paper or the executive washroom?"

"I don't put anything past dear Roger," Marcus grumbled. "And there won't be anybody there to protect you."

Toby interrupted, "It's risky, but Marcus, it's also a great idea. With all the paperwork involved in keeping Masters' business ventures going, he's bound to have dozens of employees, temp or not, who have to get those documents out in a timely fashion. He's not going to want his security team bothering anyone who can contribute to his bottom line."

Marcus admitted Toby and I had some valid points. "Okay, let's say Shiloh does this and finds something juicy on Masters, Sid, could she end up in jail?"

"Well, she wouldn't be breaking and entering and," he turned to me, "assuming you discovered papers showing illegal or just seamy activity by Masters, you wouldn't be stealing any actual paper work, correct?"

"Correct. If I happened to stumble across, oh, say a memo to a city councilman telling him twenty-five thousand dollars was going into his campaign fund and, 'by the way, be sure not to let the landmark society prevail in its efforts to keep the Rhythm Palace open and let's meet for drinks next Friday,' I'd photograph said memo and pass it on to Jim, who would protect me as his confidential source. All legal, yes?"

Sid chuckled. "Some might call it skirting the edges, but I'd call it legal. Mind you, I'm not up on the variety of loopholes in obtaining incriminating information. My specialty is Constitutional Law, not Criminal."

"Great. Settled," I stated. "Although there is a major hurdle in doing this."

"What?" came from Marcus. "Something worse when it comes to your safety? You are nuts, Shiloh Meridien. I'm crazy about you, but you're nuts."

I tried not to melt after hearing him say he was crazy about me. I focused on the problem. "I have absolutely no idea which agency Masters uses for hiring temps."

Toby lit up like Times Square on New Year's Eve. "Got it covered. We have the perfect person to find out." His expression darkened. "Assuming of course, he's okay after being tossed to the ground like a sack of compost today." He paused, then added, "Billy Don has the names and addresses of every employment agency in the city because he's not merely a great deejay and greeter at the Center, he helps vets find jobs. He's well liked by both owners and personnel at those agencies. He'd be able to find the right one in a heartbeat. We have to wait till he's up to making some calls, but after what he went through today? Shoot. If he could type, he'd be working the night shift with you."

Chapter 27

Mid-October 1975

One week later, I was standing in the upstairs reception area for the midtown offices of Roger Masters, staring at a wall clock showing the time to be 11:07 p.m. I'd checked in at 11:00 p.m. with an overweight, sleepy-looking security guard in the lobby and then ridden the elevator to the fortieth floor where, according to Von Schmidt Superior Personnel, I would find a desk with a dictaphone set up and approximately fifteen documents for me to type (error-free and no white-outs) and have ready to be sent out and delivered to fifteen clients by 7 a.m. tomorrow.

But I need to back up a bit to Monday, the day after the disastrous rally, before I dive into this night's activities. I arrived at the Am-Vets Center at eleven as usual to teach my class, but there was no Billy Don to greet me. Marcus was there instead.

"Billy Don had to go back to the doctor today," he told me. "He swears he's okay. But they wanted to check him out after yesterday's…"

"Brutal and malicious dumping from his wheelchair?" I interrupted.

Marcus nodded. "Yeah. But, bottom line, you won't have a deejay to help out with class."

"I didn't have one in Austin," I told him. "As long

174

as someone doesn't mind putting a needle on and off a record, it shouldn't be an issue. Or I'll just run back and forth to the turntable. Find longer songs to use."

Marcus stood, reached behind him and picked up a guitar. "Or how about live accompaniment?"

"Really? Are you up to it? You also took quite a beating."

"I won't get into any energetic, wild riffs. Mainly chords." He sighed. "Using a guitar that did *not* get slammed to the ground yesterday."

"What about singing? Won't it hurt your ribs taking super-deep breaths?"

He shrugged it off. "I'll be fine. We've got a microphone I can use, so I won't have to take super-deep breaths."

"Okay, tough guy, here's a plan. Instead of you straining your lungs, how 'bout we do some of the spirituals and let the guys themselves sing as they're doing movements? I'll sing, too. If nothing else, everyone can chime in on the chorus."

Marcus brightened. "Let's do it."

Having live music added an amazing extra energy to class. I scrapped most of the movements I'd thought up to have the guys do to the sounds of sixties British rock and decided spirituals called for more group swaying, lots of stretching to the sky, and spine contractions and releases, especially when we were singing everyone's favorite, "Didn't My Lord Deliver Daniel?"

We all needed a water break about forty-five minutes in. The center had a water fountain, but I always included a thermos in my dance bag, so I grabbed it and joined Marcus, who was sitting in a chair in the upstage area. I wanted to stay warm and flexible, so I marched in place, added a few "pony" steps, and chatted about music with the guys who'd brought their paper cups over and formed a small circle.

Which is when the miracle happened.

Jonah, the vet with the baby face, who hadn't spoken a word in more than three years, tapped me on the shoulder and said, "I like these spirituals a lot, especially 'Daniel.' Would it be okay if Marcus could also maybe sing 'Chasm of Darkness' at the end of class? It's such a good song."

The first impulse of all of us gathered around Marcus's chair was to jump up and down shouting "Hallelujah!" and screaming, "Praise Heaven, Jonah's talking!" But, in an innate understanding by everyone that this wouldn't be the right way to react, there were merely gentle head nods and a few remarks on the order of, "Yeah, great idea, Jonah. Love it as well."

Marcus glanced at me. I was doing all I could not to burst into tears. My thoughts were mirrored in his eyes. A veteran had overcome a barrier imposed by the horrible traumatic events he'd experienced in Vietnam. Was it the dancing? The live music? The mix? Was it being with his comrades sharing a non-stressful experience? All of the above? It didn't really matter at this moment. Jonah had broken through and initiated communication. Jonah spoke. The miracle happened right here at the Center. It was vital the place remained open, and if I had to end up committing a felony at Roger Masters' office to ensure the safety of the Center, well, give me the prison stripes, slam the cell door, and turn the key in the lock.

Fast forward to Sunday night.

Billy Don had been invaluable in setting up a way

for me to gain access to the offices of Roger Masters. Furious and humiliated from the ill treatment suffered by the vets at the hands of foreign mercenaries, and thoroughly vexed and irritated at the way the rally had gone down, he'd been thrilled when he got back from the hospital and discovered we had a plan. It wasn't a great plan. Truth be told, it was probably a durn stupid plan, but at least it was better than sitting around moaning, wringing one's hands, or punching through a wall. At any rate, the minute Billy Don returned from his second doctor's appointment on Monday, he started contacting his buddies at the top employment agencies. It took him less than thirty minutes to get the information we needed. Roger Masters—LLC, Incorporated, or whatever—had an exclusive contract with Von Schmidt Superior Personnel. Billy Don called me. I called Jim, who had this whole "how to investigate and be sneaky" thing down to a fine art and who said he'd provide me with a fake ID and a small camera and show me how to use it and where best to hide it.

Wednesday, as "Mary Smith" (who happened to be Jim's photographer at *The Manhattan Legend*) and neatly dressed in my "I'm-so-efficient-and-I'm-all-business" charcoal gray suit, I arrived early enough for my appointment at Von Schmidt Superior Personnel to provide the impression I was prompt but not so early as to appear desperate. I took the tests, impressing everyone with my skills in typing and delighting the interviewers with my quirky ability to read nearly illegible handwriting. I'm not sure where this gift came from, but I figured it was because my own penmanship stinks. I understand squiggles. If I didn't, I'd never have been able to read my own notes at school. This talent, I'd been told by more than one employer, was a real perk. It turned out tons of businessmen in top positions had a habit of jotting down memos with penmanship that could pass as ancient hieroglyphics, and if they couldn't be deciphered, financial gains could be lost. Yeah, it always came down to money.

Anyway, following the tests, I was told I was in. I was in *and* I could have my pick of firms. I used my acting skills and managed not to jump up and down yelling "Yee Howdy!" the minute I noticed one of the 'higher-end" jobs presented to me was an upcoming Sunday night shift at the midtown offices of one Roger Masters. I casually told the personnel agent that typing for Masters looked like an excellent fit for my schedule.

As soon as I left the offices of Von Schmidt Superior Personnel, I hit the nearest phone booth and called Billy Don to give him the news. He promptly contacted a different agent at Von Schmidt's and poured on the East Texas charm, chatting with her until she unwittingly revealed the layout of the offices, the number of security guards, what time most of them took coffee or cigarette breaks during a night shift, and best of all, some surprising information. Roger Masters was a slob, had never used a typewriter in his life, and tended to jot notes on everything he was involved in, carelessly leaving pieces of paper scattered across his desk. Wait. I'm taking back my comment. I'd claimed this was the best, but in actuality *one* other personality trait topped his messiness, because it could prove vital to our operation. Word had it that Roger Masters been brought up in a seedy neighborhood in Brooklyn in a tiny one-bedroom apartment, and now Roger Masters valued wide-open spaces. He was nearly claustrophobic. Consequently, the man had a huge suite of offices with no doors. No locks to pick. Finally, it appeared there was a small break for our side.

Marcus, although he'd been in pain for the last week, came to see my show at the Henske Thursday evening, which is when I told him I needed to brush up on my spy skills and I couldn't concentrate on Espionage for Crafty Dancers 101 if I was worrying about him. I suggested, with some force, he go see a doctor as in *now* and allow me to fill my head with all the different crimes we were certain Roger Masters was committing and what I might be able to find to nail him.

Shocker. Marcus agreed. He called me Friday afternoon to say he'd visited a free clinic where they x-rayed and told him he had hairline fractures of two ribs, so he'd stay home and rest over the weekend. He wanted me to phone him Monday morning when, hopefully, I'd have something viable to report concerning my Sunday night gig at the Masters Corporation offices and we could go somewhere quiet and celebrate.

Chapter 28

Mid-October 1975

Which brings me back to Sunday night, staring at a clock on the fortieth floor while waiting for the security guard (not one of Masters' goons) to inspect my bag. The man seemed amused at the variety of dance paraphernalia I'd brought with me. I wasn't thrilled I had to reveal "Mary Smith" to be a dancer, but it was important to have a reason for my alter ego to be carrying around tap shoes in her bag.

"Where's your tutu?" came the not-nearly-as-witty-as-he thought question.

"In the wash," I answered with a flirty smile. "Yeah, yeah. I get it. It's ridiculous to be lugging this thing around everywhere I go. I keep reminding myself to either be sure to dump all this stuff at the end of the week, or buy a totally different bag for business jobs."

I held my breath, hoping he wouldn't notice both tap shoes were wrapped with duct tape. This was because one of those shoes displayed an odd hole in the heel. My friend, roommate, and reporter extraordinaire Jim McLean, along with the real Mary Smith, who, as previously stated, was a photographer at the *Legend*, had devised a nifty gizmo inside the tap shoe which concealed a hidden camera. If I found anything incriminating to Roger Masters or his company, I was to snap a few pictures. As my ballet slippers were also heavily covered in tape, I figured the guard would assume (correctly) I was one of those poverty-stricken dancers who couldn't afford new footwear.

I spent the first three and a half hours doing the job I'd been hired to do, which was typing documents transcribed from the dictaphone. There were a ton of what were basically illegible contract negotiations handwritten by Masters himself, and I was forced to work my magic in deciphering each word. The friendly warning given by Billy Don's friend at the Von Schmidt agency about Masters' lousy penmanship turned out to be grossly understated. I compared his scribblings to a deranged feral cat finding a pen and a pad of paper out in the wilds and scratching out a message begging someone to come rescue him so he could get a decent meal and a warm bed.

There's no way around it—typing is boring. I'll skip the majority of the night's activities because typing really was all I was doing. Finally, around three-fifteen a.m., when the security guard hanging out in the reception area went for a coffee, donut, and cigarette break, I decided it was time to make my move. I'd earlier separated two pages from one of Masters' lengthy, handwritten letters and stashed them in my bag. I now took out one of the pages, along with the bag, and entered Masters' main office, attempting, while fighting a pounding heart and sweaty palms, to convey calmness and an attitude of "I have every right to be here."

I set my bag down by Masters' desk and placed the page on his desk. If anyone came in I was going to tell them I was looking for the other page to the letter. Which was sort of true. I began hunting through the clutter on his desk, marveling that anyone as business savvy as he was could be so ridiculously untidy. I found scraps of paper with messages ranging from what to order for take-out for lunch (pastrami on rye with a dill pickle, potato salad on the side and cream sodas for three people on Friday), to when best to meet with someone (name illegible) to discuss a proposal for high-rise luxury apartments downtown in the Bowery (following the eviction of current residents), to a list of folks invited to an upcoming party, half of whom were politicians.

A different list of names looked promising for a moment or two. It was also primarily made up of politicians (all men) and each one had a couple of comments beside his name signifying what appeared to be personal vices or events where their behavior had been less than respectable. Possible blackmail or extortion? *Give Roger what Roger wants or Roger exposes your habit of hiring very young, very male escorts to your home while your wife, who inherited the fortune used to fund your campaigns, is sunning herself in the Bahamas.* Or *Let Roger tear down a building and slap up a shoddy high-rise or your wife's divorce attorney hears about the money you have stashed in an off-shore account.* Finally, *Keep Roger happy or your constituents discover you've opted to go with a landfill instead of the promised playground near the elementary school over in Staten Island.*

I was about to take out the tap shoe and begin photographing when it occurred to me, nasty as the alleged offenses were, I didn't have real evidence of illegality. Roger was free to make his observations about any and all of his buddies and put them down in writing. Unless there was a way to prove he was making threats, offering bribes, or receiving payoffs, everything I'd unearthed so far, while fascinating, disgusting, and sleazy, was ultimately useless.

I continued searching, keeping an eye out in case the guard returned early. Billy Don's source at Von Schmidt's had mentioned the chubby Sunday night guard liked to stretch out the length of his break and word had it he'd often stay out of the office, smoking cigarettes, snacking on pastries, and drinking coffee, for up to forty minutes, sometimes as much as an hour.

Twenty minutes into the heavy snooping, I was becoming disheartened. I could tell the world what Roger Masters liked to order at the pricey Italian restaurant over on Fifth Avenue and how many city officials (not to mention a state representative or two) were currently committing adultery, but unless something blatantly illegal and incriminating popped up soon, the Rhythm Palace would be tumbling and crashing faster than the dancers who'd once graced its floors during a twelve-week-long marathon.

And then I spotted it. To be precise, I spotted *them*. Two different examples of activities I was certain warranted investigation by a certain governmental agency with a reputation for toughness (the Internal Revenue Service), with a possible and highly desired outcome…Roger Masters indicted and put behind bars with no way of buying the Am-Vets Center, ever.

I'd unearthed an oversized notebook with a cover entitled Daily Agenda sitting under a pile of papers. Nothing out of the ordinary. However, instead of events calendared in, there were carbons of checks. And the names written on the checks coincided with the names of the South African so-called bodyguards we'd tangled with at last week's demonstration. Victor Kruger. Joep Meerholtz. Johan Burgess. Pieter Van Der Merwe. Willem Nels. I'd bet money it was a crime to hire foreign mercenaries, especially if one weren't concerned with the legalities of withholding, W-2s, -4s or -9s or other forms normally required for providing employees with their weekly or monthly salaries.

There were other checks, what I'd term large checks, made out to City Councilman Gregory Campbell and Deputy Mayor Lawrence Buckley. Not to their campaigns, but to them. As in personal checks to Greg and Larry. There were quite a few notes with some kind of adhesive on the backside (moderately legible) stuck to the opposite page, with memos laying out precisely what Masters expected in return for his generous contribution.

I grabbed my tap shoe, pulled off the tape to expose the hole allowing the camera lens through, and started snapping photos of the memo and the checks as quickly as I could hit the flash button. I'd managed to wrap the tape back on the shoe and was about to toss it into my bag and scurry back to my own desk and typewriter, when one of those bodyguards entered the room. It was the same thug who'd dumped Billy Don to the ground and who subsequently ended up with my foot in his stomach. If he recognized me, the consequences wouldn't be pretty.

I wasn't an idiot. I'd made certain I didn't look anything like I had last Sunday at the rally, when I'd worn jeans and a bright blue sweater, which couldn't be seen, thanks to one of the vets lending me his military jacket after the wind grew a bit nippy. My hair had been down and flying all over my face. Tonight, I was wearing a classy business suit. I had slicked my hair down with gel, to make the red appear closer to brown, and pulled the curls back into a tight bun. I'd slathered on makeup as if I was performing on stage, which, in a way, I was. I'd also donned fake glasses (courtesy of someone at the *Legend*...I didn't ask) which hid most of my face.

Not that it would make a difference if the guy recognized me. He'd be ticked off at anyone he considered to be in the wrong place. To him I was a non-entity, a mere temp employee trespassing in his boss's office, and he was the guy who had a very large rifle slung over his shoulder.

Chapter 29

Mid-October 1975

"Why are you holding a shoe in your hand?" came the guttural, accented demand. "And what are you doing in Mister Masters' office? Is not allowed."

Oh, well, the way it is, ya see is this, I'm just hanging out here, trying not to faint or jump out the nearest window, was the response ripping through my brain. I did not say it aloud. I also neither passed out nor jumped. Advice supplied by my freshman Acting teacher at U.T. magically replaced the fear. *No matter how improbable the scene you're given, whether scripted or improvised, the actor's job is to sell it. Make your audience believe every word and every action.*

"Roaches!" I shrieked. "They came scurrying out when I was looking for the other half of a letter missing from the documents I was typing. I was getting ready to smash them with my shoe. I'm terrified of them!" Partly true. I had seen a couple of roaches munching their way through an opened carton of leftover Chinese take-out, but give me a break here. I'm from Dallas. Roaches in Texas are so big they intimidate feisty chihuahuas. Icky fact—the demonic *cucarachas* who call the Lone Star State home are actually capable of flying, so the day I'm bothered by a couple of puny Manhattan roaches lounging in a smelly bed of shrimp *lo mein* is the day I check into Bellevue for unreasonable phobias. But the huge, unpleasant guard didn't need this information. Killing bugs seemed like a valid excuse for me to be waving a tap shoe in the air, thanks to the fact, as previously mentioned more than once, Roger Masters was a slob. Personally, if I were a messy millionaire with the cash to hire multiple cleaning and pest control services, I'd do a better job of making sure they brought vacuum, mops, dusters, and a lot of lemon-scented bug spray to my offices daily, every hour on the hour. But maybe Masters didn't care about invading insects. Maybe he enjoyed chasing them and soaking them in insecticide himself to get his kicks watching living creatures die.

Mister Big Soldier of Fortune (masquerading as a legitimate security guard) Willem Nels (according to the name tag neatly sewn above his left-hand breast pocket) glowered at me. "You leave. Now. I repeat. You are not allowed in here." He aimed the rifle at me and I quickly scooped up my bag, throwing the shoe back inside.

I waved the two pages of the letter at him. "I'm going, I'm going. I found what I needed." I didn't add anything else. Some innate sense of my own safety told me less explanation was the way to play this.

Once we were back in the main office where I'd been doing my work, he marched me to my desk. The rifle was back over the shoulder, but he wasn't ready to leave.

"Hand me your bag."

He'd get no arguments from me. I handed him the bag. He dumped the contents on an empty desk to my left and began sifting through. He lifted up a variety of personal belongings which included a pair of crumpled, ready-for-laundry pink tights, pink ballet slippers (with as much duct tape wrapped around on them as the tap shoes), the tap shoes themselves, two black leotards (also in need of a wash), one pair of jazz pants (clean), one pair of leg warmers (semi-clean), a coin purse with two dollars' worth of quarters for vending machines, one dime, one subway token, last Thursday's copies of all three show biz trade newspapers, a small notebook, an assortment of pens, and one large, ancient thermos currently half-filled with water. If Willem had begun his inspection of the bag two hours earlier, he would have unearthed a veggie burrito and an apple, but I'd downed both during the one break I'd taken.

The expressions on the faces of the two other temps working in the area shifted from apprehension to amusement as each piece of dance attire or essential-to-daily-living-in-the-city item came into full view. Willem's features conveyed annoyance and anger at the bag's contents. I guess he'd hoped to find a knife or gun or something equally dangerous, which would then enable him to escort me downstairs to the building's courtyard, march me to a bench in the center, blindfold me, and shoot me full of holes, claiming I'd staged a botched assassination attempt on his boss.

A second merc joined Nels as he was emptying the coin purse—looking for a vial of poison? A miniature dart gun?—I wished I hadn't read quite so many novels of intrigue and espionage during my teens as I dove to the floor and scrambled to retrieve the sole subway token, which had bounced on the carpet and rolled under the desk. Subway fare for one crummy trip had increased to fifty cents back in September, and while I'm in terrific shape, I had no desire to hike all the way up to W. 103rd

Street from midtown once this night ended.

The other guard, name tag identifying him as Johan Burgess, joined Willem Ncls and me at the desk, asking with a surly attitude what the heck was going on.

"I found her snooping in Masters' office," was Willem's response.

Time to speak up for myself. "I wasn't snooping. I was trying to locate the second page of a handwritten letter I needed to type." I held up the pages. "Which, fortunately, I did find before I got freaked out by a party of cockroaches who were snacking on Chinese take-out."

Johann raised an eyebrow. "The cleaning crew comes in at four."

I attempted a bit of humor. "Well, I hope they bring a whoppin' big can of bug spray along with their mops and buckets."

Johan looked at my fake photo ID, stared at me for an eternity, then waved at me to go back to my desk. "Finish your work, then, Miss Smith. Stay out of Masters' office."

There were no apologies emanating from either man for intimidating and scaring the living doo-doo out of a lowly temp. I didn't ask for one. I didn't want one. I wanted to finish the job and get out and never come back. I returned to my desk and whipped out the rest of the (error-free) contracts, rental agreements, and deeds of sale. I even remembered to neatly recreate the infamous two-page, originally illegible and doubtless unimportant letter. I was finished by five a.m., and spent the next two hours practicing my typing speeds by redoing documents until my shift was over.

At seven a.m. I signed out as Mary Smith on the agency-originated job sheet provided by Von Schmidt

Superior Personnel, silently accepted the carbon copy to be handed in or mailed to Von Schmidt Superior Personnel, took the elevator downstairs to the lobby, said 'bye to the American guard manning the security station in the lobby, and was out the door. Not until then did I feel my pulse return to a rate under a hundred beats per minute—normally I'm around 47—and allow my stomach to settle somewhere near my abdomen instead of my throat.

I walked about three blocks west, found an open diner, and asked if they had a public phone for use. They did. I called Jim at the *Legend,* and told him to meet me at the diner as soon as he could and I'd swap him a loaded tap shoe for enough money to cover coffee and a muffin.

After our exchange, I decided to walk over to Marcus's apartment in Hell's Kitchen, about fifteen blocks away. I'd never been there and this really wasn't the right hour for a social call, but I wanted to see him in person and give him the play-by-play of what had just transpired.

Across the street from where Marcus lived, lounging against the stoop, staring directly at Marcus's building, cigarette in hand, was a tall man dressed entirely in brown. Brown pants, brown turtleneck sweater, brown beret, brown sneakers. His features were obscured by a brown mustache and a brown beard. Maybe he lived in the neighborhood and was being polite to a spouse or roommate by not exposing them to secondhand smoke? Maybe he'd been out for an early morning walk around the city and decided to take a break? Maybe the odd choice of holding a cigarette, without moving it to his mouth and inhaling, while looking directly at Marcus's apartment was only a coincidence?

There was nothing overtly unusual in his apparel. I couldn't see his eyes or pinpoint what led me to suppose a menace in the man's demeanor, yet the performer in me can see emotion and intent in how people hold themselves, in how they walk, in how they keep a position of stillness. I shivered as one of what Zelda called my *déjà-vu-isms* whispered "danger."

For a long moment I stood, shaking, reliving the fear of the moment when Willem Nels caught me in Masters' office. I turned around and headed for the nearest phone booth. I dug inside my bag and found a dime, then called Marcus.

"Who is it?"

"Shiloh."

"Oh, thank God! I barely slept last night worrying about you. Are you okay? Are you safe?"

I am. Not so sure about you. I didn't voice the thought.

"How did it go?"

I proceeded to tell him all about discovering the checks at Masters' offices, nearly getting caught by Willem Nels and Johann Burgess, finishing my work, meeting Jim at the diner and giving him the tap shoe with the photos inside.

"I'm sorry for calling so early, but I figured you'd want the story as soon as you could."

"I considered waiting outside Masters' building for you but was afraid it might put you in danger if anyone saw me," Marcus said. "I'm beyond relieved you're safe. We never should have asked you to do this. Unbelievable. I never imagined the man would have his mercs roaming his offices at all hours."

"Marcus, forget the mercs for a moment. I saw a

strange man across the street from your apartment a few minutes ago. It's why I'm phoning. I didn't want him seeing me go into your place."

"Why?"

"There's something creepy about him and the way he kept staring at your apartment."

"You believe he's dangerous? Not just some super fan of folk music? Shiloh, they're out there. Male and female. They send letters. They leave gifts for singers. They follow them around the city. No harm. No foul."

"Really? I didn't realize folk singers had groupies."

Marcus yawned. "Sorry. I didn't sleep much last night. Your fault. I spent a lot of time pacing and worrying. Anyway, forget this guy. He's probably new to the neighborhood and isn't watching me at all. I'm more concerned with you. Seriously, how are you holding up now that you're out of the lions' den?"

Which is when I burst into tears.

Chapter 30

Late October 1975

Four days later, the headlines at *The Manhattan Legend* screamed *Developer Roger Masters Subject of IRS Investigation for Tax Fraud and Bribery!* The byline read *Jim McLean*.

We'd done it. Jim had contacted agents at the IRS Monday morning while he and I were still having coffee. They thanked him and asked him to hold off releasing the story for a few days. He wanted the scoop and the treasured byline but, bless him, he also wanted to be sure the big notebook entitled Daily Agenda with the copies of checks didn't suddenly disappear. He agreed. Getting agents to search Roger's office as soon as humanly possible was the priority.

I almost didn't care what the IRS had seized that might prove tax fraud and bribery. Roger was about to be too busy defending himself (using his money to pay high-priced attorneys) to waste time fighting with the landmark society or the rest of the City Council over one lousy building. And, bless Jim again, in his piece for *The Manhattan Legend*, he had somehow managed to sneak in a sentence about the lawsuit filed by Sid, for actions taken by the soldiers of fortune hired by Masters that resulted in damage to persons and personal property at the rally.

I did worry I might end up as a target and have to end up in witness protection, but I was reassured by Jim that, first, Masters' security team (except for the infamous Willem Nels who apparently was an American citizen) had been deported back to Johannesburg, Cape Town, and Pretoria. If the goon squad decided to exact revenge on someone they suspected had leaked info on their boss to federal agents, to them I was Mary Smith. There were probably four hundred or more Mary Smiths currently residing in the five boroughs. And who knew how many of the ladies were listed in the phone directory? Plus, according to an unnamed source, each foreign member of Masters' team of brutes was wanted in connection to serious crimes back in their native country. Once their plane landed and they were home, they'd be too busy fending off charges and trying to raise bail to start hunting for a Miss Mary Smith, super typist, who was last seen in a city of just under two million people. New citizen Willem Nels was facing his own issues with the IRS for receiving a heckuva lot of salary under the table.

I was also afraid Masters would somehow connect Mary Smith, wielder of hidden cameras in dance shoes, with Marcus Kennedy and he'd find a way to retaliate against him. Again, reassurances from everyone starting with Jim and ending with Billy Don that the link from Mary to Marcus was impossible to connect and determining the source of the leak to the IRS would mean sifting through a long line of victims who'd been determined to see justice done for years.

So. It was now Thursday, and Marcus, Toby, Billy Don, and the rest of my dancers were sitting around following class—a class during which Jonah had spoken up twice to offer opinions about music!—cheerfully arguing about which of the vets was best at basketball free throws from a wheelchair. A discussion both innocuous and restful after more than two weeks of anxiety and stress.

"We should have a celebration," was the off-topic, out-of-the-blue suggestion raised by Toby.

"Celebration?" I asked.

"Yeah. The Center will be staying open. Masters may or may not go to jail, but even if he squirms out of the tax fraud, he won't be acquiring and tearing down historic landmarks for quite some time, especially since the councilmen he was bribing are worried about saving their own skins and making sure any other deals are strictly kosher." He glanced quickly at Jonah, then winked at me. "Miracles are happening all around. Consequently, I say it's celebration time."

Marcus perked up. "What about combining a triumph of good over evil bash with the launch party for the release of my album? The producers were going to rent some pricey space downtown, but this way the money can go to the Center instead. And I can be around people I care about instead of trying to impress folks in the music industry." He paused. "Wait. Am I being selfish? I mean, wanting to use the space for the launch? Be honest, folks."

Head shakes all around. Sid spoke up first. "It's not selfish. It's inspired. Veterans' issues will get some attention. And money. Always welcome. Do you have any idea what your songs have meant to all of us at the Center, to vets in general? You're the one who organized the benefit concert back in August. You sing for us and with us every week for several hours. This is a win/win."

****

I'd never been to a launch party before but I had a feeling this one, for the release of *Remake the Song* was, like the record itself, not exactly traditional. Marcus had told me to invite whomever I wanted. So I did. I asked Zelda, Jim, the real Mary Smith, Wyatt, Wyatt's girlfriend Cathy, and Fredda and Frank Kaufman. Some unidentifiable push in my brain got me to track down the vendor, Fiona Belle Donovan, who was delighted yet, oddly, not surprised to receive an invitation. She even promised to bring three dozen cranberry-orange scones. I couldn't wait to see what she'd be wearing.

Marcus told me he didn't want to perform more than one or two songs. Those would probably be "Johnny Has Gone for a Soldier" and "Didn't My Lord Deliver Daniel?" both of which were on the new record, and ask anyone who knew the words to join in on either or both tunes.

Everyone I invited showed up. They were having a blast circulating and chatting animatedly with the veterans, although I had a feeling Jim was tamping down the urge to interview a music producer about a payola scandal making the news this past week. I'm not much of a party person, so I hung out at the table with the coffee and Fiona Belle's scones—brought in a cute picnic basket by the baker herself, neatly dressed in her Russian Army dance costume—along with Zelda, introducing her to Toby and also to Sid from my class. Toby was delighted to tell Zelda he'd heard (from me) that she was taking his brother's class and (from his brother Terry) she was already kicking serious butt. Zelda told Toby, with much admiration how much she'd heard (from me) how efficiently he ran the day-to-day operation at the Center. From there forward, their flirting was subtle but steady.

Jonah joined our small group in time to hear our way-off-topic-from-the-record-launch discussion about the soap opera for which Zelda had snagged an audition, thanks to a producer seeing her in *Dames at Sea* and becoming instantly entranced. She was hoping to get cast as a new, villainously wicked, and blatantly seductive, character with the ridiculous name of Bathsheba Brickhouse. Jonah informed her, as we tried not to jump for joy hearing him speak, that *Exit to Eternity* was his favorite TV program. Zelda and I agreed. It was ours as well.

Marcus found me debating with Zelda as to whether or not I should audition for *Exit for Eternity* the next time they had an open call and said, "Decide later, Miss Shiloh. Time to get out of your corner. Not to sound like a whiny brat, but it's my party and I'd like to enjoy it. The producers hired a live band and I'm dancing with my lady. Fractured ribs be hanged. I've made the rounds talking to critics and deejays and other musicians from the label. Enough business for the night. And I refuse to go hawking the merchandise Angela is pushing."

"What? You're not enamored with those T-shirts displaying your handsome mug on the front?" I teased.

Marcus groaned. "Have you seen them? Angela approved the design without asking me. I wanted a simple shirt with *Remake the Song* in calligraphy-style lettering. Nothing else. No photos. I still wouldn't be happy about it, but I'd be a bit less embarrassed if she'd chosen the other option, which was the record cover. At least that one had the name of the album instead of some stupid picture of me standing there with my guitar, looking goofy."

"Well, if it makes you feel better, the cover photo is wonderful. You don't look goofy; you look very, uh, musical."

Marcus chortled. "I'm not sure what 'looking musical' means or if you do either, but for now, let's forget about merchandise and promoting and get out there and dance. Are you up for a rumba, Miss Meridien? I'd request a jitterbug, but I'm not sure I'd make it through."

"Rumba. Love it. What about you? How are your ribs? You say 'be hanged' but I'd prefer not to see you writhing in pain."

"As long as I don't lift you in the air I can handle the moves."

One thing Marcus had insisted on, as well as having the launch party at the Center, was hiring Billy Don as deejay, with a top salary. Billy Don didn't let him down. He had a knack for picking the right song at the right time. The right songs at this time featured a variety of dance rhythms, and Marcus and I happily joined the folks making use of the huge floor space. A couple of the vets from my class were enjoying the music with their wives or girlfriends. Toby was doing a unique version of a cha-cha with Zelda while Sid steered Mary Smith through his own concept of a merengue using the same song. Marcus had invited Jeremiah Henry's parents to the party and the couple were displaying some nice moves in between meeting some of the veterans.

After less than twenty minutes of nonstop dancing, Marcus declared break time for us and started to lead me to a table, but we were waylaid by Frank Kaufman.

"I took the liberty to ask your deejay if there was a

waltz tune in his stack of records. Old or new. Didn't matter. He searched and came up with a few ideas. So, Shiloh, would you care to dance with me if Marcus can bear to part with your company? We can improvise as the spirit hits us."

Marcus grinned at him. "Go for it. You can even do the lifts my ribs won't allow."

I grinned back at Marcus, then turned to Frank. "I would love to waltz with you," I replied, immensely pleased at the invitation. "And as you're aware, my middle name is Improvisation."

Frank led me back out to the floor and nodded to Billy Don, who waved at us before he dropped the needle down on a medley of waltzes composed by the king of the genre, Johann Strauss. Once we'd finished, we looked for Marcus but he was standing by the entrance of the ballroom, engaging in conversation with a blonde woman I hadn't yet met. So Frank escorted me over to a table filled with beverages so I could quench what was now quite a thirst. If I'd had the smallest inkling of what awaited me, I'd've gone back on the floor, regardless of the song.

Chapter 31

Early November 1975

I was just finishing my third glass of sparkling water when I was accosted by a woman in her mid-thirties. I recognized her as Angela Dane, Marcus's business manager, wearing a chic, black, short, cocktail dress and a far-too-solemn-for-a-party expression on her face. She'd overdone her perfume, a scent I recognized as *Gardenia Gardens* from the last time I went to a department store and was chased by a sales girl with a spritzer, who must have had a quota to fill. For a brief second I recalled having smelled the odor of gardenias when I was struggling to breathe during the ghastly attack of clairvoyant trauma down at the World Trade Center. Angela.

"Your waltz was very graceful, Miss Meridien."

"Thank you. Miss Dane, isn't it?"

She nodded. "Yes."

"Please, call me Shiloh."

She didn't return the favor of suggesting I use her given name. She didn't speak at all. A long silence ensued, while she stared at me, making me nervous and edgy.

I broke it by asking, "So, uh, do you think the party's going well?"

She shrugged. "This was not the launch I wanted,

but then again, this was not the album Marcus should have recorded."

Ouch. "Well, I'm no critic, but I've been listening to his music since I was in junior high school and I personally believe this is his best album to date," I said, trying to remain pleasant.

Angela ignored my comment and didn't attempt to continue the discussion about the record. She jumped right into her motivation for approaching me. "I specifically mentioned you were graceful as you waltzed because I would appreciate it if you will cut your friendship with Marcus with equal grace."

"What?"

"You heard me." Her tone grew progressively discordant as she rushed into a lengthy monologue, which essentially came down to belittling me while trashing her own client. "Listen, sweetie, the last thing Marcus needs right now is some wannabe chorus girl hanging all over him, encouraging him to go down a path in his music which leads to nowhere. He's very susceptible to praise, and he's not faithful. Not to his music and not to any women he might encounter, especially starstruck groupies like you. He's got an obsessive personality, and if you're on the wrong side of whatever happens to be his latest obsession, he'll run you over without a single regret. He's also stubborn as a goat, but I can usually get him to see reason if I wear him down long enough, and I can block anyone else attempting to influence him. Which is precisely what I will do. Wear him down until he sees reason. I've talked to two producers who are willing to put up the front money for another record, if it's commercial enough to actually sell, which means getting away from his latest absurd mix of musical genres. But, you, dear, are not helping. Like many before you, your presence in his life is neither needed nor required."

Her smile was fake, her expression far less than agreeable. She gestured to the corner of the ballroom, where Marcus was still talking with the girl who could have been the clone of my sister Lacey. Blonde, petite, and very animated. Ten to one she had sparkling blue eyes and either a doctorate in business or a thriving practice in entertainment law.

Angela grabbed my arm and held it. "The young lady who's captured Marcus's attention is his ex-fiancée, Beverly Collins. A woman with ambition for Marcus. A woman who understands the music business and who also understands Marcus. A woman totally unlike you. So, sweetie, enjoy the rest of the party, go home with the friends you invited who have nothing to do with the industry, and then make a gracious exit from Marcus's life."

I didn't like Angela Dane. I didn't like her cloying, gardenia-scented perfume. I didn't like being called '"sweetie"—which has always seemed like a derogatory address for any creature other than a poodle. I didn't like being called "dear" either, which has always seemed like a derogatory address for every creature, including poodles. I didn't like the way Angela talked about Marcus. I didn't like the way she wanted to control Marcus's life.

I didn't like the way Marcus appeared to be hanging on every word Beverly Collins was saying or the fact he was now leading her over to join Angela and me.

I didn't like the kicks in my stomach which were rising to my heart.

Marcus and Beverly crossed the room in record time and were now standing in front of me. Marcus was providing introductions. He was honest. There was no subterfuge or cute euphemisms to explain who Beverly was. The good news was he didn't appear to be thrilled by her presence. Perhaps I'd misinterpreted his attention when they'd been on the other side of the room. The kicks moved back down into my stomach and subsided.

"Hey, Shiloh. Look who turned up. This is Beverly Collins. We dated a bit a few years ago. Beverly, this is Shiloh Meridien, my girlfriend." He turned and glared at Angela. "Gee, Angela, fancy Beverly coming to the party. Can we say shocker? No one mentioned she was back in Manhattan."

Angela rolled her eyes, something I'd always thought was impossible, but she achieved it. "I invited her. I thought if anyone can knock sense into your artsy-addled brain, it's Beverly." Angela and the Lacey doppelganger exchanged hugs, and then the petite Beverly inspected me from my toes to the top of my five-foot-ten frame with an expression indicating clear disdain for what she saw.

We shook hands. "Back from where?" I managed to ask in as polite a tone as I could muster.

"London. I've been working with a record company, Top Tunes, across the pond for the last sixteen months, doing public relations for several of their biggest clients."

"Oh. How, uh, exciting," I said, not meaning it.

She put her hand across Marcus's arm. "I was serious when I told you they want to sign you to their label. You have a big following in England. Throughout Europe, really. Top Tunes is very anxious to set up a recording session at their new studio in Notting Hill, which is the same place numerous Grammy winners have used. But, the catch, like I also said, is they want the newer sound with the electric guitars and electronic keyboard. Much closer to disco. Zero acoustics. And definitely no protest, gospel, or spirituals. These guys are the best in the business and totally up on the latest trends. What you're doing is in the past. It needs to stay there."

Marcus stated, "In other words, they want nothing with a soul. Definitely nothing like *Remake the Song*."

Angela took over and fiercely announced, "This album won't sell, Marcus. I've used every bit of clout I've ever had with any and all industry folks to get them to even come to this stupid party, which is coming off like amateur night at the local high school. Bottom line, no one wants to promote the record. We're fighting for even a moderate distribution. It's time to cut losses and move on." She glared at me, and I was well aware moving on meant dumping Shiloh Meridien.

Marcus sighed. "Look, this is not the time or the place to have this discussion."

Angela nodded. "Well, finally, something you and I agree on. We don't need outsiders involved in any of the business."

"If you're insinuating Shiloh is an outsider, scrap the notion right now, Angela. She's very much involved. But any discussion regarding whether to record another album should be tabled until we've gotten through this launch. We're supposedly here to celebrate the release of the album I loved recording more than any other in my life."

He held his hand out to me. "So, Shiloh, let's celebrate. Let's dance."

Chapter 32

Early November 1975

Midnight. Marcus and I were sitting on what passed for a stoop outside my apartment, holding hands and gazing up at the stars determinedly shining through too many tall buildings.

"I'm so sorry," Marcus said.

"For what?"

"For Angela. Heck, while I'm apologizing, for Beverly as well, although she wasn't quite as aggressive or rude. I had no idea Beverly was in Manhattan until she showed up at the Center. I was stunned when she sauntered over to me and immediately began prattling on about the wonders of European producers. She worked with Angela a few years ago in the public relations end of the recording industry. I haven't spoken to her or communicated by letter or carrier pigeon in more than a year, and I sure as heck didn't invite her to the party. Anyway, neither of them had any business bringing you into the middle of the fray and talking about the latest scheme to turn Marcus Kennedy into the king of rock." He groaned. "Or worse. A disco star."

"You and I were kind of kidding about that a couple of weeks ago, but are they actually serious?" I didn't bother to stifle my laughter. "Excuse me, but has either of these women ever *met* you?"

Marcus threw his hands up into the air. "Apparently not. Be glad you didn't hear the first conversation I had with Beverly when she was telling me all about some heavy-hitting management company in London who have this notion that, with some tweaking and major changes to my entire personality and sound, they can turn me into a singing clown to entertain the posh high society set at La Troubadour's or Ducky's Disco in the West End. Record an album in about a week, with music composed on a synthesizer...probably *by* the synthesizer! Then whisk me back to America to perform at Les Chic in L.A. where the pay is even better."

I chuckled. "I'm sorry. I am now trying to banish an image of you wearing a gold lamé jumpsuit and swinging those hips while a crowd of sweaty dancers writhe to the beat."

Marcus laughed. "Your imagination is horribly vivid. I can visualize it way too clearly. I'm tellin' ya, Angela and Beverly are both seriously deranged, and they're making me feel like a string of taffy during the pulling stage of production."

We lapsed into silence for a long moment.

Finally, I squeezed his hand. "Marcus, I have breaking news for you. Unless there's been a drastic change in the U.S. Constitution, you're a free citizen with the ability to make your own choices." *Beginning with firing Angela and waving bye-bye to Beverly at LaGuardia as she boards the next plane with a one-way ticket to London.* I did not give voice to those last suggestions but I had the sense Marcus was well aware of my thoughts.

"Free choices. I need to remind myself you're right. And, frankly, I'm tired of bickering with Angela about every music decision I make." He paused, then added, "She's been acting weird for the last four months or so. I keep wondering if she's contacting producers behind my back and I'm going to wake up one morning and discover I've been drugged and flown to France to headline some rich aristocrat's newest disco. Now, I admit it, I love France. Paris is…well…Paris. Great food, great sights, one of the best opera houses in the world, which is the Palais Garnier. But back to the issue. Angela has been my manager for the last six years and she was great up until about a year ago. She supported my original dream to make a difference through music and didn't seem to be focused on how much money an album generated. Now her main objective is how much of a cash cow she can turn me into. But I'm having a tough time figuring out how I'd replace her. As in, with whom. Let's face it, most of the managers I've met have the same mind set. Money."

"What about hiring Sid?" I suggested. "He's two shakes away from being a full-fledged member of the bar and he's got a great business sense. More importantly, he's got a soul and he loves your music."

He brightened. "To quote the Brits, 'Smashing!' I do need to, well, fire the woman before I start running through streets screaming, 'I have free choices!'" He leaned down and tucked a stray strand of hair behind my ear. "Okay. Speaking of the devil, what exactly happened at the party? You're never a chatterbox, but you've been really quiet tonight. You've been like the proverbial mouse ever since you spoke with Angela. What did she say to you?"

"Oh, nothing important," I replied.

"Not important but doubtless tactless and pretty

ugly. Let me guess. You are wrecking my career. You are nothing. Less than nothing. You are a dancer with no real career of her own, so you're trying to horn in on mine. And I'm a faithless, stubborn goat who goes through starstruck music lovers like you as if they were tissue paper. Oh, yeah. Forgot this one. I'm obsessed with getting my way and if you're blocking it, I'll plow through anyway."

"Did you have a hidden tape recorder in the coffeepot?" I asked.

"Wouldn't be worth ruining the coffee. No, the truth is, Angela has been haranguing me about you for weeks. She started the day I met you down at the World Trade Center."

"I do seem to recall the term 'homeless groupie' tossed around while I was on the ground struggling to breathe."

"Did she also bring up the Beverly-is-perfect line tonight?"

"Not quite in those words, but close. She called Beverly your ex-fiancée."

"What! Total lie. Beverly and I went out about four times, but when we stopped seeing each other Angela was so upset she nearly went into hibernation. Shiloh, please don't buy any of the hogwash she's spewing. Although, she is correct about one personality trait I have. Stubbornness." He assumed an air of innocence. "I prefer to say I'm steadfast and determined, but I suppose if one is on the opposite end of what I want, the term cantankerous or obstinate could be easily applied."

"Well, on occasion I've personally forgotten vegan principles and gone with pig-headedness in refusing to back down." I faked a serious expression. "It doesn't harm the hogs."

Marcus stared into my eyes. "Then I hope this is one of those occasions when you'll use your hoggish tendencies and refuse to buy all the ridiculous things Angela said." He wrapped his arms around me. "Can we forget her for a while? It's horribly late, but I'd like to spend some time holding you and kissing you before Wyatt and Jim realize their baby sister hasn't come in yet and come barging out to shoo me away."

I agreed by leaning in for his kiss. His lips searched mine with both gentleness and passion. And he tasted marvelous, with a tangy, almost bitter flavor of coffee mixed with the sweetness of what I swore was pastry. Quite possibly one of Fiona Belle's scones we'd snuck out with and devoured only minutes before.

Marcus suddenly released me, but gently. He pointed down the street and grinned. "It appears more than record sales might have been sparked tonight. Look. They're perfect together."

"Who?" I peered around him and couldn't suppress my amusement and delight as I watched Zelda strolling down W. 103rd Street, her hand clasped tightly in Toby's. "You're right. They're perfect. This is great. I can't wait to get all the dirt from Zelda about the budding relationship."

"I thought Zelda lived in the West Seventies," Marcus said. "What's she doing up here?"

"She does. She's spending the night at my apartment so we can roust each other from a sound sleep and make sure she gets to her audition for *Exit for Eternity* tomorrow morning."

"Ah. The super soapy soap. Are you auditioning as well?"

"Nah. Emma Andersen Dance Theater will be back in the States in a couple of weeks and my very long-held desire has been to earn a spot with them. Plus, Zelda's audition is by invitation. I'm just going to lend support."

I felt a wisp of a feeling, or a premonition? One of my *déjà-vu-isms*? Whatever it was, it left the strong impression that when it came to becoming a member of Emma Andersen's company, I would soon be facing a decision completely unrelated to auditioning. And my choice could affect everyone I knew and cared about.

Chapter 33

Early November 1975

Exit to Eternity was filmed at a huge studio warehouse on the Upper West Side. It was much closer to Zelda's apartment than mine, but due to the furniture issue, namely there being a couch in the living room of my apartment and none at hers, Zelda had stayed with me instead of forcing me to sleep on the floor at her place. We'd taken the extra distance of thirty-five blocks into account, and gotten up at an early hour to get ready and catch a bus so there wouldn't be the slightest chance of getting trapped on a stalled subway train and missing her time slot. We'd been up the night before until around two, but Zelda remained jazzed about meeting (and falling for) Toby and had energy to spare for the audition.

"Did your agent tell you anything about the character you're reading for?" I asked her as we rode down toward the studio.

"Not much. I gather Bathsheba Brickhouse is the CEO of a lingerie company and she makes great use of their products by wearing them while sleeping with everybody and his brother. I'm not sure where she fits into the current storyline, which, I have to say, has been thrilling. Miranda has discovered she's the illegitimate daughter of Prince Rupert, who got her cousin Lulu pregnant, but he's really in love with her maid Jezebel, who's been spying on the royal court ever since she was kidnapped by the cult in Idaho, brainwashed, and installed in the prince's household a year later."

I started chortling the instant Zelda said "royal court" and was now laughing so loudly I was afraid the bus driver would ask me to leave. "Stop! I beg you! Stop! I haven't watched the show in about six months and had no idea this was going on. I'm doubling over and am now in pain. I have to get in control before I escort you into the studio and they throw me out for not taking their storyline seriously."

She tried to keep a straight face. She failed. "Well, I'll more than make up for your deplorable lack of diplomacy with my obvious passion and enthusiasm. Shoot, I can recite every plot line from *Exit*, starting from when I was ten and getting a gig with this soap became my biggest dream and ambition." Zelda sighed. "It wasn't exactly a lovely time in my life. My parents were fighting and constantly flinging around the word 'divorce,' and I couldn't handle it. I'd fake illnesses to skip school and watch soaps, but especially *Exit to Eternity*. I figured out early on that the storyline changed every thirteen weeks or so and, while the villains were on top in week one, by the last episode of a particular plot they were toast. I already knew I wanted to be an actress, but I set my sights on landing a job with *Exit*. Honestly, I'd settle for a nonspeaking walk-on as a nurse removing a bedpan from some no-name's hospital room."

Once we arrived at the studio, we were immediately ushered onto the set itself. Zelda handed her headshot and resume to a tiny, wiry young woman wearing jeans and a show jacket and sporting a spiky short hairdo and sixties-era granny glasses. She took Zelda's contact information, thrust scripts at both of us, whirled around, and marched off toward a cameraman about twenty feet away. Her attitude and bearing was clear. *I'm a woman on a mission to save the world—Do not mess with me!*

"Excuse me," I said loudly, holding out the pages. "Could you wait up a second? I need to give these back. I'm not auditioning." I pointed to Zelda. "She is. Has an appointment at nine, which was set up by her agent. But I don't, so I don't need a script."

The woman stopped in mid-stride, turned back to face us, and stared (or rather, glared) at me. "Are you literate?"

"I beg your pardon?"

"Did you learn how to read at some point in your life?"

"Age three-and-a-half," I responded, unsure where this was going.

"Great. You're reading Lilith Leatherby opposite your friend reading Bathsheba Brickhouse."

Zelda's eyes pleaded with me to comply with the request, so I agreed. I wasn't sure I had a choice. The stage manager's attitude was clearly, *I don't take no for an answer from anyone, including the show's producer, director, any and all advertisers, and especially the so-called "talent."*

I hadn't expected to be auditioning with my best friend, but the ten-minute scene, performed for the casting director three times, with scripts in hand, turned out to be the most fun I'd had in weeks, not counting dancing with Marcus, which, admittedly, was enjoyment on an entirely different level.

Back to the reading. Both characters were deliciously vicious, bitchy, and appropriately outrageous. In the scene we'd been given, Bathsheba, the ruthless CEO of Slinky Silk Lingerie, and Lilith, a black-leather-wearing dominatrix who owns Whips, an S & M dungeon, were verbally ripping each other to shreds because Lilith is having an affair with Bathsheba's lover, who is married to Lilith's housekeeper. We were dying to ask for the upcoming script when the verbal ripping would no doubt escalate into serious cat-fight shredding.

Zelda and I had met less than three months ago, yet we possessed the kind of chemistry essential to sharing a scene with an acting partner, along with a natural rhythm to how we phrased our sentences. We took advantage of our close connection and in-sync tempo, and we nailed it.

By the way, small tangent, but if anyone is scoffing and sneering at the folks who work on soaps, let me state emphatically it's one of the hardest performing jobs out there, and an actor's skills have to be top-notch. When I was at U.T. I took a theater course called Acting for Film and Television, where my instructor had been adamant about respecting the art of performing daytime dramas as if they were Shakespeare. After all, many of Master Will's plots had been as off-the-wall as those presented on contemporary soap operas. Consider *Romeo and Juliet*, the professor had stated, as a great example. Juliet's scene of, *"Oops, no poison left, so I'll stab myself while whipping off a terrific monologue before joining Romeo in forever sleep,"* was pure daytime drama. Then there was *Hamlet,* with its protagonist prince, upset over Daddy's murder and consequently coming up with the tricky and slick concept of a play within a play, the outcome of which left everybody and his brother (well, uncle) dead on the floor. In many of his plays, Shakespeare tossed in elements of the supernatural with ghosts, impish fairies, ugly but smart witches, and powerful magicians controlling the waves of the ocean. This was centuries before vampires in New England and ocean cliffside settings became the reason teenagers skipped after-school activities to race home, switch on the TV, and find out who would prevail…the seductively beautiful witch or the two-hundred-year-old brooding antihero with the cape, the fangs, and the never-ending desire to reunite with his true, chaste, lost love.

Renaissance-era audiences lapped up the Bard's plots and invested belief in them as surely as today's viewers eagerly tune in to see whether Artemis's half-brother marries their stepmother Persephone, who's the artificially cloned twin sister of cousin Demeter, whose multiple-personality disorder has her plying her wares as a hooker named Tessa Trollop by night and raising chickens in a cloistered convent as Sister Mary Mendacity by day.

Added to an actor's skill in making a character believable is the task of memorizing pages in absurdly short time periods. Multiply the stress of memorization on a daily basis and add a splash of stepping in front of a camera and making viewers either weep for your constant trials and tribulations or savor loving to hate you. Many regulars on a soap work an average of twelve hours a day, five days a week. Intense doesn't begin to cover it.

This job, with this particular soap, was the one Zelda wanted more than any other. She deserved to be cast. She deserved to have audiences all over America discussing

Bathsheba Brickhouse's nefarious schemes while drinking their morning coffee, be that in one's home kitchen, a college student union, or the office's conference room.

We finished the scene for the third time and headed out to the lobby to check out the wall of history, which featured shots of actors and actresses from the early days of *Exit to Eternity* (1955) up to the present casts. Zelda pointed to the professional photo of former vaudevillian Howard Baez, who'd played a kindly doctor for the last twenty years. "Dr. Dalton" was an elderly, old-school, home-visiting saint of a medical man who'd had the misfortune to father three wicked sons who wreaked havoc on all the women in the town of Eternity, Somewhere in New England.

Zelda was nearly swooning as she gazed at his photo. "I adored him. I wanted him to find a way to come to Illinois, swoop me up, and adopt me."

"Is Baez still with the show?" I asked. "Remember, I haven't seen it in six months."

She shook her head. "No. He finally retired about four months ago. He's in his nineties and living happily with his wife of seventy-odd years on an apple farm in upstate New York."

Before I could respond, the gruff stage manager came racing into the lobby and yelled at us to stay right where we were.

She joined us, and thrust some papers at Zelda. "You're in. You have an agent, yes?"

Zelda remained upright, although I was prepared to catch her if she fainted from shock. "I do."

"Well, take these to him, or her, whoever, and have him, her, whoever, check them out. It's a standard contract, at least for now." She turned to me. "You. Ridiculously tall redhead. Do you have a headshot and resume?"

"I do."

"I want them. We're holding off on adding Lilith until the spring and we're in negotiations with a 'name' but everyone was so impressed with your reading, especially playing opposite Ms. Zimmerman here, we didn't want to lose your contact info."

I dug into my bag and pulled out a headshot, with my resume stapled to the back, and, feeling somewhat dazed, handed it to the stage manager, who had yet to introduce herself.

The girl took it and nodded, then turned to Zelda. The barest hint of a smile emerged. "Welcome to Eternity, Bathsheba Brickhouse."

Chapter 34

Early November 1975

Zelda and I were going to grab a late breakfast after the audition, but she was anxious to get to her agent's office over on Fifty-First Street and get the contract signed, so she hailed a cab and took off.

I had a few hours before I was due at the Henske and planned to take a ballet class early in the afternoon, but that still left me with some free time on my hands this morning. I walked the forty or so blocks from the soap studios to the Am-Vets Center so I could tell Toby the wonderful news about Zelda being cast and suggest we come up with some kind of celebration. And yes, I hoped Marcus might be at the Center, perhaps doing some extra clean-up after last night's launch party.

I entered the building right as Marcus and Sid were exiting, bags draped over their shoulders.

"Hi, guys. Where are you off to?" I asked.

"Washington," Marcus replied.

"An exciting, educational visit to the Capitol or the Smithsonian?"

"I wish," Marcus answered. "Nope, this is to the Pentagon. We have managed to arrange a sit-down meeting, supposedly with a JAG officer who might be able to provide some insight."

"Into?"

Sid glanced at his watch.

"I'm sorry," I said. "Do y'all have time to fill me on what this is about?"

"Yeah. Flight's not until later this afternoon. We were about to grab lunch down the street and discuss strategy. Want to join us?" Marcus asked. He turned around and shouted at Toby, who was straightening papers scattered all over the reception table. "You coming?"

"Yeah. Hang on."

Once we were settled into a booth at some nameless diner a few blocks from the Center, Toby turned to me. "Before we get into the juicy details of the reason for our trip to D.C., how did Zelda's audition go this morning?"

"Beautifully. She's in. Assuming her agent has no grief with the contracts, she'll be seen all over America starting in about two weeks, when the character of the very seedy but very sexy Bathsheba Brickhouse is introduced."

Silence. Then laughter.

"Bathsheba Brickhouse?" Marcus chortled in unabashed glee.

I held my hand up. "Swear. I did *not* make up the name. She's the CEO of a lingerie factory, although as we were leaving, I heard someone say the writers are still torn between having the lingerie factory linked to the porn industry or be a front for a munitions factory selling bullets to mobsters and drug cartels. Possibly both. I gotta tell ya, Zelda is over the moon. Deservedly so. She was awesome at the reading." I took a sip of coffee. "Which reminds me. The whole reason I stopped by the Center was to give you the news and see if we can come up some kind of celebration."

Toby's whole face lit up. "Yes! Um, does she like French food and champagne? There's a great restaurant over on Forty-Third Street I went to about a year ago for a buddy's birthday party. Food is excellent and it has the whole 'snooty' vibe one wants when celebrating something special." He paused. "Wait. I guess you were imagining more like a party at the Center, and we can definitely do that, but I'd love to take her there on a real date first."

"Sounds perfect," I said and winked at him. "I'm sure she'd love the French food, and don't tell Zelda I told you this, but if you're the one inviting her to dinner, she'd be thrilled with simply a slice and a soda."

Toby looked as if he was debating whether to duck under the table in embarrassment or jump on top of it in sheer glee. "I'll call her tonight, from D.C.," he mumbled, staying in his seat.

I took another sip of my coffee. "Okay, guys. Enough talk of daytime drama. What's up? Why the trip?"

Marcus gestured to Sid. "You tell her. I'm so angry I'm not sure I can say anything without getting up and throwing chairs around the diner."

Toby chuckled. "Yeah. Good luck with that. Dang hard to do when they're booths. But Sid has the legal mind and can put things in order better."

"Guys? Spill, already." I said.

Sid took a breath. "For the last few months, we've had an influx of veterans coming in telling us they've been diagnosed with ailments one normally associates with much older people. Cancer, diabetes, heart disease. Parkinson's. Hodgkin's. The worst is Lou Gehrig's, often referred to as amyotrophic lateral sclerosis, but shortened to ALS since the other is quite a mouthful. And the ever-popular shell-shock everyone assumed was from witnessing and being involved in horrific events during battles."

I grimaced, then asked, "Influx leading to ask—what?"

"If these diseases are linked. And if so, how? And, lo and behold, we made a discovery. All these guys, plus a couple of ladies who served as nurses, are all either Vietnam or Korean vets. Not World War Two."

Marcus added, "Last week Toby and I sat down with a doctor who'd been treating about six vets from the Center, and he told us he'd been researching a lethal exfoliate used in both Korea and Vietnam and had major concerns regarding anyone serving who might have been exposed."

"Agent Orange," I said.

Again, there was silence, but this wasn't followed by laughter over the name of a daytime drama character.

Sid spoke first. "Where did you hear that term?"

"I'm not sure. Hang on and let me see if I can recall." I did recall but the memory veered into *déjà-vu-isms*, and I had no desire to come across as deranged. My date, Ethan Whatever, at the pub we'd gone to after the Benefit Vets concert, had talked about a deadly herbicide the U.S. government had blithely exposed soldiers and civilians to in Vietnam. The problem was I was sure I'd heard the two words "Agent Orange" inside *my* mind rather than stated by Ethan.

I said, "I've got it. Where I heard it. I was out with some folks after your August concert, Marcus. My blind date was a doctor, doing his residency in Ohio. He'd heard about this poisonous, um, exfoliate. But the conversation was focused more on the dangers in Manhattan, especially drug deals going down on public corners, and the idea of a lethal herbicide didn't really resonate with me until you guys brought it up."

All three men seemed to accept my statement, although Marcus shot me a look conveying a sense of *not the whole story, Shiloh, but we'll table it for now*.

"Well, your doctor friend was right," Toby stated. "And the effects of this herbicide are far worse than anyone imagined. No one in the military wants to admit somebody got spray happy and consequently the body count for veterans is rising."

"Aha. This explains the trip to Washington. You're hoping to get official word about the military dousing soldiers with poison?"

Marcus nodded. "Preferably much more. The government needs to provide compensation. It's not like the majority of veterans are wealthy. Precisely the opposite. And the hospital costs for treatment of almost all the diseases associated with Agent Orange are outrageously expensive."

Sid growled, "And what are families supposed to do when the thirty-year-old breadwinner trying to support a wife and three kids is confined to a bed or wheelchair and medical insurers ignore him while he waits to die? We're talking about thousands of veterans here."

"I had no idea it was this bad," I said. "Ethan, the medical resident, said it was a shame no one was aware there was an issue, because one of the singers might have been able to expose the seriousness of the issue at the concert."

Marcus emitted a cross between a snort and a sigh. "It's ironic and stupid. I had a call about an hour ago from Angela, who apparently spent most of the night following the launch party holed up in a bar with Beverly trying to figure out how best to get me to 'see reason' in how to further my career. Anyway, she informed me she'd been on the phone this morning with three of the critics who'd been at the launch and she had direct quotes from all three, who opined, 'We love Marcus's voice. As always, it's perfect. But *Remake the Song* is going nowhere because no one wants to hear such an eclectic mix and anything hinting at protest is out. Push him to something commercial before he has no career left.' End of quotes. The word of the day, according to Angela and supported by her buddy Beverly, is 'disco, disco, and disco.' "

"I'm lost. Why ironic and stupid?" Toby asked.

"Oh. Yeah. Sorry. Went way off on a tangent. Because, had I heard about Agent Orange before now I'd've skipped the cabaret portions of the new album and written several very scathing protest tunes aimed at the military hierarchy and their uncaring, secretive, greedy attitude regarding the very people they can't do without. The critics would roast me, but the word would be out." He attempted to lighten the mood. "I'm sure my manager would have been able to heat small buildings with the amount of steam rising from her head if I'd added a song about Agent Orange, although I'd've had to be very obscure with lyrics. I mean, orange is notoriously impossible to use as a rhyme. Maybe I could have gone with herbicide and homicide?"

Sid mused, "I'm pretty sure exfoliant wouldn't work either, but maybe if it's labeled what it is, poison?"

"'Poison rains on boys and sons,'" Marcus intoned.

"Not bad for a man with about two hours of sleep

and a mission to accomplish," Toby responded. "Not good, either." He and Marcus grinned at each other.

"Well, the stuff is a gas, right?" I tossed in. "Um, howzabout 'lethal gasses killing masses'?"

Marcus raised an eyebrow. "It's so bad it's perfect. You might have a new profession as a lyricist."

"If one can consider four words as constituting a song," I said. "I doubt Grammy-Award-winning producers will be knocking on my door begging me to pen the latest hit any time soon. I'm not that inventive."

Marcus managed a smile before his expression turned somber again. "Talk about inventions. Do you suppose the scientists who originally created the formula for Agent Orange had any idea it'd end up destroying more than innocent foliage?"

Sid shook his head. "They thought they were doing something helpful to farmers, finding a way to cut through undergrowth in jungles and open up land for use in crop development. I doubt they knew someone would see the opportunity to turn it into a weapon."

Toby's tone was grim. "Well, someone knew. They knew in Korea and they sure as shootin' knew in Vietnam."

"Well, no matter what kind of runaround we get in Washington tomorrow morning," Marcus stated, "One way or another, even if they have to shoot me to stop me, I intend to make sure the whole world hears the truth."

Chapter 35

Early November 1975

Marcus let Toby and Sid hail a cab and took the opportunity of giving me a kiss without interested eyes enjoying the moment. After the taxi screeched to a stop, I waved 'bye to the trio and started to head north on Broadway to get to the studio where I normally took my modern dance class.

The creepy guy in the all-brown ninja-inspired outfit was standing on the corner by a news stand down the street from the diner. This was not a coincidence. He was following me. Or Marcus. Or both. Was he one of Roger Masters' mercenaries who'd forgotten the name tag and preferred brown to black? Was he a deranged fan of folk music? I had no clue.

I turned around and circled three blocks before retracing my steps and continuing up Broadway. Creepy guy was gone. I made it to the studio, changed clothes, and added layers of leg and arm warmers and a sweater-wrap because I was freezing. Not from cold. From fear. I made it through class but realized I was executing both barre and center movements with what might best described as an automatic pilot muscle memory haze. I did perk up enough to perform *The Golden Age Revue* with honest enthusiasm, and managed to summon the focus and energy to sing and dance while shutting out the events of the day.

After the show, I walked down the block toward the subway station closest to the Henske hotel and theater and allowed a barrage of emotions—bugging me throughout class and the show, ever since the two words "Agent Orange" had been spoken at a diner in midtown Manhattan—to come to the surface. I was devastated to hear about the hell veterans were going through thanks to this poison, and confused and frustrated because of the hazy memory of the first time I'd heard the words. I was positive Ethan hadn't said them. I was also positive they'd been quite clear in my mind. But how I was hearing words I hadn't heard before had me confused and frustrated. I'm being repetitive, but too many wacky events since August 21st had left me confused and frustrated. Zelda's word *déjà-vu-ism* was silly and cute...unless odd clairvoyant flickers and flashes were hammering into the life of the person experiencing the *déjà vu* ramped up a few notches.

Agent Orange. Black Lives Matter. BFFs. Finding daily planners with messages urging me to attend auditions for shows I didn't have a chance or any great desire to be cast in. Fashionable, in-my-size clothes I didn't remember buying turning up in my closet. Reliving, with color, sound effects and sharp odors, a horrific future event. The certainty Marcus was in real danger. Zelda and I had joked about poltergeists and the oddities after I told her about my findings, but I was past considering them as intriguing exercises into the supernatural. I was frightened and I was angry.

I spotted Fiona Belle Donovan, today wearing her pink fairy godmother ensemble, waiting for me at the end of the block. She was perched on a stool in front of what appeared to be an empty cart. I walked…no, I *strode*…over to her and glared at her. Thanks to the positioning of the raised stool, we were face to face, so I couldn't intimidate her with my superior height, which made me even angrier.

I spoke first. "You."

"Me."

"Who exactly are you? Or should I say, '*What* are you?' I mean, I have this certainty you're the instigator, perpetrator, provocateur, and engineer in charge of driving the trainload of bizarre stuff I've experienced over the last couple of months, which is impossible, but there it is."

"Shiloh, lass, calm down. You seem troubled."

"Not an answer. Dang straight, I'm troubled." I laid it all out for her. The phrases, the clothes, the messages, the horror at the Twin Towers. "What is happening?"

"Shiloh."

"Fiona Belle."

"I can't give you answers," she said.

"You mean, you won't."

"This much I'm sayin' to you, lass—you'll be seein' me again, and I'll be aft ta providin', oh, let's call them…disclosures." She inhaled and then blew out a huge breath. "But, and understand me now, you'll also have a choice to make, and it's comin' soon."

"A choice? What kind of choice? Can you offer one meager, teensy little hint as to what in blazes you're talking about?"

"Go home, Shiloh. You've had a long couple of days and you need to rest." She handed me a bag filled with scones. "Enough fer you and yer roommates fer breakfast tomorrow."

I sighed. "You are demonic. I crave these suckers. Okay. Fine. How much do I owe you?"

"On the house. You ought to get somethin' out of this chat, even if it's loaded with sugar and calories."

After I got back to my apartment, I showered, then ate three scones. I called Jim at the newspaper and told him all about Agent Orange, mentioning I'd heard the term in August from a medical resident. He was excited about getting a story and I promised to get him in touch with Marcus or Sid or Toby as soon as the guys returned from Washington. Next, I tried to call Zelda, but her line was busy. Perhaps she and Toby were discussing the menu of the French restaurant he'd mentioned?

I debated about phoning Marcus, but all the guys were bunking with a former Marine buddy of Sid's at his house in Georgetown, and I didn't want to intrude. Not to mention, if Toby and Zelda were chatting, I couldn't exactly cut in on the line.

I dragged out the huge and mysterious duffel bag I'd stored in the back of my closet in August. I'd removed the clothes out ages ago to wear them, but now I pulled out the magazine clippings along with the notes I'd jotted down after the Benefit Vets concert. They weren't much help. I'd already recalled talking about Black Lives Matter with Sandra, Ethan, and Eddie, although the death-by-cop-shooting at the time had been of a teenager, not PFC Jeremiah Henry, Jr. It did appear the situation with the "greedy developer" and a bribed city councilman had been taken care of, although I wasn't sure I trusted the legal system to mete out the justice Roger Masters and Councilman Gary Campbell deserved. It wouldn't surprise me at all if, like some cartoon villain who doesn't die, the evil developer and corrupt politician would keep surfacing and causing more havoc..

The *Vegan Health News* clipping, what there was of it, was intriguing, and finally seemed to have meaning in terms of what was happening with the veterans. Half the information had been scratched out (in purple ink) but I found enough left to conclude some researchers theorized that a raw vegan diet consisting of tons of fruits and veggies and seeds containing Omega 3s (whatever they were), along with daily exercises, might stave off serious diseases exactly like the ones the vets were suffering from thanks to the herbicide. Yes, the operative word was "might," but "might" was still more encouraging than what anyone else had been offering these veterans, i.e., a whole lot of nothing.

Marcus phoned me around ten. "I wanted to call earlier, but Toby pretty much had the line tied up talking to Zelda." I could hear the amusement in his voice. "I do not want to be around when he gets the bill in a couple of weeks."

"Well, Zelda's about to become a big soap star, so I'll suggest she let Toby call collect next time."

"Doubt there'll be a next time. I foresee very few separations for those two." Marcus paused then added, "Which is where I see us, as well. I miss you, and it's been less than ten hours since we were together."

"The feeling is mutual. I wish I could have come with you. My other feeling is y'all are going to be facing a rough day tomorrow."

"Yeah. The military has a reputation for avoiding full disclosure, which is fine and desirable when it comes to battle tactics, but annoying and disheartening when one is attempting to get an admission of wrong-doing.

Anyway, I won't stay on the line long, but I had to call you. Apart from wanting you here with me, I kept having this sense all day that you've been going through something weird. Am I right?"

"Yeah."

"Can you tell me about it?"

"Yes and no. I've experienced some strange things over the last three months, and I have no plausible or rational explanation for them, but I'm fairly certain I'm not crazy. "

Marcus's voice was gentle. "Does this have anything to do with what happened down at the World Trade Center?"

"Yes." I paused, then added, "When you get back, let's find a time when we can be alone, and I'll give you the rundown on odd doin's in the life of Shiloh Meridien."

Chapter 36

Early November 1975

The following morning, I cast aside all thoughts of bizarre events, and portents of doom and gloom, and caught a bus to midtown early enough to hit Terry Travers' martial arts class. I then attended two more dance classes and added my own improvised gleeful jig after spotting a notice on the bulletin board in the lobby of the Forty-Sixth Street Studios announcing the return of Emma Andersen's company in two weeks and the subsequent, albeit tentative, scheduling of auditions sometime in December.

With three hours of free time before the tea show at the Henske, I decided to walk over to the public library and delve into whatever research I could uncover regarding vegan diets and links to cures for serious illnesses. I found an article in, of all things, *The Manhattan Legend*, from an issue dated six months ago, discussing vegetarianism and listing a whole slew of big names who espoused the philosophy of "no meat," but the emphasis seemed to be more on trends and the ethical side. Which in itself was great to see happening. After all, I quit eating meat and dairy as a kid because I loved animals and cancer wasn't exactly a big concern of mine when I was nine years old. I was now hoping for the kind of information I'd read in whatever hadn't been scratched or cut out of the *Vegan Health News*. I had yet to find the actual magazine and strongly suspected it didn't exist and Fiona Belle had written and printed out the article herself on some ancient press she'd discovered in some hidden attic in a tiny village in Ireland.

Marcus, Toby, and Sid were due back early this evening. I tamped down my anxiety about the results of their interactions with Pentagon lawyers, did the show at the Henske, then hurried over to the Am-Vets Center to greet them.

All three men were seated in the lobby, and all three men were angry and morose.

Marcus and I hugged for a very long moment. He took my hand and led me to a chair next to his in the small circle the guys had made. Before I could say a word, the door opened and Zelda hurried inside, joining Toby for a hug matching Marcus's and mine in length and intensity.

"It was not a successful trip, was it?" I inquired after we sat down.

Marcus shook his head. "Remember Angela labeling me as stubborn? Well, the military bureaucrats make me look like a compliant slug."

"I gather it's a no-can-do on getting benefits?"

Toby growled, "Benefits? We never got to a discussion of benefits, because no one will admit to the existence of Agent Orange, which means no answers as to how much was sprayed around the country from the start of the war to the end, which means how can benefits be given for something 'nonexistent'? Words of the day were 'stonewalling' and 'denial.' "

Silence.

"I'm trying to figure out a legal way to force the

military to discuss the issue and provide some information," said Sid, "but right now? Folks, I got nuthin'. I feel hopeless. Everything we need about Agent Orange, from history of invention to statistics about the amount sprayed, was stored in a file cabinet two feet from where we were all sitting. I wanted to run out, buy a sledgehammer, come back in, demolish it and haul it out of there with the goods, but I might have had a whale of a confrontation with the guards."

Marcus tossed in, "Well, I debated on grabbing the guy who was spouting a bunch of nonsense about 'classified this' and 'top secret that' and hauling him by the scruff of his scrawny neck over to Arlington Cemetery where he could explain to the families who were leaving flowers on graves that he had this whole 'importance of silence' routine about what killed their loved ones." He took a deep breath before adding, "Okay, not quite true. He didn't have a scrawny neck. It was the opposite. Thick as his thigh. After I noticed, I debated about begging Toby to grab the arrogant jerk. I swear the guy was at least six-four and must have outweighed me by sixty pounds. But, get this. He wasn't even a lawyer. Just some lackey from the communications branch. An immensely large lackey."

Toby added, "I would have gladly grabbed him. We're talkin' easy-peasy. Could have whipped him with my good arm tied behind my back."

Everyone nodded in cheerful agreement, but quickly reverted to the previous frame of mind of doom and gloom.

"Hmm. Maybe I should assume the identity of typist Mary Smith again, get a job at the Department of Defense and sneak the info out in the dead of night?" I said, partly tongue-in-cheek.

"I wish. Of course, you'd have to figure out a way to break into those files unless you could casually carry Sid's nonexistent sledgehammer in with you," Marcus said. "Sadly, the military is far more disciplined than Roger Masters and they don't leave incriminating documents lying around under delicatessen take-out. Everything is neatly stashed in steel-encased cabinets with impenetrable locks."

"Hey! I'm a fast learner. There's bound to be a vet at the Center here who included lock-picking among his activities as a misspent youth. Let me sit down with him and take a crash course in the fine art of safe-cracking and I'm on it," I responded. "Wait. Different plan forming. Mary Smith." I turned to Toby. "May I use the phone?" I asked.

"Sure."

I rose and left the others sitting in silence while I made a call, then joined them about five minutes later. "I'm not sure how much help this could be, but I contacted Jim and gave him the skinny on what happened in Washington with you guys. I'd already told him about Agent Orange and its links to veterans with illnesses, and he was definitely interested and eager to do a story. He's at the paper's office, and he said if you could stay here he'll do an interview within the next forty minutes. He promises the paper will print it, although they'll have to get other sources to verify. They love nailing bad guys, whether they're greedy corporate bosses or the whole durn Department of Defense."

"Yes!" was chorused from everyone in the room.

Jim must have run the entire ten blocks from the paper's offices because he was inside the Center in less than ten minutes. I made introductions to Toby and Sid, then glanced over at Zelda, who nodded at me. As usual, she and I were in sync.

"Guys? We're going to leave you in Jim's capable hands. Zelda agrees with me in suggesting once the interview is done you should go home and sleep for the next twelve hours. All three of you are clearly exhausted. The Texas phrase—or maybe it's from cowboys all across America—is 'rode hard and put up wet.' I'm upping the ante and saying y'all look like you've been 'rode hard and put up soaking, dripping, and drenched.' "

After hugs all around, Zelda and I left. We were also tired, although nothing like the trio who'd attempted to breach the walls of secrecy at the Pentagon this morning. We didn't want to go grab dinner, we wanted to go home and take our own advice. Sleep. We started heading toward the bus stop at the end of the street, but my attention pivoted to someone standing across the street from the Am-Vets Center. It was the man in brown, standing still, staring at the building.

I quietly said to Zelda, "Don't make it obvious, but if you can, check out the creepy guy in front of the doorway to the strip club?"

She dropped her bag on the ground, leaned down to pick it up, pretended to scoop an object or two into the bag and managed to give the man a swift perusal.

"Got him. Tall sucker. Ugly brown beret topping uglier clothes. I can identify him in a heartbeat if asked, although his features are a bit obscured with the hat and the hair. What's this about?"

"I've seen him several times in the last couple of weeks and could swear he's following either Marcus or me or both of us. I have no idea who he is, hence the moniker, 'creepy guy.' "

"I see why and totally agree. I can feel an 'ick' vibe from thirty yards away," Zelda replied. "Not sure what can be done about him, though. I guess he's free to go where he wants."

"I told Marcus about him, but he didn't seem concerned. Then again, I haven't told Marcus I've seen him twice more since the first morning I noticed him, which was when he seemed far too interested in Marcus's apartment."

"Well, if this guy does do something scary, as I previously stated, I can describe him. I have great observational skills."

We solemnly shook hands as we simultaneously said, "Acting One-oh-One. Lesson One." We boarded the bus, agreed there wasn't a rat's behind we could do about the man in brown, and then spent the rest of the ride chatting about the French restaurant where Toby was taking Zelda to celebrate getting cast on *Exit to Eternity*, and whether the critics really were going to skewer Marcus's new album as badly as his manager predicted.

Zelda got off at her stop at W. 78th Street, and I sat, thankfully next to an empty seat (no desire to make polite small talk with a stranger) until my own stop at W. 103rd.

Once I was home, I dropped my bag in the living room, washed my face, crawled into some sweats, and went to bed. It was all of eight in the evening.

I felt like I was seventy instead of twenty.

Chapter 37

Early November 1975

Twelve hours of solid sleep proved remarkably restorative. I could do nothing to force the military to release information or provide benefits due veterans. But the story would be in the paper, maybe later this week, and hopefully spark someone with some clout to push the powers-that-be into action.

Meantime, I needed to concentrate on preparing for the audition with Emma Andersen's company. I planned to hit the hardest classes in the city for the next couple of weeks, to ensure my body and mind would be in perfect shape. There was no way I was going to blow this chance. While I had no intention of making any Faustian bargains with any demons, I was determined not to let any outside forces derail me from a job I'd desired more than any other ever since I first mastered the concept of contract-and-release prevalent in all the modern dance styles.

Today was also my "healing through dance" class day at the Am-Vets Center, but I was able to attend a ballet class beforehand. As soon as I entered the lobby, I was greeted by Billy Don at the desk, who told me both Toby and Marcus had called to say they wouldn't be coming in.

"Marcus said he and Toby and Sid did an interview

with your friend at the paper about the whole Agent Orange thing. Do you have any idea when it's coming out?"

"I'm not sure. I found a note this morning from my roommate Jim—who's writing the story—anyway, it said the interview had gone really well and he was off to do some research and talk to a few doctors who might be willing to tell the truth about how deadly this stuff is. Could be a week or more?"

"Well, it can't be soon enough for everybody here who's heard about the brick wall the guys ran into yesterday."

"Yeah. Which reminds me, are you going to be able to deejay today? Marcus isn't coming in. Believe me, I don't blame him. He needs to rest. I've never seen him look so beat as I did last night. He was literally shaking, he was so tired. It's as if the same brick wall fell on him."

Billy Don nodded. "Sure. I love playing deejay for your class. Makes me feel like I'm part of it."

"Are you serious? You're half the reason the whole class works!" I started to head toward the doors leading into the ballroom, but Billy Don stopped me.

"Shiloh. Maybe I shouldn't bring this up right now, but I'm betting something more than being tired is affecting Marcus. And there's definitely a problem with Sid. More than a problem. By the way, he won't be in your class today either."

"What do you mean, problem?" I asked.

Billy Don lowered his volume even though no one else was in the reception area. "Sid's fainted at least four times, right here in the lobby, in the last two weeks. He literally toppled over. Claimed he hasn't been getting enough sleep because he's been studying for the bar exam. I told him I wasn't buying it anymore and he finally admitted he's been diagnosed with cancer. This was the day before he and Marcus and Toby left for D.C. Shiloh, he's thirty-two years old."

"Oh, no." I winced. "This is horrible."

"Yeah. And then there's Marcus."

I paused for a beat before saying, "You're talking about his hands shaking. I guess you'd call them tremors?"

"Yeah."

"I've been concerned as well, but not sure what to say or do. I mean, Marcus puts on a great show in front of everyone, but he's gone weak in the knees more than once and, much as he likes me, I doubt it's my great beauty causing it. I've been trying to attribute it to his being super-stressed about the Center, and all the business with Roger Masters and trying to help the Henry family get justice for their son and having to deal with his launch party and being constantly pushed by his manager into recording something he doesn't want to record…" I took a breath. "But Marcus is only a few weeks away from his twenty-seventh birthday. Not exactly entering old-age territory. And, regardless of all the angst and worry lately, he shouldn't be losing his grip when he's holding a glass in his hand, and he should be able to play more than a chord or two without wincing in pain. He shouldn't be forcing himself not to buckle over like he's been tackled by a giant linebacker when he's in the middle of dancing a waltz."

"He needs to see a doctor," Billy Don said.

"I agree. But, as my Texas grandmother used to say, and I'll twist the pronouns, 'I'm not the bossin' of him.' "

Billy Don grinned. "Sounds extremely familiar. We might share the same grandmother." He sobered. "Can y*ou* get him to see a doctor? The man is nuts about you and might listen. Maybe you can make him understand it's time he took care of himself as well as everyone else?"

I nodded. "Worth a shot."

The front door opened and three of the guys from my class entered. Time to put an end to our conversation. But it stuck in my head throughout class and the rest of the day. I didn't see Marcus all day Thursday. When I got home around nine p.m. there was a message for me to give him a call.

"So, Mr. Kennedy, how'd the interview go?" I asked about two seconds into the conversation. "I didn't get much out of Jim."

I could tell Marcus was beaming. "It was fantastic. Jim said he was going to connect with a few doctors here in the city who are willing to tell the truth about medical issues, and also try and get one of the local veterans' offices to respond. *The Manhattan Legend* is not ignoring us. Jim said his editor told him it'll go to print next week, or possibly the Friday *before* Thanksgiving, Supposedly, it's the perfect day for news because folks are picking up the paper to look for sales after Thanksgiving, which seems to be the start of Christmas shopping, but they're still interested in seeing something other than ads."

"Which is loony. I mean, shopping this early. But if people are taking time out from seeing the ads and actually reading about both how horrible Agent Orange is and how the government is keeping quiet, maybe it'll help the cause. Is Jim using quotes from all of you guys and naming you as his source?" I asked.

"Yes and no. Not from Toby. But, yes, from Sid and me. Sid has all the stats on his side and, embarrassing and cocky as this sounds, a lot of people do recognize my name, so hopefully folks will pay attention. Although—and I hate to sound discouraging—I'm not sure what anyone can actually do to get monetary benefits for the vets unless we get a few politicians willing to buck the system."

"Never stops, does it," I said. Marcus didn't ask what "it" was. He knew.

"No, it doesn't. Which brings up the issue of time speeding by too fast and me wanting and needing to spend more of that time with you. So, point being, this Saturday night, would you like to try the French restaurant where Toby took Zelda last night? According to Toby, the food is top-shelf, the atmosphere is elegant and sublimely romantic, and, also according to Toby, I'm an idiot if I don't escort you there as soon as possible. And before you answer, I've been very chauvinistic, and you can call me either extremely controlling or, hopefully, enthusiastic and optimistic, because I've already made reservations. I was able to speak with the owner and explain I was bringing someone wonderful who didn't eat either meat or dairy and could they accommodate her needs? Turns out, the man's wife is vegetarian and he created a special menu for her and any patrons with similar requirements. So? Whaddya say? Yes?"

"Yes."

Chapter 38

Mid-November 1975

Neither Toby nor Marcus had provided an elaborate description of *Café La Douce* but, upon entering the restaurant, the words "elegant and romantic" summed up the ambiance quite well. The restaurant was tiny, about eight tables in total. The lighting was appropriately dim but not so dark one couldn't see one's companion, or notice how beautifully the flowers had been arranged on each table. The restaurant's interior decorator or designer was clearly an art lover. From any table, one could sit and appreciate the reproductions of three of Monet's landscapes, the unusual but highly romantic *The Kiss* painted by Gustav Klimt, and the sensual *Le Printemps* by Pierre-Auguste Cot, all hanging on the walls beside brass antique-looking sconces. (For the record, I took an art history course in college, and had purchased an inexpensive print of *Le Printemps* from The Met about a week after I moved to New York and had it prominently displayed in my bedroom.)

I'm no connoisseur, but the champagne was crisp and fresh and wonderful. I'd ordered the owner's special vegan meal featuring a mix of vegetables wrapped in eggless crepes, artichokes spritzed with lemons, asparagus with a spicy vinaigrette sauce, tiny hard rolls (also eggless) and fresh fruit for dessert. Marcus ordered the same.

We skipped topics related to the veterans, Roger Masters, the military, and Angela's campaign to push Marcus into recording disco tunes. Instead we talked about us. Marcus wanted to hear more about my family in Texas.

"Well, I'm the oddity. Everyone in my family is a financial wizard except for me. My sister Lacey took dance, but strictly to help with the pageants, and she and my folks never could quite understand me choosing it as a career. I'm not sure they ever got the concept of equating Shiloh's identify as a dancer with Shiloh as the person."

"Do you get along with them?"

"Surprisingly, yes. I do. They make me crazy and vice versa, but there's an odd acceptance from everyone, and I don't feel I have to hide in the basement or something over holidays. Both my folks and my sister shared my radical views on Vietnam and supported me heading off to protest. They think the vegan food thing is pretty weird, but at Thanksgiving there's a giant salad for me. I don't go tearing around the house shouting, 'Murderers!' when they start carving the turkey, and they don't try to stuff cheese casseroles down my throat. But what about your family? I know you miss them terribly."

"I do." He told me that, regardless of opposing views on the war, he and his brother Colin and his dad had been close. His dad had worked as a cop, policing a nearby neighborhood beat, and appreciated the rewards of surrounding himself with brightness and love at home after witnessing too many families destroyed through drink or abuse passed down through generations.

"Dad was a big fan of touring our hometown,"

Marcus said. "All of it. He was not your stereotypical Irish cop. Whenever he was off work, he'd take the family to a museum or whatever show he could afford. For less cultural pursuits, the amusement park on Coney Island was a favorite. Not expensive, and a super place to unwind."

"What about your mom?" I asked. "She taught you to play piano?"

"She did. She was tough. Not in a nasty way, just very disciplined. When she realized I had a gift for music she had me practicing piano hours and hours every day. I rebelled when I was about ten and begged for a guitar, which was almost worse. I ended up with calluses so scaly and bumpy I wore gloves to hide my hands from my classmates at school. But, of course, ultimately, the guitar worked better for the folk music scene. It's a lot easier to haul a six-string down to a club in the Village, than it is a piano, and half the places where I sang didn't provide any instruments at all. It was strictly 'bring your own.' " Marcus stared at the painting on the wall. "She'd've loved seeing the artwork. *Le Printemps* was one of her favorites."

"Mine, too." I told him I had a copy, a cheap copy but a decent one, at home. "I wish I could have known her. Your mom."

"She'd've loved you. I have faith she's somewhere in Heaven and she's watching over me." His eyes sparkled with mischief. "Wouldn't surprise me to discover Mom managed to hunt down a guardian angel and pester him or her to figure out a way for us to meet."

"Maybe she did." I told him about Fiona Belle and how she seemed to be the instigator of any and all of the original run-ins with Marcus, starting with the concert and making certain I was seated so close to the stage. "I've occasionally wondered if she was sent from somewhere above, but then again, I'm not sure how a Divine Presence would feel about one of His angels charging around dressed up as a Harlequin clown, a honeybee, or a Christmas elf."

"Speaking of…"

"Christmas?"

"Original run-ins. Are you ever going to tell me what you were experiencing down by the Twin Towers the first…no, it was the second time I saw you, if you count the concert, which I do."

"Ah. No and yes. No, because I don't want to get into specifics of images and sights and smells. No, because you don't need to hear about any other horrific events, future or past. Yes, a little, because they seem to be connected to weird supernatural doin's in my life, and those I'll talk about."

Marcus's eyebrows lifted. "Go on."

I took him through all the strange things I'd experienced since mid-August and how Zelda and I had discussed them more than once and failed to come up with anything close to a sensible explanation. I did not include the "saving Marcus" directive I was sure was at the heart of all the oddities. Since I had nothing specific to warn him about, it would just muddy the whole issue.

"There is one certainty, though," I said. "Fiona Belle Donovan Winthorp, minus the Winthorp she despises, has the answers."

"But Fiona Belle Donovan, with or without Winthorp, isn't talking, right?'

"You got it."

Marcus poured us each another glass of champagne,

then lifted his. "To Fiona Belle, who might be tight-lipped when it comes to important questions in the universe, but to whom, if she really was the instigator of you and me meeting, I say, 'Thanks'!"

We toasted. We finished the champagne, talked a bit longer about absolutely nothing of consequence, then decided to walk around the city, savoring the lights, the quieter pace of the people, and the crispness of a cool, but not cold, November night.

We were kind of talked out, so we walked in silence, holding hands, gazing into each other's eyes and trying to avoid crashing into other couples who were also not paying attention to anyone else and blissfully unaware they, and we, weren't the sole inhabitants of the city.

We reached the discount ticket booth in Times Square, now deserted by all the theater-goers who'd taken advantage of great prices on top seats. Marcus gently took my shoulders and turned me to face him.

"I've been trying, honestly for weeks, to come up with the most romantic spot in New York to use for the proper setting, and I toyed with composing some kind of elaborate song, but then it hit me...the city itself is the right backdrop and I don't need elaborate words wrapped up in an exotic melody. Sometimes, simple is best. So I'm simply asking, Shiloh Meridien, will you marry me?"

I didn't need elaborate words either. One would do. "Yes."

Chapter 39

Late November 1975

I heard the sound of the telephone ringing and
thought I was dreaming. But when it didn't stop and I
realized I was wide awake, I knew. Something was
wrong. It was six in the morning. Nobody calls another
human being at six in the morning with good news. The
phone continued its insistent peal. Jim wasn't going to
answer. Wyatt wasn't going to answer. It was up to me.

I groaned, crawled out from under the cozy
comforter with much reluctance, grabbed a bulky
sweater I'd left hanging on the ancient rocking chair Jim
had found on the street last month, silently blessed the
creator of the radiator for gifting humanity with an
efficient source of heat, and staggered into the kitchen.

I lifted the receiver. " 'Lo." I coughed and cleared
my throat, which was producing sounds more suited to a
cigarette-smoking, rum-drinking, seventy-year old sailor
than a twenty-year-old dancer, and spoke again, adding
an appropriate syllable. "Hello?"

"Shiloh, it's Marcus."

"What's wrong?"

"It's Sid."

My throat, heart, and stomach plummeted to my
feet. "Go on."

"He's dead."

"No!" I gasped out. "He can't be! Cancer doesn't suddenly strike overnight, and he was fine when I saw him in class last week."

"It wasn't the cancer." He paused, then hoarsely stated, "It was a drug overdose. Heroin. The police are wavering between calling it accidental or suicide. I told them Sid hadn't touched any drug for five years, and had never been a heroin user anyway. His vices were weed and mushrooms, and there's no way he'd accidentally shoot up that crap. Which is pushing them to the suicide theory."

I was now completely awake and furious. "No. Absolutely not. Sid was a devout Catholic. We had a discussion after one of my classes about a variety of issues in the church, including suicide. He told me his parish priest had offered a Requiem Mass and buried two people in consecrated ground, although they'd committed suicide. Sid told me the priest felt God wouldn't condemn a suicide if the person had become so mentally distraught they honestly couldn't distinguish between right and wrong anymore." I took a breath. "Then Sid said he could never imagine ever being so mentally distraught he'd take his own life. He was so adamant he said he wasn't sure he even agreed with the priest about God's mercy."

"Yeah. I understand." I could hear a faint smile in Marcus' voice. "Shoot, if I ever committed suicide, Father Joe would kill me."

"I'd join him," I said. "Okay. I need coffee to process this, but—Marcus? We're sure this wasn't an accident. Sid was determined to beat the cancer and was already trying to do anything he could to be healthier, and we're both positive it wasn't suicide, which means we're talking about something truly nasty."

"Murder."

"Murder," I echoed, then asked, "I'm not totally awake, but how did you hear about Sid this early?"

There was a long moment of silence.

"Marcus? Are you still there? Talk to me."

"I didn't hear. I saw. Shiloh, I found him. Actually, Toby and I did. This morning, when we got to the Center around six. Yeah, absurdly early, but we hadn't cleaned up after a big bash last night to celebrate Calvin passing his EMT test. It was past midnight and no one felt like staying. I agreed to meet Toby to help toss trash and whatever else was needed before anyone showed up for morning basketball practice, and to keep Billy Don from having to deal with a mess." He took a breath. "I'm stalling. All right. Sid has a set of keys for the Center, and last night he shooed us out and said to go home, he'd lock up. This morning Toby and I get to the Center at the same time and the doors are unlocked. We walk inside and there's Sid, lying on the floor near the reception table. This isn't pretty. There was a needle stuck in his arm and a tourniquet tied around his arm."

I started crying. "Does, um, does he have any family?"

"No. At least nowhere near. He has some cousins in the Midwest somewhere, but no one close. The guys at the Center were his family."

"Are you there now?"

"Yeah. Toby and I decided we'd stay here and tell the guys as they come in, and phone those who didn't have anything scheduled."

"I'm coming down. I mean, I have to get dressed, but I want to be there."

"Shiloh, you don't have to. It's going to be a truly rough day."

"And I'll be with you. I feel like these guys are my family. I need to be there, if for nothing more than to show my support and listen to anyone who wants to talk."

"Shiloh, you *are* family to everyone here. Thank you."

We hung up. I rushed through getting dressed. I didn't bother with makeup, and didn't bother making coffee. I left a message on our board in the kitchen for Jim telling him what had happened, and boldly used the word "murder."

I made it to the Center in twenty minutes. I lucked out by catching a train as it slid into the station at W. 103rd Street, was able to change to the Express on W. 96th Street, and then ran from the 42nd Street subway exit.

The instant I opened the doors, Marcus was beside me, holding me. The police had taken Sid's body away, he told me, but a detective would be back later to ask more questions.

"Well, I have one," I said, "and it's probably nuts, but last night at any time before, during or after the party, was there any chance the creepy guy who's always dressed in brown, with a tacky beret, um, was there any chance he was in the neighborhood?"

"You've told me about him before, but he seems to be invisible when I go looking for him. Why?"

I sank down onto one of the shabby director's chairs near the platform inside the ballroom area. "He's part of the strange feelings I've had, and I wish I knew what they meant. There's something about him. I can't identify what it is, but it's wrong. I can't prove he's nothing more than some random guy with bad fashion sense who likes hanging out near the Center and your apartment building. I can't base anything I'm saying on facts, but Marcus, I swear he's been stalking you or me or both, and maybe people closely involved with us, as well."

"Well, when you stop and consider, there are folks who are pretty ticked off about some of the activities we've engaged in this past month or so and might have sent someone to keep an eye out in case we had other schemes in mind."

I swallowed air. "Would someone like Roger Masters be capable of—what are you saying? Hiring a hit man?"

Marcus's expression was grim. "Totally capable. And, excuse my distrust of the military industrial complex, but the people at the Pentagon and the chemical companies who provided access to millions of gallons of a lethal herbicide are not exactly happy about the interview Sid, Toby, and I did for *The Manhattan Legend*. Adding to the list, and I haven't told you because I didn't want to worry you, but I've had some calls from anonymous guys claiming to be buddies with the cop who shot Jeremiah Henry, and the calls were pretty threatening."

"Should we mention any of this to the detective when he comes back? You and Toby could be in danger. Or is that a bad idea since the cop might be more sympathetic to those threatening buddies if they're on the force?"

Marcus shrugged. "He'll doubtless call us madder than rabid squirrels, but it couldn't hurt to at least raise some possibilities for motives."

The rest of the day was a bizarre mix of sadness as veterans learned of Sid's death, some honest but brief merriment talking about the antics he'd pulled during Ping-Pong games and art classes at the Center, and total frustration. The latter was listening to an obese, surly NYPD detective flatly accusing Marcus, Toby, and me of being both paranoid and delusional in our accusations aimed at the U.S. military, the fine, upstanding citizen Roger Masters, or any cop in the city by suggesting any of the above had been out to get Sid or any of us, especially by sending a guy in a seedy brown outfit to follow us around and find the best time to strike. When he put it that way, it did sound pretty ludicrous.

Around two in the afternoon, Marcus said he needed to leave if he was going to make a doctor's appointment. I corralled Billy Don and asked if he could fire up the turntable. I invited every vet there to join in on a special dance session in honor of Sid. Wheelchairs, no wheelchairs, those who'd already taken a class with me, those who'd never danced a step in their lives. It didn't matter because we all swayed to tunes Sid had loved. We needed to share our pain and find a way through it.

Sid would have approved.

Chapter 40

Late November 1975

Something was off.

I had a sense of *déjà vu*, just the normal kind associated with reliving an experience, not one of my weird "isms." I was sitting across from Marcus at a new Italian restaurant called Piero's Trattoria on W. 86th Street and Broadway, and the *déjà vu* might be because I was dressed in the exact same multi-colored (greens and blues), four-tiered skirt and poet-sleeved sweater (forest green) combo I'd worn to *Café La Douce* the night Marcus had proposed to me. Less than two weeks ago.

I was diving into a spicy veggie-and-mushroom pasta dish, dipping bread into olive oil so fresh I wondered if they had an olive presser or smasher in the kitchen, and I was sipping a very tasty, very expensive red wine. We were nearly finished with our meal. We'd discussed his upcoming interview with one of the music magazines. We'd talked about the latest scandal rocking the city council and whether or not D.D.S. Chemicals was going to clean up its act and quit polluting half of New Jersey. We talked about whether Roger Masters was going to get a prison sentence or skate through by paying a fine but remaining a free man. We discussed what would happen now to the lawsuit Sid had filed against Masters after the botched demonstration. We debated as to whether there was chance in a million the government would own up to spraying troops with a deadly pesticide.

Marcus had griped about how badly Angela was handling the distribution of *Remake the Song* because she was doing anything in her power to push him to London to record a new record. "As though there weren't numerous reasons to mourn Sid's death, he and I had already started discussing his new role as attorney and manager. Angela was less than pleased when I fired her, and I swear she had this expression of malicious glee when I asked her to work with me again, at least for the time being. She was speechless when I told her I already had a deal with a label to record a new single which exposes some very bad sins committed by very bad people including corrupt, bigoted cops and greedy developers."

We'd moved on to other, lighter topics, laughing about the storyline for *Exit for Eternity* to introduce Zelda Zimmerman's character, Bathsheba Brickhouse, as the lingerie executive caught having sex in a hot air balloon with her mother's husband, Congressman Samson Samuels, when it gets shot down over Staten Island by a secretive organized crime syndicate from Oregon, known only as The Merchants.

Yet. Something was off.

We'd toasted in memory of Sid even as we expressed our anger that the police were treating his death as a suicide, ignoring all our suggestions of motives for murder. We'd toasted to the news Toby had received about a renewal of the lease of the Am-Vets Center for another two years.

Yet. Something was off.

"Let's go for a walk," Marcus suggested. "Work off all the starches and the wine."

"Sure."

Marcus paid the check, politely helped me with my coat, held the door open for me, and we began walking up Broadway. In silence. My stomach and brain were screaming in unison. *Something is off!*

At the corner of W. 103rd and Broadway, as we stood looking into the window of the hobby store featuring the model trains Marcus had recently become obsessed with, I'd had enough.

"Would you like to explain why we had a fancy dinner and didn't discuss our status as a newly engaged couple, and have now spent the last ten minutes strolling up Broadway without a word? Without you looking at me? Something is off, Marcus, and you need to tell me what it is."

Marcus shifted his gaze from the window display featuring the enchanting Alpine village serving as background to a Victorian era railroad, and stared into my eyes. He reached out his hand and took mine in his.

He inhaled too deeply, and when he spoke his voice was hoarse. Clipped. Like someone whose throat was bleeding. "There's no easy way to say this. Shiloh, remember, right after Sid's death I went to the doctor to see if he could figure out why I'm having these tremors? Why I'm unable to play a lick on a guitar anymore?"

"And?"

"He ran tests. And the diagnosis I finally received this morning was, and I quote, 'It appears to be some form of early onset Parkinson's, a rare disease for which there is no cure.' He said there are drugs to curb the symptoms, but no cure has yet been discovered. I get to look forward to a life of progressively losing motor skills. Crap. Forget 'skills.' 'Motor control' is closer to the truth." Marcus's tone turned bitter. "I'm three weeks out from my twenty-seventh birthday. Happy Birthday! But, hey! The good news is if I die sometime during this next year I can be part of the rock music curse of singers and musicians dying at this age a bunch of folks in the music industry have been jabbering about. Of course, they all died of overdoses or suicides. Not from some stinking disease people don't get until they're ninety. They didn't die from a disease I'd bet my entire collection of songs was caused by Agent Orange. The doctor said as much when I told him about being exposed. It's the only thing that makes sense. No one in my family has ever had Parkinson's, so it shouldn't be popping up in me, especially this early."

I tried to put my arms around him, but he pushed me away.

"No. Shiloh, it's time to stop."

"What do you mean? Stop?"

"Us. I mean stop us. We need to break up. You can't be saddled with someone with an incurable disease."

I stared at him. "No. No! I'm not listening to this. You really believe I'm so shallow I wouldn't stand by you because you've got an illness?"

He inhaled, then shook his head. "No. It's the opposite. I know damn well you'd go through the bowels of hell for me. You've got loyalty running through every vein in your body. But I can't, I won't, I refuse, to ask you to live with me. You'd end up as my nurse. My caretaker. I can't put you through the agony of being with someone who's getting progressively worse and dying. You'd probably be a widow before you're thirty. I saw what it did to my dad losing my mother, and they'd had twenty years of marriage before she died."

I started to speak, but he held up his hand. "Shiloh, I've seen them. You've seen them. The wives or girlfriends of guys at the Center who've become walking zombies; the same as their loved ones. They come and they visit guys who are in wheelchairs, or they bring by the ones who are ambulatory, and then they run away before they have to watch Joe or Johnny crying when he tries to walk to a corner but collapses before he makes it halfway across the room, or when he goes diving onto the floor, screaming, because some delivery van outside backfired and put him right back in the Mekong Delta."

"Marcus, this is different. This isn't a wartime trauma, this is an illness." I held up my hand. "An illness caused by a deadly herbicide. How this will affect you is a mystery because, as you said, it's not genetic. It's manmade."

He closed his eyes and remained silent for a long moment. Then he shrugged his shoulders. "But if it turns out Agent Orange did cause this, what does it really matter? No cure. The only thing I can do is use the time I have left to protest and do my level best to force the government to compensate all the vets and others who were exposed to it, and maybe actually admit fault. It doesn't change my stance regarding us and our future."

"Which is?" I began wiping away the tears flooding down my cheeks.

"I will not marry you with a death sentence hanging over my head."

"But—"

"No. Go home, Shiloh. Let me spend what time I

have left fighting for veterans. Go home. Forget you met me. Become a principal dancer with the company of your dreams and enjoy your life. One day find a man who won't be shaking and falling and dying in front of your eyes."

"Marcus! What are you doing? You're not a coward, yet all of a sudden you're acting like one. We can fight this together! And I'd rather be your—what did you call it? Caretaker? I'd rather be your caretaker for six months or six years or whatever than live out a sweet, boring life with some Mister Super Health somewhere down the line."

"No. You believe that now, but after a few years of dealing with my illness? No. Decision made. For what it's worth, I love you. I will always love you. Which is why I'm telling you it's over."

It was pointless. As he said, the decision was made. I had no part in it and he wasn't willing to listen to any argument to refute it. I needed to get away before I started screaming. I began walking down my block, but I was crying too hard to face Jim or Wyatt, so I passed by my apartment and headed for Riverside Park, where I could stare out across the Hudson River and curse the government, scientists, the military, and any person on the planet more interested in power and money than in the horrors they'd inflicted which had ruined so many lives.

****

Upon reflection, strolling over to Riverside Park at nine-thirty at night to gaze across the Hudson River at whatever part of New Jersey exists on the other side, ignoring the tears coursing down one's face while concentrating solely on the waters below, was not a wise move. But when the love of one's life tells you it's over and refuses to allow you to be part of whatever time he has left, well, this pronouncement turned me into one very distraught and distracted idiot.

I don't know how long I'd been standing at the edge of the river before something, I wasn't sure what, finally alerted me to another presence. Unfortunately, the warning was not in time to dodge the hand pressing over my mouth. The good news, thanks to numerous hours of training with several excellent instructors, was that my snap-to reaction time was pretty durn fast. The bad news was my attacker was wearing gloves, so chomping down with my teeth on his forefinger wasn't as effective as it would have been on bare skin.

The fight was on. I'd never been in an actual fight where my opponent was determined to inflict injury (or worse). All the matches were for points. This was different. This was brutal. I was immediately weakened by several quick slashes to my ribs with a very sharp knife. I was way overmatched. The guy had mad skills and four inches of height on me, plus probably an extra hundred pounds of solid muscle making him capable of warding off my kicks and punches as if I were an annoying mosquito.

I attempted every kick and punch in my arsenal of things learned. Nothing helped. Blood cascaded down from a gash on my cheek. I screamed, "Take my stinkin' bag and whatever money is in there!" I recalled the stupid, almost lighthearted conversation about personal thefts I'd had with Sandra and the two "E's" (Edward and Ethan) last August after the vets' concert about how New York dancers don't get mugged because word is out they have no money in their bags, just leotards and tights in need of laundry. But this was no ordinary mugger. I figured that out the instant he hurled the words, "Stay away from Marcus Kennedy!" at me as the knife raked across my cheek, and then he kicked me to the ground.

I was down and out and in horrible pain, but I managed to do one last thing after he slashed the back of the same knee and lifted his foot and slammed it into my leg. I managed to scream, "Help!" My voice might not have been filled with Tony Award pitch-perfect winning tones, but was loud enough to be heard in a 300-seat theater without a microphone.

For a moment, I thought I was hallucinating. I saw, or maybe I merely sensed, Marcus Kennedy execute an amazing flying tackle and knock my attacker away from me.

My last thought before passing out was, *"Who's going to save Marcus in December?"*

Chapter 41

December 11, 1975

My career as a professional dancer died before it was born. With the cruel slash of a knife and a strong, booted foot. Destroyed.

I wasn't in the hospital long. They slapped bandages all over me, put a cast on my knee, and sent me home with crutches and a ton of pain meds. Once I was back at the apartment, I forced myself to trust the amazing Dario Bernardi's concept of healing through continuing movement. I would never dance again but I was determined to be as mobile as possible. So, daily, I moved whatever parts of my body were not encased in gauze or plaster.

On a chilly (forty-four degrees) December eleventh, I bundled up in my parka, slowly made my way on crutches to my favorite park bench on Riverside Drive, sat, put my leg up on the bench, and stared out at the Hudson River. I was soon joined by Fiona Belle Donovan, once again attired as a buzzing bee. I now recalled our first meeting down in Texas back in August when I was a seventy-year old woman who'd worked as a professional dancer her whole adult life. I remembered that life. I also remembered my life here in New York over these last four months.

Fiona Belle asked how I felt and I shot her an, *Are*

you serious? scowl. She handed me Marcus's *Remake the Song* album with the ghost train cover. The same album I'd bought four months earlier at a flea market in Oak Cliff. Then she handed me the sheet music to "Yellow Rose of Texas" with the note on the top saying *For December, if you choose to go back.* The date stamped at the top of the music was August 21, 2025. "Okay, Shiloh, it's time to make yer decision."

"Can you give me an idea of how this would work? I mean, let's say, I choose to go back to 2025 today. Will my life be the same as it was, or had been, before you sent me into this timeline?"

Fiona Belle nodded. "Yep. You'll have danced fer twenty-odd years with Emma Andersen's company. You'll have gone home to Texas and taught. You'll marry Gerard. You'll move back to New York in the late nineties. He'll be the same cheatin' fink he always was. You'll return to Texas and get the annulment. You'll teach. You'll perform at various theaters. You'll date some nice men. And when yer roamin' Final Destination Flea Market on August twenty-first, you'll buy the skirt set and the *Remake the Song* album, but this time around it'll be the original cheery cover; not the ghost train. And ya won't be given a chance to return to nineteen-seventy-five. You'll be age seventy again and go on from there as if we'd never met. You'll have a date next week with the man you met when you were taking ballroom dance lessons. 'Six-three and dances like a dream,' I believe was how you described him."

"Wow."

She added, "I might be aft ta bringin' ya some cranberry-orange scones once ya buy the record, but I make no promises and ya won't recognize me as anyone but the vendor from Retro Records."

"Okay. I now have more questions, and they're not in any particular order of importance."

"Shoot."

"What happens to Zelda if I return to twenty-twenty-five? I mean, her life changed because we met at the audition. Will it go back to what it was before?" I grimaced. "Which wasn't great in a lot of ways because in the first timeline she married Dwayne Bunyan and was miserable."

As usual, Fiona Belle provided a non-specific answer. "You'll meet her in nineteen-ninety-nine at the Ghost Tour gig down at Trinity Church, exactly like before. There'll still be a ton of wailin' and lamentin' between the two of ya about not havin' met earlier. What I'm sayin' is she won't be aware of anything different. She won't have gone through these past four months with you."

I was silent for a long moment. "And what about the guys at the Am-Vets Center? I didn't teach there in the first timeline."

"Their lives will continue the way they were goin'. Whatever that might be."

"Oh, jeez! This stinks! I can go back to being a professional dancer with my dream company and have the life I had, which I loved every minute of apart from being with Gerard, but maybe Zelda still marries Dwayne? The Center gets torn down? And Jonah? Will he eventually speak if Marcus and I aren't there to do the class together?"

Fiona Belle stared at me. "The nineteen-seventy-five timeline will continue as it did before."

"So you're not really saying. Got it. Okay, dare I

inquire, what happens to my *own* memory about these last four months if I go back to twenty-twenty-five?"

"You'll remember the original timeline," she repeated patiently.

"Which means…?"

Fiona Belle nodded. "It means no memories of meetin' a certain folk singer. It means Marcus Kennedy dies December sixteenth, nineteen-seventy-five."

Jab straight through the heart.

"What about if I stay? How do I figure out who's trying to kill him? There's a fairly large cast of villains here. Roger Masters sending his soldier of fortune Willem Nels. The scientists who created Agent Orange. The military leaders in D.C. who are ticked that Marcus and Sid flat out accused them of not having veterans' interests at heart. The cops who shot Jeremiah Henry. How do I find the right answer?"

"Darlin', ya gotta focus. Yer lettin' yer thoughts go dancin' off in twenty different directions. Go back in yer mind to your attack. You're smart. You have your answers right there about who wants him dead, because it's the same person behind yer attack."

I thought for a long moment. "Oh, my God. I *do* have the answer. Wow." I paused, then asked the most important question. "Can I save Marcus if I stay?"

"No guarantees."

I grimaced. "Thanks a lot. Okay. Let's say I ride in on my white horse—or crutches—in time to keep him from being murdered. Save his life. Would he listen if I showed him articles from the future about how exercise and a vegan diet—along with the advances in drugs and medications being developed for Parkinson's—could actually work to, if not heal, at least put a pause on his symptoms? Would he be willing to get married? I mean, he was pushing me away because he didn't want me to be his caretaker, and now he's added a gigantic dose of blaming himself because I was attacked and he wasn't there to stop it, even though he did save me from being killed."

"No guarantees."

"Well, that's just wrong!" I exclaimed, furious. "I thought there were some actual choices here."

"Faith and Saint Bridget, Shiloh! Don't ya be havin' a fit. I told ya this wouldn't be easy. Fifty years in the future when I gave ya the option to come back, I told ya. You jumped at the chance. Remember?"

I glared at her. "Since you brought up the 'r' word, as in 'remember,' if I *do* choose to stay in *this* timeline, will I have any memories about the other me who was seventy when we met? Oh, man. This is so confusing. Pain meds aren't helping and neither are you."

She stated flatly, "It's like the first timeline never happened. And today is the last day you'd be recallin' there ever was another timeline. Any more questions?"

I shrugged. "I'd ask why my so-called options are so lousy, but you wouldn't tell me, would you? Or what the point was to this whole crazy scheme of going back fifty years from the future? Jeez, woman, why provide the whole option to travel through time if it was all going to come down to an impossible decision?"

"It's hard, Shiloh. I get it. I do. If it helps at all, I'll be checkin' in on ya now and again, no matter which time ya choose. And no one will be any the wiser about their own lives…including you. Now be quiet so ya can think and decide."

There was no reasonable response to this. I did as

she asked and lapsed into silence.

My second semester at the University of Texas (in both timelines) I'd had a teacher in her early thirties whose background had included dancing with one of the premiere professional American ballet companies. She'd suffered such a severe knee injury she'd been forced to give up a career as a performer. She was a good teacher, but there was an immense sadness and bitterness within her. She tried to hide it but couldn't. "I loved my life back then, Shiloh," she told me one day after class when I was helping put away the portable barres. "I loved the grueling schedule. I loved taking classes taught by legendary Russian ballet divas with accents so thick that half the time they demonstrated without bothering to speak. They carried large sticks in their hands and weren't afraid to use them. I even loved the bitchiness and jealousy among the dancers because once we hit the stage, it was all gone. Every member of the company gave a hundred percent in performance." She sighed. "I'll tell you something. If Satan himself came flying out of the piano bench and offered me the chance to go back in time and stop the accident and allow me to be the dancer I was again in exchange for my soul, well, give me the parchment and the quill pen and I'm signing on the dotted line in blood."

I didn't equate Fiona Belle with Satan and blood oaths. She wasn't exactly what I'd call angelic, but I was positive—during any celestial team match-ups, she'd be batting for Michael and Gabriel rather than Team Lucifer. Yet this choice, if I could call it a choice, seemed to me to be one pretty devilish bargain.

I glanced down at my knee, or rather at the plaster cast. I'd walk again, although I'd always have a limp. At some point, possibly even in a year or two, I should be able to dance around a living room or even move around at a disco without pain. But my knee would never regain the strength and flexibility I'd enjoyed for twenty years. For seventy years. The kind of strength and flexibility required of a professional dancer. If I remained in this timeline, I would never perform with a dance company. I was a decent singer and a better actress, but without great dance technique to make me a true triple threat, I doubted I could make it into a chorus, not to mention it would take a ton of stage makeup to cover the large gash already scarring my cheek. Broadway wasn't exactly looming large on the career horizon.

But, hey, forget career. According to the Irish elf, whether or not I stayed, Marcus might still end up dead on December sixteenth. I knew he hadn't (and wouldn't) commit suicide and was certain he'd been (would be) murdered, and having a goon take out my knee (along with the face cut and slicing a few chunks from near my ribs) while warning me to stay away from Marcus seemed pretty solid proof and evidence regarding the whole murder thing, but how could I actually, physically save him? My brain was pounding with all the ifs, hows, whys, and wheres. I was now fairly certain of the "who" but not sure I could convince Marcus to listen to me. The only things absolutely clear were the when and the how, thanks to my seventy-year remembrance of the news articles talking about Marcus's death, along with the liner notes on the ghost train cover, which made everything even more confusing because it was now a when and how in two timelines, and I'd just used way too many conjunctions and interrogative words to make any sense.

Added to the "no guarantee" of saving Marcus Kennedy was the big wrinkle of the Marcus/Shiloh relationship currently lying face down in whatever gutter where romance goes to die. I didn't know when, or if, I'd see him again. After saving me from the attacker and getting me to a hospital, he'd disappeared from my life. Well, not quite vanished. He'd called to check up on me, but he talked to Jim or Wyatt. Not to me. He wouldn't talk to me.

Yet...

I loved him. At age twelve, he touched my heart with his music. At age twenty, he captured my heart when our eyes met as he sat on a stage and sang. Three weeks later, he healed my heart as I relived a future horrific experience. Less than four months later, he fractured my heart with his refusal to allow us to stay together. At age seventy, in another life, I'd bought a record album and some sheet music at a flea market in Texas and tumbled into an abyss of time in order to save him.

Staying in this time was risky, unpredictable, dangerous, more than probably devoid of real love, apart from the memories of the last few months.

Yet...

There was less than one week. If I stayed but couldn't find a way to save Marcus Kennedy, he'd be murdered on December sixteenth. If I stayed, and he died, I'd be alone living through an unpredictable timeline with one certainty. If I stayed, my dancing days would be over forever. Yet...

Chapter 42

August 21, 2025

"Ooh! Nice. *Remake the Song.* Marcus Kennedy. Definitely his best. I never understood why some critics were less than kind when it first came out."

I waved to get the attention of the impish-looking vendor manning the counter of the Retro Records stall at Final Destination Flea Market, a tiny but plump woman. I put her age at anywhere between fifty and a hundred. Her short frame was swallowed inside a striped yellow-and-black bumblebee costume, complete with yellow wings on her shoulders and little yellow antennae balls popping up behind her head.

She winked at me. Her eyelid was covered in cobalt blue eyeshadow and her eyes were hiding behind absurdly long false eyelashes. The woman personified "retro." Possibly in more than one era. I was certain I'd met her before, but the memory was iffy, at best.

She stated, in a pronounced Irish dialect, "Are ya interested in buyin'? It's three dollars."

I gave her the record to ring up on a cash register so old it could have been the prototype. "I feel like I'm cheating you."

She shook her head. "Yer not, but there is a mite somethin' extra I'd be aft ta askin' of you."

"Whatcha need?"

"Do an interview for a very young journalist who needs a human interest story this month fer the Oak Cliff paper. I'll be bringin' my famous cranberry-orange scones to ya both—and before ya say anything, they're vegan."

"How did you—?"

"Don't bother ta ask."

I stared at her. "Have we met? You look familiar, but if we did, it was like fifty years ago and I can't recall anything specific, although I keep having this image of the two of us sitting on a bench in Riverside Park in New York. In the mid-seventies. Maybe nineteen-seventy-five?" I chuckled. "You were wearing the same, uh, outfit. Did I imagine this? I do get weird visions sometimes."

She sighed and gave me a non-answer while ringing up the purchase of *Remake the Song* for three dollars plus tax: "I should have worn my fairy godmother dress today. I love pink. Not to mention the tiaras. It's surprisingly cooler, even with all the tulle." She pointed at an empty table in the small makeshift cafe Final Destination Flea Market kindly provided for weary shoppers. "Now, go sit yerself down and I'm aft ta be back in two minutes with the scones and iced coffee and the young lady doin' the interview."

I settled myself at the table, tucked the album into the huge bag I'd carried around for fifty years, and tried to recall why I'd been sitting on the bench in Riverside Park in nineteen-seventy-five and why this vendor, her twin, or her clone had been with me.

Before I had a chance to process the vision, she returned, along with a girl who reminded me of me at age twenty. About five-ten, with red hair and green eyes, and a dancer's lean build.

"Shiloh, meet Cooper Perry. She's a blues singer, but also writes human interest pieces for the *Oak Cliff Monthly News*, and when I told her you were here, her exact words were, 'I want an interview. Can you make it happen?' "

Cooper and I shook hands, and she sat down across from me. The odd lady played waitress, presenting each of us with large tumblers of coffee, then plopping a basket of freshly baked cranberry-orange scones in the middle of the table. I took a bite. Amazing, awesome, incredible, delicious.

I finished chewing, then stated, "Cooper, you may ask me anything. I will freely spill any and all sordid details of my life just to sit here and eat these amazing, awesome, incredible, delicious pastries."

Cooper grabbed a scone, took a bite, finished chewing, and then responded, "I almost don't care about an interview now. Perfect scones. Perfect coffee. Perfect morning."

We ate in silence for several minutes. I took a few sips of coffee, then nodded at the girl. "Okay. Perfect scones notwithstanding, I don't want you to end up in trouble with an editor for failing to write a story, so go for it."

"Cool. Thanks. For starters, can you tell me a bit about the dance therapy you do?"

"Sure. It involves working both with people who have emotional problems generally caused by trauma, especially military veterans, and those with motor and mobility issues. The therapy is a combination of dance and music. Nutritional advice gets tossed into the mix as well."

Cooper's eyes widened. "Nutrition?"

I chuckled. "The vets especially hate hearing they need to go vegan. Most of them here in Texas were brought up in cattle country, but I show them there's been a ton of research showing cutting out animal products along with dairy and sugar and processed foods can really make a difference in healing diseases once thought of as terminal, including Parkinson's. Not to mention, if you love animals, saving some of them from the slaughterhouse is kind of a priority."

"Agreed. How did this all come about? The teaching? The healing center?"

"Oh, boy. Long story, but I did dance therapy with Vietnam veterans many years ago and saw some incredible, life-saving things happen. Miraculous, really."

We spent the next ten minutes talking about how dance and music can truly change the lives of folks suffering from illnesses, along with "everyday" people who want to feel better and lead healthier lives, both physically and emotionally.

Cooper told me she was old-school and preferred writing to recording and transcribing later, and she rapidly took pen to paper as we talked. But at one point she put her pen down and flatly stated, "Okay. Off topic in a way, but speaking of saving lives, is it true folk singer Marcus Kennedy saved yours from a mugger when you both lived in New York in the mid-seventies?"

"Loaded question, and the correct answer is yes *and* no. The 'yes' is because he did save me, but the guy wasn't a mugger. This was personal. I was attacked specifically to keep me away from Marcus."

"Wow. Ouch. I'm so sorry. Does it bother you to

talk about it? I don't want to be pushy or insensitive, and I promise won't use it in the article unless you say 'yes,' since the focus will be on your work in dance therapy."

"No problem. It doesn't bother me, but wouldn't you rather hear the full story from both of us?"

"What?"

I gestured toward the white-haired man limping toward us, a Bells 'n' Whistles canvas bag from one of the hobby stalls draped over his arm along with a second canvas bag hidden behind it. Before I had a chance to say a word, he was pulling out a small windmill from the bag and waving it at me, his hand shaking with the effort to hold it steady.

"Shiloh, check this out. They finally found the red-and-green Christmas windmill. It'll be great with the trains in the California ghost towns."

"About time," I replied. "You've been looking for that piece forever. We'll set it up as soon as we get home. But for now," I turned to the girl, "Cooper Perry, I'd like you to meet my husband, Marcus Kennedy."

Chapter 43

August 21, 2025

Marcus Kennedy.

I loved him. At age twelve, he touched my heart with his music. At age twenty, he captured my heart when he sat on a stage and sang and our eyes met. Less than four months later, he fractured my heart when he refused to allow us to stay together. Now, fifty years later, at age seventy, he filled my heart with the most intense love any person could ask for in a lifetime.

I nodded at him. "Hon, meet Cooper. She's doing a story for an Oak Cliff magazine. Or paper. Whichever. Oh. Before I forget and we devour them all, do you want a scone? They're awesome. Still warm, though how is a mystery. They've been sitting here for the last fifteen minutes."

Marcus grabbed an empty chair from a nearby table, sat and, hand trembling, took a scone out of the basket. "I don't care. Warm or hot, I love these things. Hey! Do you remember the super short lady who wore crazy outfits and sold cranberry-orange scones from a cart in Manhattan? She came to the launch party for *Remake the Song*. You said her name was Fiona Belle Donovan Winthorp but not to use Winthorp because she told you she despised him. Whoever he was. We kept looking for her all over the city after you and I got married, but we never could find her."

"Whoa!" I exclaimed.

"What?" came from both Marcus and Cooper.

"The vendor at Retro Records who just sold me a copy of your *Remake* album. For a stupidly low price. It's Fiona Belle. Well, her clone or daughter, anyway, unless she figured out a way to stay the same age. I guess the recipe got passed down. Sorry. It was bugging me. Anyway, I was getting ready to tell Cooper how you saved me from the attacker fifty years ago."

Marcus leaned over and gave me a quick kiss, then turned to Cooper. "Can I also tell you how Shiloh saved me? In so many ways." He shook his head. "To begin with, Shiloh never would have needed saving if it hadn't been for me. My fault. She was upset because I'd broken up with her…the dumbest move I ever made in my life… Anyway, she'd gone wandering into the park alone."

"Not my smartest move either, and totally not his fault," I said. "The fault lay with his greedy, scheming, evil business manager, Angela Dane, who had a plan."

"Which was?" Cooper asked.

"Well, Marcus and Angela had been at odds over his music for months. Angela wanted to kill off the *Remake the Song* record and replace it with a Greatest Hits album which would go gold, platinum, and to the moon. Tacky, but not homicidal. But that wasn't nearly enough for her. She came up with a literally killer scheme when she did the math and discovered what happens to record sales when singers die at age twenty-seven, especially from suicide."

Cooper's eyes widened. "Like a member of the so-called Twenty-Seven Club. Truly sad and pretty disgusting, but yeah, you're right, royalties for those singers and musicians who died went through the proverbial roof."

"Exactly." I nodded. "Although, at the time, specifically late nineteen-seventy-five, the coincidence of the age thing hadn't been noticed, except by Miss Dane and a few others in the music industry. Trust greedy Angela, who, since there was no internet back then, kept scouring newspapers looking for deaths of singers like some kind of rabid undertaker. She discovered that if the death was a suicide, all of an artist's previous records, especially 'greatest hits' records, would skyrocket in sales. Drug overdoses were a gold mine. And as Marcus's business manager and agent, she'd be able to manipulate which records were distributed."

"So she hired someone to kill Marcus just so she could get her hands on the royalties?"

"Pretty much. But we're talkin' big, honkin' royalties. Much more money than Angela would make even if her proposed 'greatest hits' album went gold. Marcus was in the process of firing her because it was clear they had different ideas for his career. It turned out Angela had a half-brother she'd never mentioned, who was devoted to her. To the point of obsession. He was creepy. He stalked Marcus all over the city for a couple of months, trying to decide where and when to kill him. Then Angela got the brilliant idea of having it appear that Marcus committed suicide on his twenty-seventh birthday. Turn him into a legend and her into a millionaire."

"He murdered Sid because of her," Marcus said, his expression as stricken as it had been the day he discovered our friend dead.

"Who was Sid?" Cooper inquired.

"He was a kind, smart, funny, wonderful man, a veteran. We both met him at the Am-Vets Center in Manhattan," I replied. "He'd recently passed his bar exam, and Marcus was in the process of hiring him as his new business manager, saying bye-bye to Angela. She and her creepy bro couldn't let that happen. They tried to make Sid's death look like either an accidental overdose or a suicide."

Silence for a few moments as both Marcus and I thought about Sid and the evil behind his murder.

Finally, Cooper gently urged me to continue. "What happened at the park?"

"Ah, mister brother creepy guy attacked me and pretty much disabled me. I never saw his face. Marcus came flying in like some super hero and tackled him."

"How'd you figure out Angela was behind everything?"

Marcus glanced at me and then stated, "*Gardenia Gardens.*"

"Beg pardon?"

I chimed in with, "*Gardenia Gardens.* Angela's very distinctive, and to me, very overpowering and very gross, brand of perfume."

"Explain how the scent connected with the creepy half-brother?"

Marcus took up the story. "When I managed to tackle him…knocked him cold six ways to Sunday, which blessedly ended his assault on Shiloh, he ended up in a coma, but unfortunately for less than a week. Obviously, he couldn't talk or offer up who'd hired him, and he managed to sneak out of the hospital practically the instant he woke up. But, back to the attack, even as

277

Shiloh was fighting for her life, her senses, including smell, remained on full alert."

"When I woke up in the hospital I could still smell it. *Gardenia Gardens*. Gag. And I thought, 'I'm sorry, but no self-respecting mugger is going to douse himself with that garbage.' He might, however, carry the scent if he'd recently been around a person who did douse themselves. I'd had this feeling for at least a month—call it a premonition—about Marcus being in danger. Just before I passed out, the guy hissed, 'Stay away from Marcus Kennedy!' Mix those words with smelling her perfume, the certainty that Angela hated me, recalling how she wanted to totally shift Marcus's career, and Marcus wanting to fire her? Well, it all added up to *she's going to try and kill Marcus.*"

Cooper shook her head. "This is awful in so many ways, and yet it's got kind of a daytime-drama vibe. I'm a huge soap fan. I have to confess, one reason I wanted to do this interview is because I loved watching you as Lilith Leatherby on *Exit to Eternity*."

I grinned at her. "My best friend is Zelda Zimmerman. Has been for fifty years."

Cooper gasped. "As in the same Zelda Zimmerman who played Bathsheba Brickhouse from late nineteen seventy-five to nineteen-ninety-seven when it went off the air?"

"Yep. Zelda told me once she thought Angela's plotting and scheming was as bad as some of Bathsheba's on the soap, except it didn't involve incest or cloned presidential candidates or a mix thereof."

Cooper beamed at me. "I'm so glad they've got *Exit* streaming on the SUDSY channel. Zelda was marvelous. Bathsheba was such a wonderfully evil character. It was a blast to watch because she looked like this cute, sweet, innocent pixie while she was plotting murder and government coups in between turning her lingerie factory into a sweatshop. And the two of you together those years you played Lilith Leatherby? You guys had such incredible chemistry."

Marcus chimed in with, "Did you see the episodes where Bathsheba and Lilith agreed to bury the hatchet so they could kidnap the mayor's dog, Horatio, and hold him for ransom unless the mayor admitted he was the real father of Desmond Dixon, but then Lilith decided she wanted to keep the dog and Bathsheba had to hire the leader of the sun-worshipping cult from North Dakota to snatch the dog back?"

I coughed. "Uh, not to interrupt, kids, but maybe we should wrap up the *real* life crime?"

"Shiloh is too embarrassed to admit she misses her days with *Exit to Eternity* and watches every soap still on the air, not to mention she bought a lifetime subscription to SUDSY about two seconds after they were available."

Marcus winked at me, then at Cooper. She grinned at him. At age seventy-seven, the man could still charm a fourth wish off a stubborn, surly genie. He charmed me, daily.

Cooper turned back to me. "Okay. Real life. You're in the hospital and you remembered the scent of your attacker. You're alive, Marcus is alive, but the threat is still ongoing."

"Yep. And, actually, I was back at my apartment by the time I recalled the odor and what it meant. I was able to navigate, albeit very poorly, with crutches, and I had no vital organs missing, so there was no reason to stay in the hospital and rack up outrageous medical bills.

Anyway, I kept having strange visions about Marcus, including seeing him riding on a train with a group of musicians and everybody is obviously dead. I told Zelda about them. She's the one who came up with the term *déjà-vu-isms* which is a kind of 'reverse *déjà vu*.' We were never sure it made sense, but we liked throwing the word around. Weird though, right?"

"Not to me. I've experienced some *déjà vu* moments I also can't explain, so I'm definitely not judging. Did the visions help you figure out who was behind the attack, or was it something else about them?" Cooper asked.

I took another sip of coffee. "It was less a help about the 'who' than smacking me in the face with a very broad hint Marucs would die on December sixteenth unless I could find a way to stop it. I almost failed."

Chapter 44

December 16, 1975/August 21, 2025

As I began telling Cooper the story, I felt as if I was experiencing one of the old *déjà-vu-isms*. Like I was reliving events in real time.

Early Sunday morning of December 16th, I tried calling Zelda, but her phone was busy. I was panicking because my visions were screaming, *This is the day!*

Jim and Wyatt were out doing an early morning jog. I scratched out a message telling them to please call Zelda and have her get hold of Toby and both meet me at the Am-Vets Center, added *Pronto!!!!!* (with five exclamation points).

I threw on my sweats and a jacket, grabbed my crutches, and hobbled out of the apartment and over to Broadway in hopes of snagging a cab. Amazingly, luck was with me and one was cruising down the street with the roof light on, meaning the car was available.

I told the taxi driver I'd give him an extra twenty dollars if we made it from my street to the Am-Vets Center in less than fifteen minutes, preferably without accidents. I told him, aware I sounded silly and trite, that getting there fast was truly a matter of life or death.

The driver could have made a career as a professional racer. We screeched to a halt in front of the Center in ten minutes. He helped me maneuver out of the taxi with my crutches and reach the entrance. I gave him the fare, plus the bonus cash, thanked him, and asked if he could perhaps either call or visit the nearest police station and tell them a murder was in progress. I was about to check if the Center doors were unlocked when Zelda shouted at me as she exited a cab which had just pulled up behind my departing one.

"Shiloh! What's going on?"

I turned in time to witness Toby slamming the door on his own taxi.

I greeted them with, "Guys! It's Angela Dane—she's going to kill Marcus—with her creepy buddy who apparently woke up from his coma and left the hospital two days ago. He's vanished, and since he has yet to be identified, he's impossible to find."

Zelda didn't hesitate. "What can I do?" She glanced up at Toby. "What can *we* do?"

"My *déjà-vu-isms* are telling me this is all going down right here, today. Angela wants to do a repeat of Sid's murder. We're going to stop her."

"She's responsible for killing Sid?" Toby's tone was a mix of shock and rage.

"I'm positive she and creepy guy are the ones who gave him the overdose."

"Wait. Is Marcus even supposed to be at the Center today?" Zelda asked.

"Oh, yeah. Today's his birthday, and he plans to celebrate with the guys here. At least this is what he said weeks ago. I haven't talked to him since I was attacked. Anyway, he told me he'd be at the Center early to set things up for a party."

Toby nodded. "He called me last night. Said he'd be here around eight a.m."

Zelda glanced at her watch. "It's like a minute past eight."

"I hope he's late for once," I said. "Or Angela is late."

"How does she know he'll be here? Who spilled the beans about the party?" Zelda asked.

"Marcus. But, like I said, it's been in the works for more than a month. Before my attack. Before Marcus told Angela he was going to fire her and hire Sid. Now, how she knows what time he'll be here this morning is beyond me, but then, her creepy, murderous accomplice in brown is great at stalking. He probably started tailing Marcus the minute he snuck out of the hospital."

"Okay. I'm checking the doors," said Toby.

They were unlocked. Which meant people were inside. People meaning Marcus. Or Marcus and Angela. Or Marcus, Angela, and the creepy guy.

The three of us nearly fell into the lobby in our haste to find out who was there and whether we were too late. I let Toby and Zelda enter ahead of me. My crutches were somewhat of a hindrance, but I managed to get inside barely a second or two behind them.

Marcus was sitting in a chair away from the reception table. He was groggy, not moving, and, along with the annoying scent of *Gardenia Gardens*, I smelled something chemical, yet sickly sweet. There was a white cloth on the floor beside his chair. Doused with ether? Something to knock him out long enough to get him onto a chair, tie a long rubber band around his arm, and pump him full of what I assumed would be heroin. Like Sid.

Angela and the creep—I really needed a name. Calling him 'creepy guy' was getting old and beyond redundant—were standing in front of him. Angela appeared to be preparing a syringe. She was quite chatty, explaining how she was already set to release a *Greatest Hits* album the week after Marcus's funeral, already had the record pressed. She mentioned something oddly familiar about musicians dying at age twenty-seven and how deaths, especially suicides due to drug overdoses, were quite a boost to record sales.

Toby didn't waste a second. He charged in and, using his one arm, flung Angela half way across the room. The needle was still in her hand. She somehow managed to land on her rear, but hit the wall with her head. She was stunned and out of action.

The battle was won.

But the war wasn't.

In our haste to save Marcus, we failed to notice the guy who'd attacked me was holding a gun. He watched Angela half fly, half slide across the room, turned, and immediately shot Toby. Thankfully, his aim wasn't great and Toby was hit in his shoulder rather than his chest or stomach. Zelda dove to the floor beside him and began applying pressure to the wound.

He wasn't finished. I don't know diddley-doo about guns, but I was vaguely aware one had to again pull the trigger after one shot to fire off another. Zelda needed to stay where she was to stop what, to me, seemed way too much blood gushing from one human.

The guy hesitated. Maybe he was trying to figure out how to salvage the situation and still make the scene look like a suicide. But, for whatever reason, he didn't immediately pull the trigger. I didn't care why.

I took advantage of the brief pause and swung one of my crutches at the gun with all the force I could muster, sending both gun and crutch sailing under the table before crashing to the floor myself. There was no way I could get back up on my feet. Zelda was dealing with stopping the blood spurting from Toby's shoulder, and Toby was trying not to pass out. Angela was writhing in pain in the corner, although I couldn't tell which body part she'd injured when she landed following her slide across the room. The creepy killer was scrambling around on the floor, seconds away from retrieving his gun.

The moment he found it, it would all be over.

I glanced over at Marcus. His face would be the last thing I saw on this earth.

Marcus wasn't in the chair. With superhuman effort, he'd risen and now reached down to scoop up my crutch. He swung it at Angela's hit man's head. He didn't miss.

The police arrived about five seconds later. I spent months trying to track down the cab driver who'd granted my insane request to tell the cops a murder was in progress, but I never found him.

I jolted my mind back to the present and said to Cooper, "Marcus hadn't killed the creepy half-brother, so he and Angela were both arrested. Toby was rushed to the emergency room. The bullet was a through-and-through, and he was out of the hospital in a day. He and Zelda got married about two weeks later, as soon as Toby was able to get the license."

Marcus added, "Shiloh and I waited, because I was a stubborn coot, but she finally convinced me she would take out her own hit if I didn't hold to my original intent of marrying her. Took about a month. She also convinced me to change what I was eating and be sure I did some kind of movement daily. Fast forward. With her help, along with some advances in medicine, I've managed to live much longer and with a much better quality of life, even with Parkinson's, than I ever thought was possible. It's one reason we started the healing center. We want others to at least try the same methods. And to never give up. Continue moving."

Cooper beamed at us both. "It's brilliant. And your story is very romantic and dramatic. I do have one more question for Shiloh, if you don't mind. But it's more personal and possibly brings up some very painful memories."

"Go on," I said.

"After the attack, you believed you'd never dance again. But could you?"

I paused for a long moment. "Not really. I spent months and years and did regain some function of my knee. My technique was never as it'd been before the knife-wielding creep slashed me, but it was passable. Definitely not for a professional dancer. But it honestly didn't matter because, by the time I was up and prancing around, two things had happened. One was I married Marcus and we began focusing on *his* healing. The second was the realization that my life would have more meaning if I was helping others regain their own mobility, their own health...be it mental or physical. I also got the part in the soap, which was marvelous and paid well, but when I wasn't working there, Marcus and I were both still heavily involved at the vets' center."

"Y'all are both remarkable and very special. I'm so glad I got to meet you. Thank you. Thank you both so much for sharing the story with me." She rose. "May I come by *Oak Cliff Healing* sometime and watch a class?"

"Of course. Or, better yet, and *take* a class," I said.

"You look like you can move. We love having people join us."

"I will. I better be off now if I'm going to get this to my editor this afternoon. Again, I'm so very glad I got to spend some time hearing your story. Hopefully, some folks in need of healing will read it and reach out to you for help."

We exchanged hugs and Cooper trotted off toward the parking lot.

I sat back down, took one more scone from the basket, and was about to bite down when Marcus leaned down, then handed me a bag he'd stowed under the table.

"What's this?" I asked.

"No clue. I didn't want to interrupt before, but Fiona Belle's doppelganger or daughter or whatever came racing over to Bells 'n' Whistles as I was leaving and told me to give this to you. Then I got engrossed in the tale of 'Shiloh and Friends Save Marcus' and, of course, chowing down on those fantastic scones. I forgot I had it."

I opened the bag and pulled out a copy of *Remake the Song*. A very different and bizarre copy. The cover was exactly like the odd visions I'd had in my head back in nineteen-seventy-five. Instead of the photo of Marcus smiling and holding a guitar, this one depicted the image of a train. It was eerie, a ghost train with figures representing singers and musicians who died at age twenty-seven from whatever curse the conspiracy theorists had created sometime in the eighties. It was ninety degrees out, but I suddenly couldn't stop shivering.

I flipped the album over and read the liner notes, which claimed Marcus Kennedy had committed suicide via a heroin overdose on December 16, 1975.

I remembered sitting on a bench at Riverside Park a week or so after I left the hospital. My crutches lay next to me. I saw myself handing a page of sheet music for "The Yellow Rose of Texas" to Fiona Belle, declaring, "Take it! I choose to stay."

A flicker of...something...passed in front of my eyes.

Vanished.

I glanced down, bewildered, at an eerie photo serving as the cover on a copy of Marcus's *Remake the Song* album. A photo featuring ghostly images of singers riding on a train. Lying beside the record album was sheet music to "The Yellow Rose of Texas" with today's date and something written at the top in purple ink. I read it, then read it again, trying to make sense of the nonsensical. The note was sparse: *For December, if you choose to go back.*

I could swear I'd never seen either the album or the sheet music before. I stared at two other words, also written in purple ink, down at the bottom of the page. A red stain (possibly from a smushed cranberry?) was positioned like an exclamation point at the end of the short phrase.

"Good Choice!"

Author's Notes

Much of *Remake the Song* is about healing using the power of movement and music.

I discovered when I was still in college that movement and music combined could work miracles and used my experiences teaching dance during my college years at a Veterans' Hospital in Texas as the true basis for "Jonah's" story.

The man who deserves a huge credit for recognizing, and using, movement as an incredible healer is Eugene Louis Faccuito (Luigi) (March 20, 1925-April 7, 2015) whose mantra, *Never Stop Moving*, has echoed through the minds and hearts of decades of dancers. In 1946, following an accident, he healed his own nearly paralyzed body, eventually creating a dance technique that included the goal of preventing injuries. He was a gentle teacher (who delighted in calling me "Texas") and all of us who were ever privileged to take his classes never left without feeling better, both emotionally and physically.

Francis Roach, artistic director of the *Luigi Dance Centre* in NYC, rightfully calls Luigi a "special human being" as he continues his legacy. A link is provided to the Luigi Dance Centre website:

https://www.luigijazz.com/index2.html

~*~

References used to research the effects of diet on diseases including heart, cancer, diabetes, Parkinson's, and other diseases affecting motor disability, include:

"Goodbye Lupus" by Dr. Brooke Goldner

"How Not to Die" Dr. Michael Greger

"The Engine 2 Diet" Rip Esselstyn

https://nutritionguide.pcrm.org/nutritionguide/view/Nutrition_Guide_for_Clinicians/1342007/all/Parkinson_s_Disease

https://davisphinneyfoundation.org/plant-based-diet-for-parkinsons/

https://parsonshouseaustin.com/can-a-plant-based-diet-help-parkinsons/

~*~

I took a few liberties with dates (one can do that in a time travel!) regarding the dates when the deadly effects of Agent Orange became public knowledge. It appears that the military knew in 1975, but word of the lethal herbicide didn't find its way into the media until the late '70s and early '80s.

The Veterans Administration formally recognized exposure to Agent Orange to be associated with Parkinson's Disease in 2008, with a "Final Regulation" on the issue taking effect on October 30, 2010. In 2022, the PACT Act was signed by Congress, providing more benefits to veterans who served in Vietnam as well as subsequent military operations.

https://www.history.com/topics/vietnam-war/agent-orange-1

https://www.ncbi.nlm.nih.gov/books/NBK236351/

https://www.va.gov/disability/eligibility/hazardous-materials-exposure/agent-orange/

A word about the author…

Flo Fitzpatrick was born in Washington, D.C. and spent her first years living in a chateau in France (as an Army brat). Flo received a Bachelor of Fine Arts In Dance from Southern Methodist University and a Masters in Theater from Baylor University.

She is multi-published in romance and mystery, with a great deal of genre overlap and often adding paranormal elements and/or humor. Her second novel, Hot Stuff, was nominated as Best Romantic Suspense (2005) by RT Book Reviews and optioned for film.

Following too many moves in the last 15 years, Flo is now living in Alabama with her extremely mixed-breed mutt Juniper and doing most of her dancing around the living room.

www.flofitzpatrick.com